SOMEWHERE
IN-BETWEEN

SOMEWHERE IN-BETWEEN

DONNA MILNER

Caitlin Press Inc.
8100 Alderwood Road,
Halfmoon Bay, BC V0N 1Y1
www.caitlin-press.com

Text design by Tania Cran.
Cover design by Vici Johnstone.
Cover photo from Arcangel Images. MI-5794, photographer
Mohammed Atani.

Printed in Canada

Caitlin Press Inc. acknowledges financial support from the Government
of Canada through the Canada Book Fund and the Canada Council for
the Arts, and from the Province of British Columbia through the British
Columbia Arts Council and the Book Publisher's Tax Credit.

Library and Archives Canada Cataloguing in Publication

Milner, Donna, 1946-, author
        Somewhere in-between / Donna Milner.

ISBN 978-1-927575-38-3 (pbk.)

        I. Title.

PS8626.I457S66 2014   C813'.6   C2013-907875-4

In memory of my mother
Gloria Jonas

1

Virgil Blue came with the land. Along with two draft horses, four cow-ponies, one hundred range cattle and a barn full of haying equipment, keeping the reclusive tenant, who occupied the old trapper's cabin on the six-hundred-acre ranch, was a non-negotiable condition of sale.

Sitting in the overcrowded Tim Hortons on the highway outside of Waverley Creek, Julie O'Dale watches her husband's reaction as the real estate agent across the table from them brushes over this little detail.

"You won't even know the old guy's there," the fresh-faced young man says, oblivious to Ian's body language.

Julie raises her mug and holds it in front of her lips to hide her involuntary smile. *Well, there's a deal killer.*

The salesman is new since Julie left the business in October, over six months ago. He shuffles through his information package until he finds what he was looking for. "You can't even see the tenant's cabin from the main house," he continues, retrieving a stack of letter-sized photographs from the papers. "Only the million-dollar view of your own private lake." He passes the glossy photos across the table to Ian. Julie recognizes his technique, this sleight-of-hand minimizing of a negative fact by placing the prospect purchasers on the property. No matter. She lets the rookie realtor, Richard-something—she can't remember his last name—continue selling illusions. After all, this is Ian's dream, not hers.

Even the realtor senses this and is directing all his comments to her husband. She might as well not be here. At one time this would have bothered her.

She sips her lukewarm coffee while Ian admires the photographs and Richard extols the virtues of the mini ranch. *Mini ranch?* Julie would describe this remote six-hundred-acre section of land, with its one-thousand-acre range permit in central British Columbia, as anything but mini. Better adjectives, such as isolated, secluded and wild, come to mind. She is vaguely familiar with the property.

Twenty years ago, when she herself was a newly licensed agent, the previous owners had contacted the office about selling. Julie had taken the call. Full of beginner's confidence, certain one could learn anything, she had made an appointment to meet with the owners to discuss listing the ranch. How different could selling rural property be from selling houses in town? She would drive out, view the ranch, compare it to the current market, to competitive listings, to recent sales, then come up with a price. It had all seemed so simple.

Early the next morning, armed with statistics and her black leather briefcase—a gift from Ian after she passed her real estate exam—she had followed the owner's directions west into Chilcotin country. She returned to town that evening, her new white Ford Taurus caked in mud and cow dung, and handed the information over to the office's ranch expert, Leon Walker.

The seasoned realtor had leaned back in his chair, propped up his polished, yet carefully worn-down-at-the-heel, cowboy boots on his desk and given Julie a paternal smile. He could have warned her, he told her, if only she had let him know she was going to attempt to break into 'his market.' Her fatal mistake had been wearing open-toed high heels, forever reducing her credibility in the rural property market to zero.

Pushing back his wide-brim Stetson, Leon had said, "Ranchers expect you to look the part." The next morning, wearing a snap-button Western dress shirt stretched over his wide girth and tucked into crisply ironed Wranglers, a fist-sized bull rider's belt buckle at his overhung waist, he took a float plane out to the ranch. Knowing that Leon, a fellow transplant from the city of Vancouver, had moved to Waverley Creek only five years before she had, Julie was certain that he had never ridden a horse, much less a bull. Yet, late that afternoon he had returned to the office with the signed listing in hand. In time, after overhearing his conversations with the local ranchers and cowboys about the weather, cow-calf units, range permits and leases, after witnessing him hold court behind his enormous burl-top desk, his blue heeler curled up at his feet, Julie had come to respect his art for staging. 'It's all in perception,' was his motto and he played it to the fullest.

His young protégé, sitting across the coffee shop table wearing a black bolo tie, matching black cowboy hat and out-of-the-box-new boots, has yet to perfect it. He's no Leon Walker, but Julie recognizes many of the tag lines of his veteran mentor. Leon, who is still in the business, but by his own definition, getting too old to traipse out into the countryside, had offered to fly them out in a float plane, a trip that would have taken less than half an hour. Julie had refused. She wants Ian to be aware of the reality of the long drive, the vastness of the Chilcotin country.

"Well, let's have a look-see at this little piece of paradise," Richard says, slapping his hands on the table and rising. On the way out, Julie follows closely behind Ian, her eyes locked on the back of his brushed suede jacket. Meeting here was a mistake. She had momentarily forgotten that, like every other Tim Hortons she has ever been in, this one on the outskirts of town is the gathering place of the locals. As usual, ranchers wearing dusty cowboy hats huddle in one corner, loggers and truckers in grease-stained John Deere caps occupy another. The odd tourist, passing through or stopping to investigate the western flavour of this Cariboo town smack in the middle of British Columbia, have found seats among grey-haired retirees and local businesspeople. And in the corner by the door, a group of local First Nations have claimed their own territory.

Weaving her way through the crowded tables Julie feels the furtive glances and ancestral eyes following her exit. She has only herself to blame; after all, she's the one who insisted on meeting Leon's stand-in here, instead of at the office. After six months she still can't bring herself to go near Black's Real Estate.

Outside, the May morning sun warms her face as they walk over to their Jeep Cherokee, which is parked right in front of the coffee shop. Opening the passenger door, Julie catches a reflection in the building's plate glass window. It takes a moment to recognize herself. Has she really changed that much? She's noticed the changes in Ian over this last winter. His shoulders are more rounded, and his tall, solid frame now appears lanky and thin. His once grey-streaked Irish black hair is almost completely silver. Still, anyone looking at the two of them today would never guess that at fifty-five Ian is ten years older than she is. Julie's round baby face, which once served her so well in her career, has thinned; the short sporty hairstyle has grown out. Gone too, is the lipstick and mascara, along with the business suits and the high-heeled pumps she once believed were vital. She climbs into the car with an inward smile. There is a certain freedom in no longer caring that at five foot two she looks dwarfed walking beside her six-foot-two husband.

They follow Richard's silver Dodge crew-cab out of the parking lot and onto the highway. As they turn west at the 'Y' intersection, the local DJ reads an announcement for a meeting of the high school 2008 Dry Grad committee. Julie leans forward and switches off the radio.

"Can they really do that?" Ian asks suddenly.

"Do what?"

"Can the owners really force us to let this old guy stay if we buy the place?"

"A seller can set any conditions they choose. Including accept-ing an existing tenancy." She considers leaving it at that, but after a moment adds as if it's an afterthought, "But unless it's registered on title, and that's unlikely, once a sale is complete there's nothing to pre-vent the new owners from finding a reason to evict."

"Good," Ian says with finality.

On the outskirts of town Julie spots one of her old red-and-blue real estate signs on a fence above the roadside.

FOR SALE. JULIE O'DALE.

"Rolls off the tongue like butter," Ian used to tease in a feigned Irish accent, which had probably disappeared from his family genera-tions ago.

No one has bothered to remove the orphaned real estate sign from the ten-acre parcel. Julie has no idea if the property has sold or not. Nor does she care.

A few miles later they cross the Fraser River and start the steep ascent to the Chilcotin plateau. When they first moved here Julie would have turned around at each hairpin switch-back to look down at the 'mighty Fraser' flowing through the deep gorge below. She used to love this drive west. How many times over the years had she and Ian hopped in the car on a whim to drive out to one of the time-warped country cafés, simply for a piece of homemade pie? Not once during those Sunday drives, as much as she enjoyed giving lip-service to the legendary 'lure of the Chilcotin,' had it ever occurred to her that either she or Ian would one day consider moving out here. For a brief moment she feels a surge of panic that she has indulged him, even slightly, on this whim, that she has let it go this far.

As the patches of forests give way to the rolling grasslands of the Chilcotin plateau, she opens her window to allow the spring air with its fresh scent of sage and juniper to blow in.

Lulled by the warmth of the sun, the hum of tires, Julie feels her eyelids growing heavy. Without warning, she is suddenly flung against her seatbelt restraints and jarred awake as the Jeep takes a sharp turn off the paved highway. On the road in front of them, Richard's truck fishtails on the loose gravel. Small stones shoot up from beneath its tires like bullets, strafing the hood and windshield of the Jeep. Julie grabs the armrest as Ian, swearing under his breath, slams on the brakes. Their vehicle skids across the washboard surface and comes to a stop in a billowing cloud of dust. Simultaneously she and Ian press their automatic window buttons to seal the interior against the thick invasion.

Julie clamps her mouth shut, resisting the urge to blurt that he was following too close; to protect him or herself she isn't quite certain. Criticism of each other is no longer a luxury they can afford.

Ian waits for the pickup's tail lights to disappear before following at a distance in the settling dust. The first week of May and already the Chilcotin countryside is drying up.

On either side of the road fir and pine saplings dot the landscape of an old clear-cut. Sun-bleached stumps, the remnants of trees cut long ago, lay like hulking animal carcasses in the new growth. Not a pretty sight. But then, growing up in Vancouver, Julie knows she has been spoiled by the majestic cedars of the coastal rain forests.

Ian slows down even more for a white-faced Hereford that ambles along unconcerned in front of them, her udder swaying between her legs. A stiff-legged calf runs beside her, its tail straight up. At the sound of their horn the calf veers off to scurry up the low bank. In no hurry, the cow follows, swinging her head, her huge eyeballs rolling a white-edged warning at the Jeep inching by.

Half an hour later they come to Richard's truck, its silver paint dulled by a layer of dust, stopped on the side of the road waiting for them. As the Jeep pulls up alongside, the salesman rolls down his window and sticks his head out. With his black hat pushed back on his forehead, he flashes a grin that says, "Isn't this great?" He points to a narrow side road leading off to the right, "Almost there, folks."

They fall in behind his vehicle once again. As they head west the grasslands gradually turn into trees, then into dense forest. Although it has been many years since her ill-fated trip to the ranch, Julie suddenly remembers her surprise even then at seeing so much untouched timber. Taking in the towering trees all around she admits that this old-growth forest very well might measure up to the coastal forests. At the next junction she recognizes the fenceline where the ranch property begins. Old instincts kick in and she is about to point out the white survey peg on the bank, then decides that she'll leave all that up to Richard. Let him do his job. Glancing at her watch, she wonders if Ian has noticed that they have been driving for over two hours.

They round another bend, the downhill grade increases and the roadside drops away on the western facing slope. After a series of hair-pin turns, the realtor's truck slows and pulls over to park on a widened area of the road. The driver's door flies open and Richard jumps out, waving them to park behind his vehicle. "This is the best view of the place, folks," he hollers. The sales pitch is back on. Julie has to hand it to him though, the guy is enthusiastic.

Ian is out of the car and standing on the edge of the road before Julie has opened her door. The last, and only time, she passed this way, she was driving and so had missed this vantage point completely.

"Beautiful, eh?" Richard asks when she joins them. She follows his gaze down over the treetops reaching up from the hillside at their feet, and gasps at the sight.

Below, a valley stretches from north to south as far as the eye can see. A willow-lined creek meanders lazily through natural hay meadows. On either side of the serpentine creek, the fresh spring grass sprouts through the dull yellow of winter-killed stubble. A hip-roof barn and a cluster of weathered outbuildings rise like silver-grey islands in the greening landscape.

To the west, a steep granite ridge rises straight up to the Chilcotin plateau, where in the blue distance, a haze of coastal mountains cuts into the horizon.

Richard directs their attention north, to the glistening waters of the lake, which dominates that end of the valley. "Spring Bottom Lake," he says. "The entire lake is on the property."

Directly below, an enormous ranch house—new since Julie was here—overlooks the lake's southern shore, its polished logs a golden glow in the mid-day sun.

"The tenant's cabin is out on that point," he adds, indicating a small bay.

Julie thinks she can detect the faint outline of a roof through the treetops. If so, the cabin in the shadows is, just as Richard promised, a good distance from the main house.

"Other than the cabin, the ranch house is the only home in the entire valley," he announces proudly.

Julie turns to Ian, and sees in his eyes that he will have this place. She sees that, with or without her, he will make it his own. It's just a matter of time, perhaps days, maybe even hours, before he tells her that he is going ahead with the purchase. He will ask her to give up her home, her life in town, and come with him. And she knows that when he does, she will say yes.

2

Instead of a grieving widow, bowed under the recent loss of her husband, a vibrant woman opens the ranch house door when they pull into the yard. Wearing knee-high leather boots, designer jeans and a silk shirt, Elke Woell flashes a brilliant smile and strides across the back porch to greet them.

Julie feels the woman's energy even after her hand is released from her firm grip. She recognizes the widow, remembers when she and her husband purchased the property through Leon Walker years ago. The couple were two of many German vacationers who had fallen in love with the Cariboo Chilcotin country, and then returned when the Deutschmark was so high that it was easy to buy into their cowboy dreams.

Over the years Julie has spotted Elke shopping in Waverley Creek every now and then. She's hard to miss. In her expensive European clothes and carefully coiffed sun-blonde hair she was a head-turner whenever she showed up on the streets of the decidedly casual town. She still is, even though she has to be at least ten years older than Julie.

To the salesman's obvious discomfort, the owner insists on accompanying them as they tour the ranch. In an accent heavy with guttural consonants, she does most of the talking. Following her through the outbuildings, Julie feels a twinge of sympathy for Richard, who is being so firmly usurped from his role, until she notices his twitches of plea-sure at Ian's obvious buying signals. The novice realtor actually rubs his palms together while answering Ian's telling question about the equip-ment in the sheds and barn being included in the sale. Julie can almost see the salesman mentally calculating his share of the commission.

Outside, she joins Ian as he strays over to the horse corral where he leans on the wooden fence, resting one foot on the bottom rail. "Beautiful," he says to himself, as two enormous chestnut workhorses plod across the dirt towards them. Their hides reflect the light in a coppery sheen; jet-black manes sway across arched necks. In stark contrast, the markings on their long faces and legs are snow white. Their feathered stockings, which look freshly combed, splay out over platter-sized hooves as they rise and fall with each heavy step.

"They must be at least eighteen hands high," Ian says.

Julie glances over at her husband, surprised that he knows this term for a horse's height. But, why not? He's a numbers man after all.

"Clydesdales," Richard says as he and Elke join them. "They're included along with the four saddle horses out in the field."

The two workhorses walk up to the fence and lift their massive heads over the top rung.

"Yah, they are Virgil's babies," Elke says reaching up and stroking the heavily muscled withers of the closest one. "His gentle giants, he calls them. At least that was what my husband told me. I wouldn't know. I don't see Virgil so much. He did business *mit* Helmut." At the mention of her husband's name something changes in the woman's eyes. She quickly blinks herself back to the moment and points to the far side of the meadow. "The west side of the property goes to the top of the plateau," she says, then begins to describe the boundaries.

"I have all the maps and overhead forestry photographs," Richard announces in an attempt to take the lead.

While the verbal tug-of-war over property lines, hay production and timber values continues, Julie scans the countryside. Across the

valley, below the western ridge, dense forest hugs the hillsides, a tapestry of variegated greens with rusty brown peppered throughout, as
if Mother Nature has prematurely arrived with a hard autumn frost.
From a distance it looks beautiful. But Julie knows exactly what causes
this effect. The dead pine trees stand like tinder dry skeletons, remnants of the unchecked pine-beetle infestation, which continues to
devastate the province's forests.

"This is one of the few properties in the area that hasn't been clear-
cut," Richard says as if following her thoughts.

"Helmut would not do this." Elke strokes the velvet muzzle of the
other horse. "He did not want to ruin the view."

"The beetle-killed timber will have to come down," Julie says, surprising herself.

Ian's head jerks up. He smiles at her, and she is glad to see his
delight at her joining the conversation.

"Virgil will log it *mit der...*" Elke stops. "*With the* horses," she corrects herself.

"There's a market for those dead trees now," Richard interjects.
"The lumber dresses out nicely. Denim pine they call it, because of the
streaks of blue grain that the beetles cause. I did the wainscoting in my
kitchen with it. Looks great."

He turns away from the corral fence, effectively ending the conversation. "Now let's see the rest of the property." He directs them toward
his crew-cab and Julie climbs into the back seat beside Elke. A few
minutes later they turn down onto a driveway flanked by mountain
ash trees.

"The rental cabin is just down here," Richard says nodding ahead.
"We'll have a look at that first."

Elke leans forward, shaking her head. "No. No. We cannot go inside."

"You didn't give the tenant notice that we were coming?" Richard
asks slowing the truck to a crawl.

"Why would I? It is his home."

The back of the cabin, nestled on the water's edge, comes into view. Typical of the ancient settlers' homes sprinkled throughout the Chilcotin, the weathered, square-hewn log cabin has a low slung roof and few windows. Except for the dented, road-weary pickup truck parked behind it, there's no sign of life.

"I'd like to see inside," Ian insists.

"There is nothing to see. It is just a small cabin, of no value. I have never been in it. Just my husband. No." Elke sits back. "We must leave."

"Sorry, folks," Richard says, the frustration evident as he throws the vehicle into reverse.

During the jaw-chattering drive to the northeast fields, in answer to Ian's questions about the tenant, Elke explains that Virgil was already living in the cabin when she and her husband bought the ranch. "He was here before we came, and he will be here when we are gone." Her husband had promised Virgil Blue he could live in the cabin as long as he wanted. She means to keep that promise.

"He does so much work around the ranch," she adds firmly. "You will be glad."

Uncharacteristically, Ian does not press the point. Another tell. Julie watches in amazement as he nods in agreement. He turns to face the road and she studies the back of his head. For the first time in months he is sitting up straight. Lately it seems as if he is shrinking, that the essence of who he once was is diminishing, and the solid walls that once made up his defences are caving in. She is afraid that something beyond weight and size is being lost. Even his neck looks different, like a turtle's retreating into its shell to shore itself up from the outside world. Is it possible that this crazy idea of his, this getting away from it all, might be their saving salvation after all?

Inside the ranch house Ian's buying signals escalate. Even a wet-behind-the-ears realtor can't miss Ian's need to touch things, to run his hand along the smooth logs, the polished wooden doors, as he wanders from room to room. In the prow-shaped living room he stops to admire the massive central rock fireplace, and then walks over to the floor to ceiling windows. Beneath the high open beam ceiling, he stands in front of the plate glass staring out at the lake. "Amazing, just amazing," he says to himself, before heading to the next room. Julie follows silently, skirting the glossy black bear rug splayed out in front of the fireplace. An involuntary shiver grips her at the sight of the bear's enormous head, its fierce open-mouth display of carnivorous teeth.

In the large office adjoining the living room, Ian paces off the floor, measuring the space. Julie can see him mentally placing his desk and furniture to take advantage of the views from the wall to wall windows. She walks over and opens one of the French doors that overlook an ambitious garden on the east side of the house. The smell of freshly turned earth wafts in with the breeze. Feeling the need for counter measures, finding something negative to balance Ian's overly positive enthusiasm, she closes the door. "Mosquitoes? Black flies?" she asks, eyeing the screens.

Elke shrugs. "Not so bad. The wind from the lake helps."

"Yes, I imagine that the north wind must be brutal in the winter. I'm surprised you built the house at the head of the lake instead of in the shelter of the trees."

"Yah. Virgil, he tells Helmut the same thing, not to build here. But," she shrugs again, "the view."

She leads them to the den on the opposite side of the living room. "Look at the light in here, Julie," Ian says. "Don't you think this would make a great office for you?"

An office for what? she wonders, then not wanting to dampen his enthusiasm any more than she has she nods and returns his smile. But something about the view of nothing except the barn and empty meadows stretching south makes her cringe. Mental isolation is one thing, but physical isolation? Could what was left of their marriage survive it?

Heading upstairs Julie tries to ignore the stuffed animals, the deer, mountain goat, and moose heads gazing down from the log walls. Ian doesn't ask if they stay, and like herself she senses him avoid their glass-eyed stares. While they tour the upstairs bedrooms, she feels him checking her reaction every now and then. It's difficult not to be impressed with the opulence of the house, the oversized master suite with a private balcony overlooking the lake. Back downstairs, she concedes, "You have a beautiful home, Mrs Woell," as they follow her into the kitchen.

The widow opens a maple cabinet and takes out four pottery mugs. "Yah. It is beautiful," she says, placing two of the mugs under the coffee machine spigots. "I tell my husband he is spending too much." She turns to face them. "I say, 'Helmut, you will never get your money back.' But it didn't matter he says, he wants to live here for the rest of his life." She leans against the counter, crossing her arms in front of her. "*Und*," she says, "he did."

Richard clears his throat and places his briefcase on the table. "You couldn't build this house today for the list price of the entire ranch," he says, gesturing for Julie and Ian to take a seat.

"Yah, the price is good. Firm," Elke announces, oblivious to her agent's slumping shoulders. "Everyone tells me, it is too soon, you must not sell so fast. You must give it some time. Virgil will look after the ranch. So yah, I could stay." She places steaming mugs in front of Julie and Ian. "But no." She shakes her head and straightens up. "Now, I go to the city. This was Helmut's dream, not mine."

Hearing the woman's statement—so similar to her own thought earlier today—Julie watches for Ian's reaction to her words. But Ian is too intent on studying his surroundings to notice.

Sipping her coffee, Julie, too, looks around the immaculate stainless steel and granite kitchen. It would be impossible not to admire the imported European appliances, the gleaming wood walls and beamed ceiling, the wood-fired oven built into the kitchen side of the rock fireplace. And, Julie has to admit, the comforting aroma of baking bread wafting from that oven, is the perfect touch. Through the bay window over the sink, Julie catches a glimpse of the lake's sun-sparkling surface. At that moment a loon glides past the shallow reeds near shore. It lifts its ebony head and releases a warbling call, a haunting plea to some unseen mate.

A professional house stager could not have planned it better. Beside her, Ian tilts his head and listens with an appreciating grin as a volley of answering cries echo across the water.

In another life Julie would just as easily have allowed herself to admire the beauty of it all. She envies Ian's ability to do so now.

3

"Purging?" her sister asks from the kitchen doorway.

Julie looks up from where she is sitting on the family room floor attacking the lower shelves and drawers of the wall unit.

"Something like that," she says straightening up and arching her back. Even with the professional movers there is still so much to do. Such a nasty job.

"I've finished cleaning the fridge," Jessie says, snapping off her rubber gloves. "Why don't I start packing the kitchen dishes?"

"No, the movers can do all of that. I'm just finishing up the personal stuff."

"Well then, how about I make a pot of tea?"

"That would be great. I'm almost done."

Watching her sister head into the kitchen, Julie says, "Jess, I know it couldn't have been easy leaving the girls in Vancouver with Mom. Have I thanked you yet for coming?"

"Only a half-dozen times," Jessie calls over her shoulder.

Julie smiles at her retreating back then returns to her final task in this room.

Moving forces a sorting of the bric-a-brac and dust collectors of life, forces a culling of the past. The last time she did this job was twelve years ago, when they moved from their first modest home across town to this executive home above the Waverley Creek golf course.

Back then, it was so much more difficult to pick and choose which 'stuff' to hang on to and which to let go. Darla, who was four years old at the time, hadn't made it any easier. While Julie had sorted and packed, her daughter had followed behind rescuing most of the discards.

This time Julie finds it easy to chuck anything and everything. There's nothing to prevent her from sweeping the tacky travel souvenirs off of the bottom shelf into the share-shed box, and she does so with morbid relish. One at a time she pulls sales awards and wall plaques from the drawers to toss them thumping and clattering into the recycle boxes.

Opening the end cabinet she is stopped short by the sight of the collection of pink albums, standing spine out, labelled from one to thirteen. She still hasn't put together Darla's fourteenth and fifteenth years. She wonders if she ever will. The neglected and unsorted photographs are stored in the shoebox on the bottom shelf. Her hands shake as she slides the box out now and places it on her lap. Unable to stop herself, she removes the lid. At the sight of the top photograph, a bittersweet memory of the moment Ian took the picture of her and Darla on Darla's fourteenth birthday floods through her. Now she is glad that she had swallowed her shock and kept her opinion to herself about her daughter's new haircut that day. Staring down at Darla's Irish black hair—shaved to the scalp on one side of her head with a long careless swatch hanging over a mascara-laden eye on the other—Julie wonders why she had hated the style at the time. It was so much better than the purple and orange spikes that would follow.

She places the shoebox on the floor, pulls a tissue from her pocket and blows her nose. It's the dust, she tells herself. Picking up the photograph again, she studies the image of Darla standing beside her, their arms around each other's shoulders. She tries to read the thoughts behind her daughter's 'say-cheese' smile, searching for any clue, any hint that things were about to change. She detects nothing in the round-cheeked face, which looks so much like her own had at the same age, minus the haircut and make-up.

When Darla was a little girl, Julie remembers other mothers warning her about the terrible teenage years to come. She had laughed off their stories about living with mother-hating she-monsters. She had sympathized when a co-worker's seventeen-year-old daughter ran away and ended up on the streets of Vancouver, but secretly she had felt immune from it all. Julie believed that her and Darla's relationship was different, special, too close to follow that route. Unlike her friends and female co-workers, she had only one child—not from lack of trying, but simply the way it turned out—and so she could focus completely on her daughter. She had foolishly believed that was all it took.

Then Darla turned fourteen. From that exact day it seemed, the little changes, small shifts in her personality, started. The changing-hormone moodiness was to be expected, certainly, but the silences, the irritation at most things Julie said, the rush to criticize or challenge her values, where had that come from? Where had her little girl gone, the one who had brought home a heart-warming Mother's Day essay from school, which concluded 'and when I grow up I want to be just like her'?

How could it all have changed so quickly? During her fourteenth and fifteenth year the only thing her shape-shifting daughter ever gave her was the dreaded shoulder shrug in response to the simplest of questions. Still, it hadn't been all bad; there were the odd moments when she forgot her rebellion, the moments that brought out the little girl excitement, and exposed the wears-her-heart-on-her-sleeve daughter. Through it all, Julie always knew that, beneath the trying-to-be-tough teenager was her same sweet Darla. She just had to wait the stage out, she had told herself. And then last year there were signs that it was coming to an end when Darla had taken a sudden interest in the American presidential race.

"Do you believe it's possible, Mommy," she had asked while watching Barack Obama's declaration speech in February of 2007.

"Of course, anything's possible," Julie had replied, more thrilled at the 'mommy' slip than the question.

Overnight it seemed, Darla turned into a news junkie, watching and taping everything she could find concerning the Illinois senator. Her bedroom walls became a shrine—like to the rock stars of Julie's youth—to the presidential candidate. She and some of her friends started a 'Canadian Students Supporting Obama' group at school that graduated to the Internet and mushroomed to other schools across the country.

Julie picks up another photograph and smiles at the image of herself, and a very different-looking Darla, both wearing matching *I've got a crush on Obama* t-shirts. Using a time delay Julie had taken that photo herself last summer. At fifteen Darla was already five foot two. She had begun to tease her mother that she would soon be looking down at her. Yet in this picture Julie appears so much taller than her daughter, who never felt the need to exaggerate her height with high heels. How well Julie recalls the night when she took the photograph. The evening of the Democratic presidential candidates' debate. June 2007. Was it really almost a year ago? It seems like yesterday, and it seems like another lifetime. A lifetime in which Julie had foolishly thought that she had everything under control again. She knows only too well now that no one, and nothing, ever is. Like the difference in their height in the photograph, it was all an illusion, the life she had built, her marriage, her family.

But on that June night, two months before Darla's sixteenth birthday, it was easy to believe everything was as it should be. After watching the debate on CNN together, they had worked side by side preparing dinner. While she diced cucumbers, Darla had gushed, "Wow, this could really happen, couldn't it?"

"It certainly could," Julie had answered, giddy with relief that they had finally found something to share, something to be passionate about together.

Darla dumped the cucumber into the salad bowl. Popping one into her mouth she pushed her stool away from the island. "I'm going to call Gram," she said jumping down. "See what she thought of the debate."

While Darla retrieved the phone, Julie had tried to ignore the twinge of regret—or was it jealousy?—at losing her daughter's attention. How could she be jealous of her own mother? Julie forced a smile as Darla climbed back up on the stool and pressed the speed dial for the Vancouver number. As Darla's interest increased in the US election, she had spent hours talking on the phone with her American-born grandmother. From the other side of the island Julie could hear the joy in her mother's voice when she realized who was calling.

"Did you watch the debate, Gram?" Darla asked excitedly, turning on the speakerphone. For the next five minutes Julie remained mute in the background, listening while the conversation segued to her mother sharing her teenage memories of the very first televised presidential debate, between Nixon and John Kennedy in the 1960s.

"Everyone I knew hopped on the bandwagon for Kennedy, after that," she reminisced. "It was all very exciting, the same excitement over the possibility of a change I suppose." Then without waiting for a response she asked, "But what about Hillary Clinton?" changing gears in a way so typical to her. "Wouldn't it be just as interesting to see a woman become president?"

"Yeah, sure, but it has to be the right woman," Darla said, reaching into the salad bowl for a piece of carrot. "Anyway, I think Canada's more likely to have a female leader before the States."

"We already did. Kim Campbell," Julie interjected just to prove she was in the room.

"I mean an elected one."

"Well, either way, Dear," her grandmother said without commenting on Julie joining the conversation. "With both a woman and an African-American running for president, we've come a long way."

"Someone's gender? The colour of their skin?" Darla rolled her

26

eyes, as if in silent conspiracy with Julie. "Just the fact that we're talking about it means we still have a long way to go."

Later, while they ate dinner alone, because Ian was working late, Julie asked Darla if all this interest in the American election might be leading to an interest in Canadian politics.

"*Très* boring," Darla replied. At her age, nothing was more tragic than boredom.

"Well, don't have a cow," Julie said, causing Darla to roll her eyes once again, this time at Julie's use of the outdated expression. Still she forged on. "What about the old adage that 'if you don't like the way things are, then be part of the change'?"

"Maybe I will," Darla shrugged. "Hey, ya never know."

You certainly don't.

Moments like that evening had convinced Julie that the worst was over. Darla's rebellious stage had been nothing more than a tempest in a teapot. A minor blip, compared to the storms many parents had to weather. Julie had slowly let down her guard last summer. Then in the fall came Darla's 'Big Lie.'

"Tea's ready," Jessie calls from the doorway.

Startled, Julie drops the photograph. "Be right there." She retrieves the picture, places it back in the box with the others.

In the kitchen, the china teapot and cups are set out on the island. Jessie fills Julie's teacup as she climbs up on her stool. "I know you like it weaker," she says, then slides a plate of cheese and crackers in front of her.

Julie smiles, silently blessing her sister for not mentioning her weight loss. Their mother would have no such reservations.

"Thanks again for talking Mom out of coming up. I don't think I could bear her criticisms right now. Or to have her and Ian in the same room."

Jessie nods with understanding. Their mother has never held back her opinion, and right now her opinion is that what Julie and Ian are doing, 'moving further out into the "boonies" of British

Columbia,' is 'downright insanity.' It took Jessie's pretence that she had no one to stay with her five- and eight-year-old daughters—Emily and Amanda—while she and her husband, Barry, helped Julie and Ian with the move, to convince their mother not to come.

Julie appreciates what a sacrifice it is for Jessie, who hates to leave her girls behind whenever she travels. The truth is that there is no need for anyone to help. They have hired professional movers. Except for the sorting of personal things, which Julie refuses to allow anyone else to go through, there is little to do. Still, Jessie had insisted. And Julie has to admit that having her sister and her husband here these last two days has been wonderful. Right now Ian and Barry are out inspecting the ranch before the lawyer releases the funds this afternoon. Julie didn't bother trying to assure Ian that an inspection was totally unnecessary, that in her experience German clients, with few exceptions, left their properties in good condition, their houses eat-off-the-floor clean. She knows the trip was just an excuse to show off the place to Barry. From the moment they had a solid contract of purchase and sale, Ian found similar pretences each week to run out there. Neither Elke Woell, nor the realtor assured of his commission, objected. Today Julie is glad they are gone. It allows her time alone with her sister.

"Will you miss it?" Jessie asks over the rim of her teacup. "This house? Town?"

Julie sets her cup down in the saucer. "You know, I felt like a fish out of water when we left Vancouver and moved to Waverley Creek, twenty, no, twenty-one years ago. God, has it been that long? Anyway, I couldn't stop hearing Mom calling it an 'overgrown cow-town in the middle of nowhere.' And for the first year, I never enjoyed working at Ian's accounting firm. But after I got my real estate licence and started working with people instead of numbers, this town started to grow on me. I felt at home. By the time Darla was born," she hesitated, looked down at her hands for a moment before continuing, "I knew I wanted to raise her here. When we bought this house twelve years ago, I thought it would be our last. I imagined her growing up here, graduating, marrying…" her voice cracks and she swallows. "So I guess the answer is yes, and no."

She picks up her teacup. "At any rate, it's too late to even think about that. The truth is right now I'm just following Ian's lead." She holds up a hand. "I know, don't say it. Mom already did. That I'm just letting life happen to me now, not making it happen. She says this move is all about what Ian needs. What Ian wants."

"Yeah, well Mother never liked him too much from the beginning, did she?" Jessie asks. "Remember all those ridiculous predictions she made about your marriage? None of which materialized."

Julie lowers her eyes, unwilling at this point to let her sister, who knows her so well, read the truth in her eyes.

Back in the family room she feels like a fraud as she wipes down the cabinet shelves. Yes, this move is all Ian's idea; he believes it will be their last. For him, perhaps it will. She is less committed to it, to anything right now. Her mother's right. She is like a leaf on the water, allowing the undercurrents to carry her along at will. Still, she will go along with it right now, see where it leads. Why not? She has nothing but time now.

Her cloth brushes over a thick paper on the bottom shelf. She reaches in and slides out the unframed portrait. Wiping the dust away, she studies her twenty-two-year-old face, smiling so brightly in spite of the agony caused by the six-inch high heels hidden beneath the satin gown. On her wedding day Julie had believed that the spike heels, the puffed-up back-combed hair and tiara made her look so tall and sophisticated standing beside Ian. Now she sees that she looked like nothing more than an over-made-up child playing dress-up.

4

Oh, Mom, it's not so bad. Okay, yeah, well maybe it is. All those puffs and ruffles look kinda cheesy now. But even with all that silly frou-frou, I've always loved Mom and Dad's wedding photograph. When I was a little girl I would imagine myself wearing her dress when I was grown up and getting married. But that little girl is gone now. And me, walking down the aisle wearing a white gown? Not gonna happen.

Still, I wish Mom would not be so hard on herself—and Dad. I wish she could find a way back to the place they were on the day that photograph was taken; back to the place where all that matters is love.

A person would have to be blind not to see the electricity between my parents in that picture. Daddy looks like a movie star—no really he does, kind of like a young Tom Hanks—in his black tuxedo, standing beside a princess in a frilly satin gown.

Maybe all daughters believe their fathers are handsome and their mothers are beautiful. I don't know, but I truly believe mine are. Inside and out. Sappy, I know. But I think I'm allowed that, after all.

When I was growing up, I never got tired of hearing Mom tell the story of how she and Dad met. She repeated it so many times, embellishing the details as I got older, that I believe I can tell it even better than her. Yeah. No doubt from my point of view now, I can.

She was only nineteen when he plunked down in the seat beside her during her first Statistics class at UBC in Vancouver. Glancing up from her notebook, her first thought was, "What a hunk." The next was, "Tilt!" when he pushed back a lock of coal black hair from his eyes, and she saw the gold band. With a polite smile she turned back to the lecture. She wasn't on the prowl for anyone, anyway. She was determined to stay uninvolved while she studied for her commerce degree. During grade school and high school, numbers had always intrigued her, she said, had always come comically easy to her. Becoming a chartered accountant appeared to be the natural choice.

Dad was older than most of the other students. "Changing careers midstream," he told her after they became friends. Study-buddies, Mom swore, was all they were. Yeah, right! Still there must have been some truth to that because his then wife didn't seem to mind the arrangement. In fact, when exams where looming they took turns studying together late into the nights at his Kitsilano condo, while his wife, a practising orthodontist, slept down the hall. The few times Mom met her, she was surprised that the solemn-looking woman was someone Dad, who could find humour even in numbers, would choose to marry. I saw her in an old photograph of Dad's, and I have to admit she looked like a pretty unhappy camper.

At any rate, after a year of sort of hanging together, Dad called Mom one night, sounding really upset, asking if they could meet. Her parents were away in Europe, so she invited him to her home in Point Grey. Hard to imagine her doing that, but, hey, she was old enough to make her own decisions, and like I said, he was, and still is, pretty much a hunk.

At her parents' place he had sat on the living room couch with his head in his hands and wept—Mom's word not mine—because his wife was leaving him. I never could imagine my dad crying. Now, after all that's happened, no problem picturing that.

I'm guessing that they ended up in bed that night, although Mom—who believe it or not, hoped I would buy into the old-school stuff about saving myself for marriage—would never 'fess up' on that one. She did admit, though, that they started dating afterward. Whatever.

Gram, of course, went ballistic. I can just see her, pulling her shoulders up, all huffy and ready for battle, when Mom announced they would be getting married as soon as his divorce was final. Gram must have seen right through the 'just dating' thing because she came right back with the accusation that she couldn't believe that a daughter of hers would have an affair with a married man.

Mom protested, did for a very long time, that things were not that way. "They're not really together, not living as husband and wife, anymore. They're just sharing the condo until it's sold. They don't sleep together," she insisted. Gram latched right on to that little fact, asking how she could possibly know that for certain. "Because I believe him," Mom told her. "I trust him." She should have stopped there, but I have witnessed their arguments and they both seem to think they have to get in the last word. "At least they don't have any children," she told her mother. "He's just trying to do this whole thing in a civilized manner." Wow! I can just see Gram's right eyebrow arching up into that devilish V of hers at that one.

"If a man will cheat on his wife," she had prophesied, "he will cheat on his wife—no matter who she is." Even looking at it all from where I am now, I still have a tough time with that one. •

Anyway, the wedding dress was Mom's concession to her mother. So in her wedding photograph there she is, lost in the puffy sleeves and billowing Gone With the Wind *skirts, forever captured as the little girl trying to appease her overbearing mother.*

All my childhood, Mom always swore that our relationship wasn't going to be like hers and her mother's. She believed we could avoid falling into the trap of mother, daughter, criticism and bickering. And mostly we did. But then there were those few nasty years. I didn't hate her exactly, it just seemed at the time that everything she did bugged me; the way she was so proud of me, always wanting to be my friend; even being the kind of woman who put her family—Dad and me—first, seemed lame somehow. I know. Not cool.

There were moments, I admit, when I was a perfectly horrible daughter and I gave her some pretty rough times back then. Now, I need her. I need her to do something for me. Something really big. I believe she would. I believe she would do anything for me—if only I could ask her.

5

Moving day comes too soon. One by one, the three vehicles turn west onto the highway in the fused yellow light of sunrise. Ian, driving the new Ford pickup truck, which they'd traded Julie's Taurus in on last week, leads the parade. Behind him is Barry in his Lincoln Continental, followed by the moving van. At the wheel of the Jeep Cherokee, bringing up the rear, Julie glances over at Jessie in the passenger seat with what she hopes is a smile. "Well, this is it," she says and pulls onto the highway.

She's grateful to have her sister's company, to have someone to talk with on the drive out to the ranch. Not so long ago she would have looked forward to driving alone; she used to enjoy her solitary time behind the wheel that allowed her head to clear out all the business clutter. Now the trouble with driving in silence, like any repetitive or thoughtless activity where she lets her guard down, is that it allows her mind to wander to places she would rather not go.

"I wonder how much Mom is spoiling the girls," Jessie says.

Now there's a reliable subject. Julie and her sister can waste hours talking about their mother and never exhaust the conversation.

"Strange how she adores her granddaughters, isn't it?" Jessie muses. "Given how you and I just seemed to be an inconvenience, a distraction from her life with Dad, while we were growing up. Making up for lost time, I suppose."

"Yeah, I guess. Lucky her. A second chance," Julie says, surprised by the harsh edge to her words. She thought she'd let go of all that. She believed that she had long ago forgiven her mother for all the times she'd chosen to accompany their father on his business trips, leaving the mothering of her children to a succession of housekeepers and babysitters.

Determined not to commit the same mistake, Julie had taken a break from her career for five years after Darla was born. That had been one of the bonuses of switching from accounting to real estate. It had allowed her to stay home for her daughter's early years and then to set her own hours after Darla started school.

"Dad was Mother's career," Jessie says, in tune as usual with Julie's thoughts. "Her job. Much of the time it felt like we were just a by-product of that."

"Ha! You think?"

"It must have been worse for you, being the oldest. I was fortunate. I had you."

"Yeah, until I abandoned you when I was twenty-two," Julie says wryly.

"You couldn't shake me that easy, if you recall."

Julie remembers. After she and Ian married, Jessie would often show up at their Vancouver apartment. And then when they moved inland she had spent her summers with them in Waverley Creek. "I couldn't wait for the end of school every June so I could hop on the bus and come up to your place."

"And I loved those summers," Julie says, then adds with a laugh, "I certainly understood your need to get away."

"Oh yeah." Jessie reaches for the Thermos at her feet. "You know I used to imagine Mom being handed me as a newborn, taking one look at me and saying 'What do I need another one of *these* for? I already have *one*!'" She snorts at her own joke.

35

Julie glances quickly at her sister's profile. Unlike Julie, whose appearance and height favoured their father's side of the family, Jessie resembles their mother. Growing up, the eight years difference in their ages had left little room for jealousy or competition between them; and there's none now. Still, Julie envies her sister's model height and elegant figure, her slim face and high cheekbones. Although lately Julie has noticed that her own thinning face is beginning to resemble their mother's as well, but not in a flattering way.

"She's lucky you can laugh about it," Julie says concentrating again on the road.

"Oh, it took a while, but after Dad died, I just stopped expecting her to be something she's not. A good mother. And then she became something I didn't expect her to be. A friend. And you have to admit she is a doting grandmother. Who knew?"

Yes, who knew? A friend though? Julie isn't certain she would put her mother in that category. They are more like adversaries who have come to an unspoken truce. There is nothing better than a child, which you both love, to soften previous transgressions in a relationship. The volatility of their past still makes Julie shudder. Visions of herself as a teenager screaming, "I hate you," at her mother, filled her with shame even though she had come to recognize it for what it had been, a bid for attention, anything to have her sit up and take notice. It never worked.

"Someone who didn't know her then would never believe how selfish and self-centred she was," Jessie says. "She puts on such a great sweet-little-old-lady act now."

"Oh, yeah," Julie agrees, as the procession winds up the hill above the river. "She puts on a good show for the cheap seats, but those of us who paid the price know what a great actress she really is."

Jessie laughs out loud at the analogy. After she regains control she pours coffee into the Thermos lid and offers it to Julie, who shakes her head in answer.

"Anyhow, it's a good thing she's not here." Jessie leans back in her seat. She takes a sip of coffee then turns her head toward Julie. "Jules?" she asks. "Are you and Ian okay?"

"Okay?" Julie replies. "What's okay?"

"I don't mean all this stuff… the moving. I mean you. Are the two of you okay?"

Julie swallows, then says, "That obvious, huh?"

"Anyone would have to be an idiot not to notice the guarded way you two treat each other now. I'd be less concerned if you were out and out bickering."

Julie's hands grip the steering wheel tighter.

"Do you want to talk about it?" Jessie asks.

Julie shakes her head.

"Well, when you do," Jessie reaches over and squeezes her shoulder, "you know that I'm only a phone call away."

Not trusting her own voice, Julie nods. After a few moments of silence she turns on the Sirius radio. She keeps her eyes on the road while a panel of CNN voices dissect Barack Obama's Democratic Nomination Victory speech.

An hour and a half later the Jeep follows at a distance while the moving van crawls down the switch-back road leading to the ranch. Near the viewpoint where Ian and Julie had stopped with the realtor, Jessie rolls down the passenger window to peer down into the green valley. "God, what a view," she exclaims.

"Yeah. It's really something isn't it?"

Suddenly a vehicle takes the corner ahead a little too fast and fish-tails on the gravel. The pickup truck rights itself and continues up the road toward them. Julie recognizes the dusty old truck as the one that was parked behind the tenant's cabin. A dog's large grey head hangs out of the passenger window, his tongue flapping in the wind. Julie keeps her eye on the driver's side of the cab as the truck approaches. It passes by, spewing dust in its wake, but not before she catches a glimpse of a shadowed figure wearing a cowboy hat—and the slight raising of the hand on the steering wheel in the universal country-road greeting.

"Who was that?" Jessie asks.

"Oh that's the tenant we inherited with the ranch. I've never met him. According to the owner, the old guy doesn't have much use for women."

"Is he staying?"

"Looks that way. Ian's decided that he'll be a great help around the place."

"So, Ian really intends to become a rancher?".

"Gentleman rancher is more like it. And I don't really know how far even that will go. He's already thinking of selling off the cattle in the fall. Doesn't want to winter feed them. Everyone tells him though, that if he gives up the cows for too long he'll lose the range permits. Who knows? This is a learn-as-you-go project for him."

"What is it for you?"

Julie considers the question. After a moment she shakes her head, and says quietly, "I don't know."

As large as their home in town was, the ranch house swallows up their furniture, leaving the oversized rooms wanting more. Once the movers leave, Ian and Barry spend the rest of the day setting up Ian's office and going over the solar system and back-up generator. Julie and Jessie unpack the linen boxes and make up the beds in the master bedroom and guest room. Leaving her sister to tackle the kitchen dishes, Julie starts on the boxes left in the foyer, which everyone else has skirted around all day. One by one she carries them upstairs and carefully stacks the boxes of Darla's treasures, her doll collection, her favourite clothes, unopened, in the spare bedroom. Ian can insist on 'letting go,' making a clean break from the past all he likes, but there are some things she can't leave behind.

After the sun goes down everyone sits exhausted in the midst of the remaining boxes in the dining room, their picnic dinner haphazardly spread out on the table before them.

Jessie and Barry carry the conversation, filling in the awkward silent spaces with the comfortable chatter of a happily married couple.

Ian reaches over and refills Julie's wineglass. He raises his own in a toast, "To our new home," he says. "Here, here," Jessie and Barry join in, clicking their glasses against his, then Julie's. She takes a long sip of the soothing red liquid, watching the implausible candlelit scene play out in the floor to ceiling windows in the living room. Beyond their reflections, the darkness outside is complete until suddenly the rising moon casts its long reflection across the lake. She leans back and watches the stark display while the alcohol's lulling effect allows the whispers to seep into her unguarded mind. *What have I done? How did I allow it to go this far?*

She squeezes her eyes shut, refusing to allow the doubts to take hold. *One year. One year,* she repeats the silent mantra. *One year.* She has committed to one year. She can do anything for a year, can't she? Then she will see.

In the morning, her head pounds with an after-wine ache as she hugs Jessie goodbye. She wants to tell her to come back up when the girls are out of school for the summer. She wants to say that she misses her nieces, and ask her to bring them for a visit soon. But she finds no voice for the words.

After she and Ian wave them off, when their tail lights disappear around the corner, he asks, "Would you like to go for a walk? See if the land looks any different now that we own it."

She turns and forces a smile to her lips. "Yes, that would be nice." It will be good to do something physical together. Ian is right, let this be a fresh start. One day at a time. She changes into her hiking boots in the mudroom then goes outside and joins him on the back porch. Closing the door behind her, she asks Ian for the key.

"Don't bother," he says offhandedly. "You don't have to lock out anyone here."

Julie's hand freezes on the doorknob. Her heart thudding in her chest, she turns to meet his eyes. She can see that his remark was not malicious, that it was just a thoughtless slip, and meant nothing, yet even Ian recoils at his careless statement. The words in themselves are harmless, but the underlying significance is pitiless enough to wrench apart her fragile heart.

6

The Chilcotin summer wears on as Chilcotin summers do, without the promise of freedom from overnight frosts, or relief from a scorching noonday sun. Throughout the Cariboo, suppression crews and water bombers fight raging wildfires. The constant winds keep the valley free of smoke for the most part, but whenever they let up, an acrid burnt smell hangs heavy in the air. On many days the sun is nothing more than a large red ball behind a yellow-grey haze. Julie keeps a nervous eye on the western ridge, half expecting a wall of flame to appear at any moment and race down into the valley. Ian assures her that it isn't likely since there is nothing on the plateau above the ranch to feed the fires except miles of sparse grassland and volcanic rock.

In the valley, meadow grass grows knee high, waist high, shoulder high. The haying crew shows up during the last week of July, parking their trucks and vans over at the tenant's cabin. Julie steers clear of the fields and meadows while they work.

The crew, mostly local Natives, are anxious to leave, according to Ian. There is far greater money to be made fighting forest fires. "They're only here thanks to Virgil," he informs her. In an effort to be done quickly they work every day, from first light until darkness, which, although the days are already growing shorter, is still well after nine at night. To Julie's surprise Ian works in the fields with them. She isn't certain whether he is a help or a hindrance out there, but he returns home each evening—smelling of freshly cut meadow grass and sweat—with a satisfied look on his dust-streaked face.

The haying is finished in record time and the crew pulls out in the middle of August. One morning not long after they leave, Julie finds herself kneeling in the potato patch outside of Ian's office. Keeping a garden is a first for her. If only her mother could see her now. She would either be horrified or impressed.

While Julie works, the morning mist rises like steam from the lake's rippling surface. The only sound is the water lapping against the stones near shore and the drone of mosquitoes and black flies. The sky is clear and the smell of smoke no longer fills the air, so that the insistent insects are back in full force. Julie alternates between waving them away and attacking the weeds with her hand trowel. As the morning wears on, the sun's rays warm her back and the mosquitoes dissipate in the heat. Rooting around in the freshly turned earth beneath a drooping plant, Julie retrieves a handful of nugget-sized potatoes. She rubs them between her gloved hands then drops them into the basket at her side. Her bounty smells of warm soil and the promise of a hot summer afternoon.

This is the love part of the love-hate relationship she has developed with this inherited garden. The hate part is the commitment to someone else's project. So in retaliation, all summer she has weeded and hoed Elke Woell's forsaken garden on her own terms, which is giving it as little time as necessary. And it shows. Today, guilt has forced Julie to pay attention to the neglected plants. Still, a part of her resents it. Now that she's free to, now that the sky is clear of smoke and the crews are gone, she would rather be hiking, following the serpentine creek that winds through the empty meadows or exploring the forests. She has to admit though, that the garden serves the same purpose. It forces her outdoors in spite of herself. It would be too easy to hide inside the house, too easy to get lost in it. It certainly is large enough. Large enough that she and Ian can keep their distance.

She glances over her shoulder at the French doors. Inside Ian's office, the top of his silver head is bent over the computer screen; files are piled high on either side of his desk. For a man who was so anxious to 'go back to the land' he spends very little time enjoying it.

When they first moved out here, he often joined her on her daily hikes. Before long he started begging off, claiming he was snowed under with paperwork. After a while he stopped altogether. Now, the furthest he ventures from the house is over to the tenant's cabin to collect the rent and have a cup of coffee. Coffee, which she notices, takes him a while to drink. After the first month, Ian had decided not to charge Virgil Blue rent, given all the work he did around the ranch. His offer was refused. The tenant insisted that, as with the previous owners, he would continue to pay the two hundred dollars a month rent as well as helping around the ranch. In return he expects unrestricted use of the ranch draft horses to log his woodlot. It's a fair exchange, according to him. More than fair, according to Ian. All this negotiation, Julie has learned second-hand from the scrawled notes she sometimes finds tacked to their back door. Here it is almost mid-August and she has yet to meet their elusive tenant. The only proof of his existence has been his shadowed outline behind the wheel of his pickup, and the distant figure she saw guiding the massive team of Clydesdales through the chest-high meadow grass during the haying season.

The hired crew had worked with the machinery, the mowers and rakes, which had come with the ranch. But just as Elke Woell said, it appears Virgil trusts no one with the horses, not even their rightful owner. Ian's only too happy to keep things this way. Haying for him has been a novelty, a diversion from accounting. Now that it's done, Julie worries that he'll go back to sitting in his office getting lost in his numbers. She fears that the only physical exercise he'll have now is walking as far as the old cabin.

She attacks the roots of another plant, wondered what her husband and their tenant can possibly find in common to talk about. Whatever it is, every time Ian returns from the cabin his step seems lighter, as if a burden has been shed on the short journey. Perhaps it's just that the old guy is so completely removed from their former life. It must be a relief to spend time with someone who knows nothing of their past, their circumstances, and who expects nothing except to share a cup of coffee.

Maybe she'll invite him over for dinner one night. She smiles at the thought of trying to win over the old curmudgeon. There are signs, after all, that Virgil Blue is aware of her existence. The first week he sent two hand-carved walking sticks home with Ian. Later, after her excursions became solo, she discovered a pocket book, *Identifying Animal Tracks of British Columbia*, out on the back porch railing one morning. Not long after there was an information pamphlet on how to react to wild animal encounters.

Last month, when Ian came back from collecting the rent he told her, "Virgil thinks you need a dog."

"Oh, he does, does he?" she had replied bemused. "I think I'll pass on that."

Then, last week, Ian had returned from one of his bi-weekly trips into Waverley Creek and handed her a black leather case. "What's this?" she'd asked. Ian was not one for unannounced gifts.

"Bear spray," he said. "Obviously Virgil is trying to tell you some-thing."

"I've never seen any bears," she said, sliding the can out of the case and inspecting it.

"Yeah, well I guess Virgil thinks that they see you."

Now, during her hikes, Julie feels the eyes of the forest following her, and sometimes wonders if those eyes belong to their tenant.

Secretly, she can't imagine having the presence of mind to remove the can from the leather case, pull out the little red tag and point the nozzle the right way, if a bear were to actually get close enough to her to spray. Yet to reassure Ian, and perhaps Virgil, she tries to remember to strap the bear spray to her waist whenever she goes hiking.

"Quite a bossy old fellow," she mutters. Yet here she is on her knees digging in the dirt all because of the advice of a complete stranger. The day after the hay was all in, she had found one of his yellow notes on the porch railing. She hadn't needed Ian to decipher the scrawled message advising the harvesting of some of the potatoes now, while they were small and sweet tasting.

She tosses another handful of the baby spuds into her basket just as a shadow falls across it.

"Look at this, Ian," she says raking her hand over the potatoes in the overflowing basket.

"This is only from a couple of plants. I can't imagine why anyone would keep such a huge garden for just two people."

When there is no response, she looks up, shielding her eyes from the sun's glare. Instead of her husband standing above her, Julie finds herself squinting into the shadowed form of a stranger.

"Oh," she says pushing herself up, "you must be Virgil."

The broad-shouldered man standing before her is not nearly as tall as Ian, but he still towers over her. He removes his dust-covered black cowboy hat, revealing the grey sheen of close-cropped hair in sharp contrast with his dark scalp. A wide-set face, neither smiling nor unsmiling, looks back at her with a neutral expression that she cannot interpret.

He's not as old as she had imagined, perhaps only a few years older than Ian. It's hard to tell. The crinkled crow's feet around his dark eyes, the high cheekbones, the clean-shaven copper-hued skin, smooth except for a faint trace of ancient pockmarks, make for an ageless, surprisingly handsome, face. She has seen this face before; it is not a face you would forget, although she cannot remember where. Julie reaches out to take the hand being offered, but hers stops mid-air as her gaze travels from his expressionless eyes down to the red bandanna knotted at his throat—and to the carved pendant hanging below. The moment passes in frozen silence, in heartbeats that stretch time like taut elastic, which snaps as the French doors behind her swing open.

"Hey, Virgil," Ian calls out. "It's about time you met Julie."

Julie's arm drops to her side, the hand trowel falls to the ground with a soft thud. "I'm sorry," she says, her voice coming out a choked whisper. Willing herself to lift her leaded feet, she turns and walks out of the garden, each step a weighted trudge.

Ian reaches out to her as she comes up the steps. "Julie, what…"

She shakes her head and pushes past him and hurries across the wraparound porch toward the back of the house. At the corner, she glances back to see Ian rush down to where their tenant remains standing, his hat in his hands, in the garden row. Without a word, Virgil reaches into his pocket, pulls out a roll of bills, and hands his rent money to Ian.

In the mudroom, Julie closes the door behind her and with shaking hands pulls off her garden gloves and tosses them on top of the washing machine. Dirt skitters across the smooth white metal and falls to the floor. She shakes off her rubber clogs and kicks them into the corner. The back door opens.

"Jesus, Julie, what the hell was that?" Ian demands.

She whirls around to face him. She does not want to have this conversation, but there is no avoiding it, no way not to break their unspoken truce. For the last nine months they have both become adept at the careful manoeuvring around the minefields of words. They have fallen into a polite routine in dealing with each other, any conversations between the two of them now about the housekeeping of life, about the day-to-day details of existence while skirting the edges of the reality. Well, reality has just exploded in her face and she can't hold back.

"The pendant. Didn't you notice his pendant?" The words sound so much harsher, more accusatory than she intends.

Ian shuts the mudroom door with a soft click as if suddenly aware of how loud their voices are, as if the subject of their first verbal conflict since moving here might hear them.

"Pendant? What pendant?" His expression changes from anger to confusion. "What are you talking about, Julie?"

"The crow! It's exactly like the one..." she stops mid-sentence as the truth strikes her. Of course the pendant would mean nothing to Ian. He had no idea that Levi Johnny used to wear an identical carved crow—his spirit guide—around his neck.

Ian hadn't seen him take it off that night and place it around Darla's neck for good luck. Ian couldn't have, because he wasn't there the night Levi Johnny killed their daughter.

7

Every single day, whenever Julie allows her thoughts to stray there, whenever she lets down her guard and imagines a different conclusion to that October night, she spirals into the futile never-ever-land of what-might-have-been.

Standing behind the locked bathroom door she splashes cold water on her face in a futile effort to tide the flood of memories. She hears the back door close as Ian leaves the house—most likely going over to Virgil's cabin. To apologize? To ask him to leave? She doesn't know. What she does know is that she could not share the real reason for her strong reaction to their tenant. So she had told him she was simply startled by Virgil's crow pendant, a pendant similar to one that Levi Johnny wore. It would be too cruel to tell him that Darla was wearing it the last time she saw her alive.

"Couldn't he just go?" she had asked Ian.

"Why? Are you going to blame everyone who reminds you of Levi Johnny?" Ian's eyes narrow into a V. "Is it because he's Native?"

No. No of course not. She couldn't blame an entire race, any more than she could blame every teenage boy, every hockey player. And yet, Ian's accusation rang true. Because yes, she wants, *needs*, someone, something to blame, otherwise she is condemned to spend the rest of her life reliving every detail, all the mistakes, the little missteps and wrong choices that were made that night, including Ian's. And hers.

Would her world, her family, still be intact if she hadn't rummaged through her purse to answer her cell phone while she was driving to the opening performance of *Grease*, Darla's high-school play that evening?

Already anxious because Ian was late on their daughter's big night, she had looked down at her cell phone's call display expecting it to be him, but saw only the 'undisclosed number' message. Letting the car slow to a crawl she had flipped open the phone and held it to her ear. Nothing but static. She was about to close it when she heard an angry male voice demand: "Do you know where your husband is?" She braked with a jerk, pulled to the highway shoulder and stared down at the illuminated face. *Call ended.* The sound of her windshield wipers filled the silence.

"Some kook," she said out loud, then pressed the speed dial for Ian's office. After one ring a recorded message announced office hours. She tried his cell phone and got the same response. That meant nothing, she told herself as she pulled back onto the rain-soaked highway. Like herself, Ian might be on his way to the school right now. He refused to answer his cell phone while driving. Probably delayed by an anxious client, she reasoned, even as the hot stone of suspicion thudded into her stomach.

Inside the school she stood on the top landing of the amphitheatre cradling the cellophane-wrapped yellow rose she had brought for Darla. The building was new, a modern open institution. Still, as she scanned the audience below, Julie imagined she could detect the universal high-school odour of metallic lockers, sweaty gym shoes and chalk dust. Seeing no sign of Ian's salt-and-pepper hair, she headed down the centre aisle toward two empty seats at the end of the second row. She took the aisle seat, placed her coat on the other to indicate it was saved, and smiled 'hello' at the couple sitting next to it. She didn't know their names but the faces were familiar. Being a realtor in a town of less than ten thousand meant most were. While she waited for the play to begin she glanced around, exchanging greetings with waves and smiles. This was one of the many things she loved about living in a small town; no matter where you went you saw friendly faces.

By the time the lights dimmed Ian was still a no-show. Feeling the guilt of hoarding a seat while others stood on the top landing, she removed her coat and arranged it on her lap with her purse and Darla's rose while the first off-key notes of the school orchestra pierced the darkness.

During the opening scenes she had to restrain herself from turning around every few minutes to survey the audience for Ian, but the moment the Rizzo character, the ringleader of the Pink Ladies of Rydell High, appeared on stage Julie's attention was riveted. If she hadn't heard Darla and her best friend, Kajul Sandhu, rehearsing their roles in the family room week after week, she might not have recognized her daughter.

For the last few months Darla had let her hair grow for the part. Now it was pulled back and tied up with a pink chiffon scarf. The satin 'Pink Ladies' jockey jacket, rolled-up blue jeans, saddle oxfords and bobbie-socks, along with the heavy greasepaint make-up and exaggerated gum chewing, made the transformation to the '50s wannabe-tough girl startling. When her daughter sang "Look at Me, I'm Sandra Dee," displaying a talent that surprised Julie, she had to blink back tears of motherly pride. As the room darkened at the end of the scene and the audience exploded in applause, Julie was filled with a sadness that Ian was not there to share this with her. *Damn him*, she thought as intermission arrived and he did not, *Darla will be so disappointed.*

She remained seated while others around her rose to file out for the break. The young man sitting in the seat in front of her stood up slowly. Things hadn't changed much from the '50s, Julie thought, noting the familiar red-and-white lettered school jacket. As the boy turned to join the line-up in the aisle, Julie recognized the thick black hair worn just a little too long and the handsome young profile already set in the serious countenance of a First Nations Elder.

"Hello, Levi," Julie said, surprised to see it was her daughter's friend. But then why should she be, he was the one who had picked up Darla and Kajul earlier to drive them to the school to get ready for the play. Before they went out the door she had watched him transfer the carved crow pendant from around his neck to Darla's for 'luck.'

Now he turned to Julie, his dark depthless eyes meeting hers, and he smiled. The change never failed to amaze her. The solemn mask was replaced momentarily with a flashing white-toothed smile punctuated by cavernous dimples. As quickly as the expression appeared it was gone, the muscles of his square jaw returning his face to the chiselled lines of seriousness.

"Hey, Mrs O.D." His voice was barely audible under the din of surrounding chatter. "That play's pretty good, eh?"

"It certainly is," she said, then asked, "So when is your next game?"

"Saturday, up in Prince George."

"Well, good luck."

"Thanks."

Watching him retreat up the aisle Julie smiled. That was probably the longest conversation she'd ever had with Levi Johnny. Still, she liked this shy young man and was glad to see that he had stayed to watch Darla's play. Levi had been part of her circle of friends ever since he moved into the high-school dorms years ago. His mother lived out on the NaNeetza Valley Reserve; the boy stayed in town for the school year. Hockey practice and games took up most of his free time. According to local rumours, and to Darla's proud declarations, he was NHL material and being scouted by a number of universities. From the beginning Julie's instincts told her that Levi was a good boy. She believed that he was the settling influence during Darla's attempted rebellion, which she had thought was over—until early this month.

Seeing Levi reminded Julie how deeply disappointed she still was with her daughter's shocking deception. The boy had unknowingly played a part in it. And perhaps she had herself when she so blindly accepted Darla's plans that Friday evening. It never occurred to Julie to question her daughter when she said that she was meeting her best friend, Kajul, at the arena to watch Levi's hockey game and so would be home late. In fact Julie had driven her downtown and dropped her off in front of the arena doors. Only later, when she thought back, would she recognize that the parking lot of the sportsplex was not nearly full enough for a hometown game. She and Ian learned the truth watching the late-night news. The visiting team, *Levi's team*, had defeated Cranbrook on their home ice that evening six to one, Levi scoring a hat trick. A hurried phone call to Kajul's home made it worse. Darla wasn't there. Kajul had not been out all night. Frantic, Julie and Ian drove around for hours checking every possible spot that teenagers were known to haunt. It was Ian who decided to drive down to the 'Hollow.'

The sandy patch of beach along the Fraser River was a local hang-out, difficult to drive to, and far enough away from town for privacy. But it was dangerous. A few years ago two teenage boys, emboldened by alcohol, had played chicken, wading deeper and deeper into the swirling river in the darkness. They were both swept away by the treacherous current, their bodies not found until the following day.

"Darla would never go there," Julie had reasoned as they bumped down the steep narrow road leading to the river valley. "She knows it's out of bounds. She promised… she promised." She wasn't sure if she was trying to convince Ian or herself.

"She's a teenager," Ian said, braking on a sharp turn. "But let's hope you're right!"

She wasn't. As they came to a skidding stop, their headlights illuminated the group of teenagers milling around a huge bonfire, scrambling to hide beer cans. She immediately located Darla's shocked face in the crowd.

All the way home a hysterical Darla swore it was the first time she had ever gone there. She had just wanted to see what the big deal was. She'd only had a few sips of beer. She would never be invited anywhere ever again after her parents had barged in and broken it up. "How could you do that to me?" she had wailed. They grounded her for a month.

Despite her whining protests, the punishment stood. Except for school, play rehearsals and performances, she was confined to the house for one full month. She had a week to go.

While the audience filed back in, Julie turned once again to check the landing to see if Ian had come in during intermission. Beyond disappointed, she was closing in on furious to see no sign of him. Two aisles over she spotted Kajul's parents, reclaiming their seats. Acknowledging Mrs Sandhu's wave, Julie couldn't help noticing the bouquet of flowers that overwhelmed the woman's lap. Their daughter Kajul, whose name always sounded like 'Casual' to Julie, was anything but. The dark-haired, doe-eyed teenager, playing the part of Frenchy tonight, had taken on the role of the beauty-school-aspiring, high-school drop-out, as if the character was written especially for her. The proud bouquet suited her.

Julie glanced down at her own small offering and smiled inwardly. It too was just right. The single rose marked a special occasion in their family. Ian had brought one to the hospital the day Darla was born. Every year, along with the yellow candles, Julie placed a single yellow rose—Darla's favourite colour—on her birthday cake.

At the end of the performance, after the final curtain call, the cast formed a reception line in front of the stage. Darla gushed over her flower, accepting it with a formal curtsy, and then throwing herself into her mother's arms and jumping up and down as if she were ten years old again. "Wasn't it wicked, Mom? Did you like it?"

"Like it, my God, I loved it," Julie shouted to be heard above the din. She stepped back and held her daughter by the shoulders to look into her eyes. She knew her own were filling up but didn't care. "You were so good... so... so wonderful... I'm so proud of you."

"Thanks, Mom."

"I'm sorry your dad didn't make it, he must…"

"It's okay," Darla said offhandedly, her gaze straying beyond Julie's shoulder. "I knew he couldn't make it tonight. He called before you got home. I thought you knew."

"Oh."

"He's coming tomorrow night," Darla said, reaching past Julie to grab a white leather sleeve, and pulling Levi between them. She stood on her tiptoes and whispered something into his ear, and he nodded a silent reply.

"Mom," she said, turning back to her, "there's a cast party after we're cleaned up here."

Julie raised her eyebrow; she didn't want to have to say it out loud. Darla knew she was still grounded.

"Pleeease, Mom. Just this once. Please, please. The whole cast is going."

Julie hesitated. "Where is it?"

"At Wade Morrey's, the guy who played Danny. He lives up on Cottonwood Drive," Darla's eyes pleaded. "Kajul's going. Honestly! Her parents are letting her. You can ask them. They're right there."

Julie glanced over at Kajul, standing between her parents, beaming behind her wild bouquet.

"Levi will drive us," Darla said. "Say it's okay. Pretty please, Mom."

Julie was aware that she was being played. Still, she had to trust Darla again sometime. She checked her watch. It was just past nine thirty. Not that late. The entire cast was going. How could she say no? She had hoped to share this excitement, this moment, with Darla and Ian. She had envisioned the three of them cuddled in front of the TV with a bowl of popcorn and a blanket while Darla rehashed every nuance of the evening.

"Come on, Mom, it's only ten minutes from our place. We'll be home by midnight." Darla tugged on Levi's arm. "Won't we?"

"Yeah," he said. "I've got a hockey practice tomorrow morning."

Looking from her daughter's hopeful face to Levi's, Julie shook her head, half in exasperation, and half in surrender. "All right then," she said, holding his gaze, "but promise me you'll see her home safely by midnight. I'm counting on you."

"Yes!" Darla gave her a quick hug. Then as if afraid she'd change her mind she turned away pulling Levi with her.

As he allowed himself to be tugged away, he glanced back over his shoulder. "Don't worry Mrs O.D.," he said, "I promise I'll bring her home before midnight."

Watching them disappear in the crowd she wondered if Ian would have caved in so easily. Probably not. It might be difficult to explain to him why she had let Darla off the hook, before her grounding period was up. But Ian wasn't here, so whose fault was that?

Outside the school doors, Julie pulled up the collar of her coat and wrapped it tighter. The cold night air smelled crisp and clean. The rain had stopped, and she looked up at the full moon in a star-filled sky as she made her way to the car. The temperature had dropped in the last few hours leaving a crystalline sparkle on the asphalt parking lot. She hoped that this weather would not last until Wednesday like it had last Halloween when all the trick-or-treaters showed up at her door shivering in the frigid wind.

Pulling out of the school parking lot she turned right, instead of left to the highway and the shorter route home. She would just spin by Ian's office; see if he was finished, she told herself. Maybe they would have a nightcap together. Downtown she slowed the car in front of his office, a renovated two-storey Heritage home on the corner of Pinewood Street. The windows were dark.

Was this why I gave into Darla's request so easily, she wondered, because of some anonymous voice on the telephone? Was that all it took to turn her into a madwoman who chases around town late at night checking up on her husband?

She turned into the alley. Two vehicles were parked in the empty lot behind the office—Ian's Jeep and a silver Lincoln Towncar. Pulling up beside the Lincoln she switched off her motor. She stared at the familiar vehicle, could almost smell Valerie Ladner's heavy-handed Tabu perfume. In all the years she had worked with Valerie at Black's Real Estate, they were never close friends. But they were cordial business associates. Just that afternoon, as she rushed out of the office, Valerie had given her a message to pass on to Darla to 'break a leg' tonight. Julie knew that she was going through a difficult divorce and Ian was her accountant, but at this time of night?

Staring up at the unlit office Julie struggled with the burning sensation rising in her throat, then threw her car door open and climbed out. She had a key to the office. Slamming the door behind her she strode over and stomped up the back steps. But as she approached the landing she slowed down. What was she thinking? Exactly what was she going to do? Burst in and throw all the lights on, hoping to discover… what?

She stopped, spun around and fled back to the car. Inside, feeling like a fool she resisted the urge to bang her forehead against the steering wheel. She shoved the key in the ignition. Then, not caring that the motor screeched, she gunned it and sped out of the parking lot.

On the ten-minute drive home she practised deep breathing, while she talked to herself. *Drive slowly. Don't jump to conclusions. There are multitudes of explanations for this.* She just had to take the time to figure it out. He had phoned, hadn't he? She hadn't had the chance to ask Darla the details of their conversation. Perhaps he and Valerie had worked late and then walked to a nearby restaurant for dinner. That made sense. Realtors' accounting can be complicated, even more so during a marriage break-up. *There's probably a message on the phone at home explaining everything.* But there wasn't.

By the time Julie was ready for bed at 11:30 there still was no call, and no Ian. Fighting her growing anger she locked all the doors. Darla had her own front door key, and Ian had an automatic garage door opener. If he doesn't have his key to the inside garage door, that's his problem.

Upstairs, brushing her teeth in the ensuite bathroom, she spotted a bottle of Ian's sleeping pills next to his sink. Unlike Ian, Julie had never felt the need for them, but tonight she was so keyed up. This weekend was going to be busy, with two open houses and a buyer transferring to town. Her day would start early tomorrow and she needed sleep. She picked up the bottle. One should do the trick. Ian always took two, but he was used to them. She shook out one of the tiny pills and placed it under her tongue, letting it dissolve as she climbed into bed. Darla would be home in less than half an hour. Even if the sedative kicked in before that, Julie had always been able to sleep with one ear listening for her daughter.

Opening the nightstand drawer she retrieved the eye mask her sister had given her. She rarely used it, thought of it more as a joke, but when she wanted to give Ian a message not to disturb her she donned the black silk mask. She did so now, securing the elastic strap behind her ears and blocking out any light. She didn't want to face him tonight; didn't want to think about any of this. She liked her life exactly the way it was and a part of her suspected that beneath her anger was a growing panic that things were about to change. To divert her mind while she waited for Darla, she laid in the false darkness and reviewed her pending sales, mentally opening each file, checking the subjects, closing dates.

She drifted off into a dreamless sleep, while out on the highway, her happily-ever-after world was about to shatter with the unheard metallic scream of steel against concrete lamppost.

Less than two hours later she had clawed her way up from oblivion to Ian's hands digging into her shoulders, shaking her like a rag doll— the scent of Tabu perfume filling her nostrils.

8

Dad saw me. I wish he hadn't, although there wasn't a whole lot I could do about it. I watched his car come up the highway, then pull over on the side of the road. Who wouldn't stop to see if they could help at the scene of an accident so close to home? Certainly not Dad. But he got more than he bargained for, an image that will stick in his mind forever. The police had arrived only a few minutes before. He would have heard their sirens on his way home.

The blue and red flashing lights illuminated his face as he climbed out of his car. He took a few tentative steps, froze, and then bolted past the vehicle wrapped around the lamppost on the side of the highway. He pushed his way between the officers and dropped onto the ground beside Levi, who was hunched over, shoulders heaving as he held me in his arms. But how could that be? How could I be there, and here—wherever here was—watching?

Both Dad and I looked down at the same motionless face. In the same breath of time, we took in the smudged greasepaint that the cold cream had missed at the temples, the diamond-shaped glass shards imbedded in the bloodied forehead, and in the limp hand lying on the ground, crushed yellow rose petals spilling out of the open palm. In the same instant we both knew. Dad shoved Levi aside and pulled me into his arms. I could hear him moaning my name over and over again, but I heard it from another place.

For Dad the pain was so unbearable that a part of him shut down right then. To protect himself, I guess. Probably a good thing because what he really wanted to do was smash somebody's face in, and the closest living person to him was Levi, and a couple of police officers. I sure didn't want to see him hit Levi. And punching out a cop, not so good.

For me the realization was simply a surprise, like, Oh, okay. So this is how it happens. There was no pain. And no feeling of sadness, no fear. Just curiosity. Like, where am I, and how did I get here?

The last thing I remembered was Levi cursing, and then white light. Yeah, white light. Just like all those creepy movies.

In that absence-of-sound-and-colour place, I relived the past. To say my whole life flashed before me would be wrong, because it was like, just that evening, which seemed to play out in real time, starting with Levi driving us to the high school earlier to put on our make-up and costumes before the play. Wedged together on the front seat of his rusted old blue Chevy Malibu, Kajul and I had hammed up our characters. Levi, as always, concentrated on the road, ignoring our giggling and ad libbing.

Every now and then I would check out his profile from the corner of my eye. I was still certain that, with his dark handsome face, he would have made a better Danny than Wade Morrey. I had even tried to talk him into auditioning for it. There hadn't been any real hope behind my prodding, but hey, ya never know. Still, Levi acting? Pretending to be anything other than who he was? Not a chance. Anyway, hockey was more important, and I knew that. He was good, really good, at it.

Grease turned out to be totally sick. It made no difference how many times we had rehearsed the play, or even the final dress rehearsal, the real thing just blew me away. When I was up on that stage in front of an actual live audience, I suddenly realized that I could do this. I was good at it. Maybe I had found something that I could practise and learn to love as much as Levi loved his hockey. Hey, I even thought that maybe I would become an actress, a singer. Why not? Mom and Dad had always drilled into me that everything was possible, that I could do, become, anything if I wanted it badly enough.

At the party everyone was still on a natural high from the first performance, rehashing the mistakes, the improvising, and breaking into our favourite Grease songs every now and then. I still had on my Rizzo costume, *wanting to hang onto the character for as long as I could. With the yellow rose from Mom pinned behind my ear, I knew that I probably looked dorky, but I didn't care.*

Someone had brought beer. I popped one open and offered it to Levi, who looked from the can to me, his face remaining passive as he silently turned it down. I took a sip, just to look cool. It wasn't real drinking. Just a beer. I had Mom's permission to be here, so what she didn't know wouldn't hurt her. Right? How wrong that turned out to be.

Some of the guys from the play said, "Hey, Dude," to Levi as they passed, but no one hung with him except Kajul and me. I'm pretty certain it was for no other reason than they were in awe of him. He was something of a hero, a local celebrity in our town, after all. He could have been playing for one of the Canadian Junior teams already, but wanted to finish high school in Waverley Creek. He was that good. Although you would never know it from the way he acts. Anyone who doesn't know him might take it from his expressions that he's an angry guy, but nothing could be further from the truth. He's a little bit shy, yeah, but mostly, Levi never says much. Yet when he does speak it's usually worth hearing. My mother told me there is something to be said for a quiet man and repeated another of her old-school sayings that she was so fond of, but I had to admit this one fit, 'Still waters run deep.'

It is true though, that sometimes the way Levi looks at, or more likely beyond, someone, it would be easy to think he's judging them, but those of us who know him, know that isn't true. His mind is just on other things: school, his hockey, his mom out at NaNeetza Reserve. And lately, I believed, maybe even me. I have reason to think that because when we left the party before midnight—just as he promised Mom—he took Kajul to her house first, even though it meant he had to double back to my place. Before I climbed out of the car I pulled his pendant from where it hung beneath my blouse, lifted it over my head, and gave it back to him. He put it back on, and then without a word, he leaned over and placed his left hand on my cheek, tilted my face up, and kissed me, kissed me so lightly that my lips tingled. He leaned back and the dimples that I am so crazy about showed up for a brief moment.

Then he said, "You make my heart come glad."

Wow, Dude, I thought, that's just about the best thing a guy could ever say. But I didn't tell him. I kept silent, knowing that with him that was the best thing a girl could do. So I just smiled back at him as I jumped out of the car. He waited while I ran across our driveway to the front door. He always stayed until he saw that I was safely inside. By the time I reached the porch though, I remembered that I had left my backpack—with my house key and cell phone—backstage at the school. I looked under the rock beneath the juniper bush, but the extra key wasn't there. Waving back at Levi, I gave the doorbell a few quick jabs. Even after I hammered on the door, the house remained dark and silent. I shrugged and walked back to the car.

"I'm locked out," I said, leaning into his window. "Do you have a cell phone?"

Levi's expression said it all. Of course he didn't carry a cell phone. I knew that.

"My folks must either be asleep or still out," I said. "Could you take me back to the party? I can use the phone there."

It was almost midnight and Levi still had hockey practice in the morning, yet he didn't hesitate. We drove back up Cottonwood Drive. The party was still happening. More people had shown up, and more beer. The house was crowded. That's how it is in a small town. Word spreads. I wondered if it's the same in a big city. I thought that someday I would find out. Not too long from now, two more years of high school and I was off to UBC. Anything less would make both my parents freak.

I used Wade's phone and called home. Pressing my finger to my ear to block out the party noise, I left a message telling Mom to mark down the time because I deserved brownie points for keeping my promise to be home by midnight, but that I was locked out. "I guess you guys are out since you're not picking up," I added, and left Wade's number for them to call when they got home.

"Sorry, Levi," I said turning back to him in the hall. "Hey, I can get a ride home from someone else. You don't have to wait."

He said no, he would wait and drive me home, which of course was exactly what I wanted him to say. Then, just in case I got too smug, he leaned against the wall and added with a grin, "I promised your mom."

Someone shoved a can of beer into my hand. I passed it to Levi and went to find the washroom. When I returned he was still leaning against the wall watching the partiers who were getting louder and louder. He handed me the full can of beer and I took a few gulps, then teasingly shoved it back, daring him. This time he took it, lifted it to his lips and took a long swallow. When he passed back the can his dark eyes held mine as if to say, 'There, are you happy?'

Suddenly the laughing and singing, all the forced excitement around us, was nothing but noise. I grabbed Levi's arm. "Let's go," I said. "We can wait in the driveway. My parents can't be much longer. Or I could try the basement and patio doors."

Walking out to Levi's car, he raised an eyebrow but said nothing about the unfinished beer I brought with me. Outside the rain-slick street had tuned frosty in the frigid night air. Levi drove cautiously down Cottonwood Drive, and then picked up speed out on the highway. Just before we reached the turnoff to our street, the rose fell out of my hair. I unlocked my seatbelt to grab for it and the beer can slipped from my grasp, splashing foam across Levi's lap. He jerked back, hitting the brake. Suddenly the motion of the tires changed, becoming weightless, soundless, as if sliding across air. "Shit!" Levi swore. "Black ice!" Now this is where it starts to get fuzzy. As the world spun out of control, I lifted my head up to peer over the dashboard just as a lamp-post headed toward me at an odd angle. Then the white light, white noise, with no sense of time or space.

The next thing I knew Levi was carrying me away from his crumpled car, screaming at someone who was jumping out of their vehicle to call an ambulance. He laid me down on the side of the road and placed his jacket under my head. Kneeling over me, his hair and the crow pendant, hanging in my face, his tears falling onto my cheeks, he lifted me gently and held me in his arms. Crazily I was watching all this from above, and all I could think about was how upset my mom was going to be. I kept trying to tell Levi to let her know that I was okay, but my lips wouldn't move. And then my father was there, pushing Levi away from me. As Dad hugged me to his chest, the truth hit us both at the same moment. Just as an even crazier thought occurred to me—who will play Rizzo's part in the play tomorrow night?—two of the RCMP members grabbed Levi by the elbows. His arms were forced behind his back.. When the handcuffs clicked on and they led him to the patrol car, I knew he wasn't going to make his morning practice.

9

Out on the lake, sunlight shatters into a million tiny fragments across the wind-rippled surface. Julie stands at the kitchen sink rinsing the nugget potatoes and staring out of the widow. The undisturbed view, the absence of anything other than what Mother Nature placed there eons ago, is calming. Something she needs right now.

The cold water washes over her hands and swirls down the drain with the garden soil while she contemplates her reaction to Virgil Blue. Remorse over her outburst is already seeping into the sliver of space left for any feelings other than ungenerous grief. Was Ian right? Was her reaction so strong because Virgil, like Levi Johnny, was Native?

All her life, her life before the accident, Julie had believed that the term *bigot* applied to others, not to her. When she was a child, whenever she and Jessie misbehaved, her father would tease them, saying, "Guess we'll have to give you back to the Indians." Back then, her dad's playful threats had conjured up images of red men with painted faces, bows and arrows.

Growing up in an exclusive community in Vancouver and attending private schools, Julie's exposure to other cultures was from a distance, to say the least. It wasn't until she was an adult, and particularly since moving to Waverley Creek, that she realized that there was worse big-otry than her father's thoughtless words. Now she is as guilty of it as anyone she has ever judged, because in her heart she has to admit there was a dark seed of truth in Ian's accusation. It wasn't only the crow pendant that had thrown her for a loop. Still, her reaction is puz-zling even to herself. It's not as if she hasn't encountered other First Nations people since Darla's death. Unless she had never left her house when they still lived in town, she was bound to, even out here. Most of the haying crew this summer were from a local band. She'd simply avoided them. The truth was that Virgil's height and colouring, his facial features, aquiline nose and flared nostrils, were unlike any of the Chilcotin people she's ever encountered.

She suddenly recalls where she saw Virgil before. It was last sum-mer, when her world was still intact, outside of the Waverley Creek Hospital. Why had she gone there that day? A blood test? Visiting a friend? She can't remember. But she does remember the unusually large crowd of First Nations, Elders and young alike, milling around in front of the hospital doors. The parking lot was full, forcing Julie to find a spot out on the street. On her way back, the people gathered at the hospital entry neither noticed her, nor ignored her. They con-tinued smoking or talking quietly as she wove her way through. Near the main entry someone was helping an old woman climb out of the passenger seat of a van parked in a visitor's stall. The woman, tiny and bent, a weathered map of wrinkles defining her face, wore a pink cardigan, despite the warmth of the day, an ankle-length skirt and fluorescent green socks. Julie smiled in spite of herself. She'd always admired the brilliant shades of clothing, a quiet celebration of colour, which elderly First Nations women seem to favour.

As the woman moved slowly through the respectfully parting crowd, Julie couldn't help but notice the tall man helping her inside. At the time Julie had no idea who he was, but she remembers being struck by the handsome face and the coppery hued skin that made him stand out in the crowd. Only now does it occur to her that the man escorting the woman that day was Virgil Blue.

Later, inside the hospital, Julie had asked the woman at the reception desk what was going on outside.

The woman rolled her eyes. "Oh, one of their Elders up on the third floor is dying," she said with impatience. "Whenever one of them dies, the whole damn tribe shows up."

Taken aback by her words, Julie had replied, "How wonderful to have so many people who want to say goodbye."

She had turned and headed to the elevator, feeling the colour rise in her cheeks, and shame at her own initial reaction—that the gathering was some kind of protest. Even worse was the fact that she had avoided Levi Johnny's eyes in the crowd, that she had not said hello or acknowledged him as she passed by.

The sound of the door in the mudroom opening and closing breaks into her thoughts. She remains at the sink when Ian enters the kitchen.

"Virgil will leave," he says behind her.

Picking up the dishtowel from the counter she turns around. She studies her hands, drying them with measured movement as Ian walks over to her. He hands her a slip of paper. Recognizing another of Virgil's scrawled notes, Julie takes it. Ian backs away and sits down at the table while she reads the short message.

If it will help her heart to heal, I will go.

She takes a deep breath, lets it fill her lungs then slowly releases it, imagining it as a black poison escaping from her body, an exercise she had learned from some forgotten book on spirituality and personal growth, books left behind in another lifetime. "He doesn't have to leave," she says, quietly. "You need him around here."

"If you want him to go—"

"No. It's fine. Really. He should stay." She looks up. "I'm sorry, Ian. You're right, I behaved poorly. It's just that seeing him made me think of Levi Johnny, of Darla..."

The sudden shock of their daughter's name hangs in the air, the absoluteness of her death filling the silence. Ian's face hardens into an emotionless mask.

"Don't," he says in a tone she has learned to recognize as a warning.

She drops the note on the table. "How do you do it?" she asks.

Immediately regretting the sharp edge to her words, she touches his shoulder and adds quietly, "Sometimes I wish I could be like you. Just move on with life as if nothing has happened."

Ignoring her hand, Ian stands up. Without meeting her eyes he asks, "What choice do we have?" and heads to his office.

"Choice is an illusion," she says to his back.

10

Outside, Julie sits on the porch steps lacing up her hiking boots. She doesn't even know what she meant by her parting shot at Ian. Other than the helplessness of knowing that if she, if he, had made other choices the night Darla died... No. She can't go there. Just as Ian can't talk about their daughter, she can't let her mind dwell on the 'if only.'

Rising from the porch step she walks across the yard, intent on burning off some of her pent-up angst. At the corral the Clydesdales' giant heads hang over the top rung. They snort a greeting as she opens the gate into the field. The warm scent of horse manure and summer dry hay fills the air. Cutting across the empty pasture she heads toward the western slopes. Although she has yet to run into Virgil on her hikes, she doesn't want to chance it today.

Out on the lake a loon lifts its heavy white chest, unfolds its wings and lets out a warning yodel. Nearby, its mate, riding low in the water, veers away. Their adolescent offspring bobs along weightlessly behind. Up close the adult birds appear so much larger and heavier than they do through binoculars. Julie has spent hours watching them nest in the marshes all summer, felt a thrill when two downy chicks appeared hitchhiking on their mother's back. Now she sees only one. She stops on the edge of the field to scan the surrounding area, searching the reeds and lily pads in the shallows, but there is no sign of the other young bird. Sadly, she wonders what has happened to it. A predator, an eagle or the osprey that nests in the treetops? She'll never know. The loons glide out into deeper water, moving soundlessly across the surface unconcerned, their loss forgotten. Memory. A bitter-edged blessing.

Julie makes her way across a narrow spot in the creek and walks over to the far side of the field. Shimmying through the bottom two logs of the snake fence she heads toward the woods below the western ridge. The thick forest hugs her as she enters the dappled shadows. A carpet of weathered brown needles and moss covers the ground. The earthy aroma of fungus and dried pine needles fills the air. Not bothering to wave away the black flies and mosquitoes, she follows the winding animal path through the dense undergrowth. The first few times she hiked this way she had had to watch each step for the obstacle course of roots and rocks that could trip her up. Now she's familiar with the terrain. She no longer shivers when she brushes a cobweb from her face, or feels repelled by the strings of black moss hanging from branches like witches' hair.

From somewhere behind her comes a low groan. Startled, she stops short and turns around slowly. In the slanted light on either side of the empty path, every dark shape, every shadow takes on an ominous quality. But there is no sign of movement, only a maze of tree trunks, tangled brush and decomposing logs. Another creaking moan followed by an answering screech sounds from the other direction and she spins around again, her heart racing. A gust of wind rushes through the forest canopy above, followed by an even deeper groan. Julie glances up and discovers the source of the strange animal-like sounds. High above her, a group of trees lean against one another, their thick trunks at odd angles as if knitted together. Their intertwined branches supporting each other, they rub together moaning and creaking as they sway with the wind. Julie lets out a nervous laugh of relief.

She presses on, aware as she goes of other 'talking trees.' On every side of the trail, the evidence of ancient deadfalls, whose root systems had not held during a windstorm, litter the landscape. Lacking the support of nearby trunks and branches the fallen trees lie like rotting skeletons on the forest floor. Isolation equals vulnerability. Everyone needs support, even trees, she thinks wryly.

Yet she has spurned it. Who is there anyway? In the last year she has come to the realization that while she was in town her friends were either colleagues, business acquaintances, or clients. The circumstances of Darla's death have alienated them all, in one way or the other. Out here her isolation is complete. Except for Jessie, who is so far away, who is there to lean on?

Ian? Ian is more rootless than she is. He was an only child. His parents are gone. Julie is all he has left. She longs to be able to lean on him, to have him lean on her. He is the only one who can possibly understand the pain she feels, the pain that threatens to bring her to the ground. But the lines of communication between them—where Darla is concerned—are severed.

At first they had clung together, shell-shocked, their keening wails rising as if from a single voice. Then later, after the horror of discovering Darla's message on the phone, the questions, the searching for a 'why' had escalated into a string of ugly reproaches. There was no taking back the accusations made in the hysteria of finding out the unthinkable.

"She was grounded! What were you thinking letting her go to a party?"

"You weren't there! Where were you?"

"How could you have locked the bloody doors?"

"If you had been there... What was so damned vital that you missed her play?"

"Why didn't you answer the door, or the phone for God's sake?"

"Why weren't you home?"

They threw their tortuous barbs at each other, as if the frenzied screaming, the desperate search for reason, for fault, could reverse the outcome. And then silence. And then it was too late. The night after the funeral, the first time they found themselves alone, Julie listened in stunned silence to Ian's business-like confession. He would tell her once, he said, would not discuss it ever again. The night of Darla's play, after working on Valerie Ladner's taxes, he had explained, he went with her to the restaurant down the block for a late dinner. They both drank far too much wine, had stayed even later for coffee. In his pragmatic manner, he admitted that after walking back to their cars, in a moment's indiscretion, they had shared a kiss. It went no further, he swore. He wouldn't lie and say he wasn't tempted, if the time had been right... if...

"I have no excuse," he offered, without meeting her eyes. "But I want you to know it was nothing more than a moment of weakness. I swear that nothing like this has ever happened before in our entire marriage. I give you my word it never will again. I'm sorry." He did not ask for her forgiveness, yet Julie felt his need for it.

"It doesn't matter," was all she could give him. She left him sitting alone in the darkened living room while she went up to the guest bedroom. She didn't want to know the details. His transgression meant nothing, neither did his mea culpa. The worst that could happen had happened. Nothing else mattered.

They no longer reach for each other in the night. Sleeping alone is the new norm. After moving out to the ranch they had each staked out their territories in the house, coming together only to share forced and halting conversations with their meals.

Ian has chosen to bear his sorrow alone and in silence, shutting out any discussion about the very thing that binds them together. Julie feels helpless, there is nothing she can do for him. The best she can do, the only thing she can do, is to stay with him until he no longer needs her. He's Darla's father, after all. But she has given up trying to speak to him about her. And so she goes on replaying the last day of their daughter's life over and over again, unable to forgive Levi, or Ian, and most of all herself.

11

Here's the thing, Mom, until you do I have to hang around here.

I wish I could tell her that, but I can't. At least that's what Mr Emerson says. He's the one who met me here.

Mr Emerson used to be my English teacher. Behind his back we always called him Waldo. No one really knew his first name, but he would spout Ralph Waldo Emerson lines like, 'I hate quotations. Tell me what you know.' That one always made us groan because he was forever quoting philosophers and writers.

He looks just the same to me as he did then, with his black-rimmed glasses, thick hair and goofy smile, just like the character from the Where's Waldo books. I think he was on to us calling him that, because in winter he often came to school wearing a silly white knitted toque with a huge red pom-pom.

Maybe because he was one of the few teachers who didn't take himself so seriously, I really liked him. Everyone did. Then last year, he died. Just like that, he was gone. Something burst inside his brain; he went to bed one night and never woke up. All my friends went to his funeral, for most of us it was our first real up-close encounter with death. I was devastated and felt guilty about calling him Waldo behind his back. I wouldn't have felt nearly so sad if I had known then what I know now.

Anyway, he said he was here to meet me because he was someone I knew *in life who had passed on before me. I wondered why not my grandfather, but then he died when I was so young that I never really knew him. Maybe I would have recognized him from Gram's photographs. Still, meeting him might have been a little scarier than meeting Mr Emerson, so it makes sense. I could always talk to him. Although I wouldn't call how he and I communicate here talking. It's just a sort of knowing. An understanding of the meaning without speaking out loud. Mr Emerson says I only see him the way I do because it's how I knew him on earth and that when I understand more I won't need to see his earthly form to recognize his presence.*

When he died it was his dead wife who met him, so it was real easy for him. Although there were people still on earth who loved him, they hadn't held him back because in their hearts they believed he was with her. They were right. But for me, until everyone I love lets me go, I can't move on through the white light, to whatever is next.

In the meantime, I get to watch. That's all I get to do. I found that out right away. At my funeral service.

Being there, and not being there, was pretty strange and cool at the same time. The whole school turned up, even kids I didn't know. Probably some just grabbed the opportunity to skip classes. Who knows? My real friends, especially Kajul and Levi, clung to each other, shaking as they walked in to take their seats. No one really wanted to be there. I knew that.

My mother insisted on the casket being closed. It was covered in white lilies and of course yellow roses. I think if she knew the truth, if she really needed to blame something, she could have blamed the yellow rose she gave me, the rose that I undid my seatbelt for. Probably a good thing she didn't. She would never be able to look at one again.

I hoped that they would bury me in my Grease costume. How cool would that have been? But Mom let Aunt Jessie go into my room to pick out my outfit. She chose a dress that looked brand new, that was because I always hated it, so had never worn it when I was alive. It didn't matter now though. No one saw it except for my family, and if it made them feel better, I'm down with that.

The funeral parlour wasn't large enough for everyone. They brought in extra chairs. Even then most of the kids had to stand out in the receiving area. I felt really bad for the cast of Grease, because they were not only sad because of me, but because the play was cancelled. That was just wrong. It didn't make any sense, and from where I was looking I would have liked to see it go on. I tried to get into our drama teacher, Mr Reid's head and tell him so, but like Mr Emerson said, that was not possible.

Just as it was impossible to comfort Mom and Dad. Through the entire service they never touched one another. I could feel their hurt. They cried silently, the tears spilling down their cheeks unchecked, especially when my friends got up to speak.

Gram though, now she doesn't know how to cry quietly. She wailed with great body-shaking gulps. Her moans and sobs punctuating each speech. Aunt Jessie tried to console her, but I could hear her thinking how dramatic her mother was, how her loud crying sounded insincere, that she cried like someone who needed attention, not someone who felt real sorrow. But Aunt Jessie was wrong. I was afraid Gram was going to have a heart attack right there, she was in such pain, for both me and for Mom.

I wanted to tell her, to tell Mom, Dad, Levi, Kajul and all my friends that it was all right. That I was okay. But unlike all those television shows now, where everyone is talking or whispering with ghosts, I can't find a way to communicate with the living. That's just not the way it is, Mr Emerson says. Still, like everything else now, that's perfectly all right. Funny, as I watch what Mom and Dad are going through, there's no judgement, no opinion. I can only feel the love for them, and sadness that they have to hurt so much. At the same time there's no notion of right or wrong, good or bad. I asked Mr Emerson about all that.

He replied with his own question, asking me what I thought the white light was.

I don't know.

Yes you do.

I do?

Yes. But don't worry. You'll remember.

I wanted to ask him if it was God. But in our family the Bible was nothing more than a very long and complicated storybook. It was truly hard to imagine a Supreme Being that was so human-like, including having the capacity for jealousy, vengeance and murder. I agreed with Mom's view that the warfaring, eye-for-an-eye God of the Bible, who commanded the smiting of enemies, along with their women and children, did not jive with the loving and forgiving turn-the-other-cheek God. According to her, that was one giant plot hole in the Bible. There was just too much war and mayhem brought on by blind belief in religious books written by men.

Jesus Christ—now him she believed in. Not believed in as in 'worshipped,' but believe that he existed—that he was a man who once lived on earth. A man, like Buddha, Confucius, or Allah, and now the Dalai Llama, all spiritual men, peaceful men, who had something to teach the rest of us but who time and other men had turned into Deities. My parents never bought any of the worship part, and neither did I.

But I have to say that when you're dead your whole belief system is in doubt. I suddenly wanted there to be a God, but not the one in the Bible. I didn't want to tell Mr Emerson any of this because I had my suspicions, so I asked: Are you God?

He smiled at me with such warmth that I felt it in my heart, even though technically I no longer had one.

It's all semantics, he said. But, yes. Everything is God.

His words brought a wisp of memory. Like smoke, the harder I tried to grasp for it, the more it eluded me. It doesn't matter; Mr Emerson promises that in time I'll get it. Time. It isn't the same here. There's no possible way to explain that in earth terms. Just as there is no way I can influence what happens there. I only wish I could tell Mom that I'm okay with hanging here for as long as she needs.

12

An unseasonal arctic front sweeps through central British Columbia at the end of August. The black flies of summer, along with the annoying mosquitoes, disappear from the valley. Thunderheads boil up in the west. A week of chilling wind and rain on the Chilcotin plateau washes away the last threat of forest fires. The low elevation and the mountain ridges surrounding the ranch protect it from the extreme drops in temperatures common to the rest of the Chilcotin. Those same conditions cause the valley to turn into an oven of oppressive heat after another about-turn in the weather as the month winds down.

Unable to sleep Julie tosses and turns, trying to find a cooler spot on the sheets. The digital clock on her bedside table casts a green glow in the room. She glances at it again. It's ten minutes later than when she last checked. One thirty in the morning, and she's still awake. Her cotton nightgown clinging to her sweat-soaked body, she rises from bed. Bathed in moonlight streaming in through the living-room windows, she creeps downstairs and makes her way to the kitchen. Pouring herself a glass of red wine, she takes it, along with the rest of the bottle, out to the front patio and settles on the chaise lounge. The outside air is cool, but not nearly as chilling as some nights she's experienced this summer. There isn't a hint of wind; the air in the valley still clings to the day's heat.

Lifting the crystal wineglass to her lips, Julie takes a long sip, only then noticing the eerie glow in the northern sky. She lowers the glass and studies the jagged horizon at the end of the lake. Above the tree-tops, spirals and wispy fingers of colour undulate and dance against a black star-filled backdrop. Julie recognizes immediately that for the first time in her life she is witnessing the aurora borealis, the northern lights. Stunned by the unexpected display, she sits back to watch the brilliant colours and changing shapes in the night sky. Like an electrically charged curtain, ribbons of greens, fuchsias and yellows lift and fall, arch and intertwine, in an ethereal light show across the northern horizon. *Spirits dancing in the night*, she thinks. In another life she would have hurried upstairs and dragged Ian from sleep to see this. And in their other life he would have come, laughing at her childish excitement. Perhaps they would have gone skinny dipping to cool off, then made love. He probably would now if she could bring herself to go up to his room. This is what she misses most about him, his laughter, and his willingness to embrace any experience for the sheer thrill of sharing it with her. For a moment she is tempted. Forcing her thoughts away from there, she refills her suddenly empty glass.

When the bottle is finished, drawn by the brilliant night sky, and perhaps by the power of the wine, she rises and makes her way down the patio steps and across the lawn. At the water's edge, she tugs her nightgown over her head and lets it fall to the ground. Wading slowly into the water, she cringes at the cool temperature. The water climbs up her legs, to her waist, to her chest. Rather than shrink away from the numbing cold, she embraces the sensation, letting it pull her forward. She imagines herself continuing out to the middle of the lake, walking underwater until her breath is gone, and then her lifeless body floating in darkness, her hair fanning above her. Without warning the lake bottom drops away, and she is sinking, sinking into nothingness. She surrenders, lets herself go, feels herself smile at the simplicity of it. A painless way to end an endless pain. But her body, her exploding lungs, betray her. Against her will her arms and legs fight her inertia. Her head bursts through the surface, her mouth gasping for air. She beats her traitorous arms against the water with a choked cry. Treading water she catches her breath, and then, forcing herself to relax she turns over and lies on her back, her arms outstretched. She is tired, so tired. She feels as if she can float like this forever. Overhead, a million pinpoints of light glow above the dancing colours. The eerie sensation of the world being turned upside down, that she is looking down upon the universe instead of up, magnifies her feeling of insignificance. She closes her eyes. Beneath the surface, her ears pick up the distant vibrations of a loon's lonely call. She remains as still as possible, listening to the sound waves travelling through the water. Is anything more plaintive than the sorrowful call of the loon? Yes. The silence of a childless father, unable to say his daughter's name out loud.

The answering warbles turn into music. Julie lifts her head and shakes the water from her ears. A volley of echoing cries fills the night. And something more. Behind the mournful chorus she imagines she hears the strings of an accompanying violin. She even recognizes the melody. The haunting music sounds just like the strains of "Moonlight Sonata."

A movement on the edge of her vision forces her to right herself in the water. She is further out than she thought. Treading water again, she turns toward the illuminated shore. There in the small bay to her right, silhouetted by the light from the tenant's cabin, is a dark figure swaying, moving in liquid rhythm with the music. Julie quickly sinks lower into the water. Unless their tenant has company, it can only be Virgil Blue, standing out on the end of his dock playing the violin.

13

In the morning Julie struggles to keep the shroud of slumber wrapped around her. The harder she tries to hang on to it, the more it eludes her. It lifts, as weightless as mist, taking with it the sensation of holding a delicious secret in her fragile grasp. Reluctantly she opens her eyes and reality sweeps in with the daylight. The pleasant feelings evaporate, replaced by the now familiar hollowness, and the scratching hair-shirt accusations. *How could you forget, how could you feel anything but pain when Darla is dead?* As if on cue, a headache blooms inside her skull.

Turning over slowly she squints at the clock. Nine thirty. Why hasn't Ian called her? He must be wondering why she's slept so late. She forces herself to sit up. She needs a drink of water. Her mouth tastes like fuzzy mold. Then she remembers the wine. Sudden fragmented visions of last night fill her aching head. The incredible night sky. A swim in the lake? The figure on the dock? Flopping back down on her pillow she massages her aching temples. Exactly how much was real and how much a dream? Or a result of all that wine? She runs a hand through her damp hair and groans. It's true. She was in the lake last night—drunk. She wonders if their tenant saw her.

Well, so what if he did? Isn't she allowed to swim in her own lake, in the middle of the night, naked, if she wants to?

Rising slowly she plods into the washroom, wondering if it really had been Virgil playing the violin. It just doesn't seem to fit the image she has of their tenant somehow. But then she knows very little about Virgil Blue—an arrangement that suits them both, she is certain. Yet, she finds herself curious. Whoever it was out on the dock last night, not only plays, but plays well—if her water- and wine-logged ears were any judge. It will remain a mystery though—there is no one she could ask, least of all Ian. The topic of their tenant is probably another off-limits subject.

She changes and goes downstairs to find the house empty. Then she remembers that it is the last Friday of the month. No wonder Ian hadn't bothered to wake her. He's gone to town; he won't be home until late tonight.

His twice-monthly trips to the office in town are strictly for the benefit of his clients. He never stays overnight. Even though the office has a small suite upstairs, he returns home no matter how late he works. His way of proving his fidelity? It isn't necessary. Julie isn't even certain if Valerie Ladner is still one of his clients. She won't ask. He won't say.

After fortifying herself with aspirin and coffee, she goes out to the front patio to clean up the evidence of her solitary drinking.

The morning air is crisp, fall creeping in on slow baby steps. The lake's motionless surface reflects a perfect image of the bordering trees and an unbroken blue sky. She glances to her left, to the pastures at the end of the lake. She has often spotted deer in the stubbled fields since haying season. They show up in herds to graze on the new shoots of grass. Sometimes, from the kitchen window she watches the bolder ones who, twitching their white tails, come right into the yard to munch on the front lawn.

A movement in the marshes at the mouth of the creek catches her eye. She squints into the light until a hulking brown form standing knee deep among the reeds, lifts a heavily antlered head. Water streaming from his bearded jaw, the moose chews unconcerned while staring in her direction. Julie remains unmoving as they keep a mutual eye on each other. The massive animal offers no threat at this distance, yet she feels her heartbeat quicken, the blood pounding in her ears.

Out of nowhere, last night's dangerous thoughts surface in her mind. Had she really tempted death out on the lake? Although she's not religious in the conventional terms, Julie has always held the belief that taking your own life is a cop-out, a selfish option. She has always believed that everyone has an obligation to life itself, to see it through, no matter what. After Darla's accident, the doctor had given Julie sleeping pills. But regardless of how sleep eluded her, since that fateful night when she had not woken to Darla's call, she has been unable to swallow one. Only now does she ask herself, why then, is she still hanging on to those pills?

Across the way, the bull moose turns and climbs up the creek bank. Sure-footed in his lumbering grace he crosses the meadow to clear the far fence without effort and disappears into the woods.

Julie goes inside to the kitchen and, still lost in thought, pours herself another cup of coffee. Staring out the window, she decides that, like the moose, there really was no danger last night; it was just the wine, that was all. She will have to be careful, though.

She forces her mind away from there, imagines herself telling Ian about the moose, which she had found strangely beautiful and ugly at the same time. She suddenly wishes she'd had a camera to capture that image.

When she was selling real estate, she had always been proud of her listing photographs. "You have an eye," she was told more than once. A spark of something close to excitement ignites somewhere inside her. She is spending so much time outside now she might as well make use of it, capture some of these images. She could send them to Jessie and the girls. And to her mother, let her see that things are not completely bleak out here. An involuntary chuckle rises to the back of her throat at the idea of sending her a mother a photograph of a bull moose so close to her door.

She makes her way upstairs to the spare room, the room where her former life is stored. A room she has avoided. Ian refuses to go in there at all. When he had caught her packing up Darla's possessions for the move, he had accused her of hanging onto them as if she believes their daughter will return. But she can't let go of the dolls, the clothes, even the bedding that still carries the smell of Darla. And yet, after they moved in, Julie found herself unable to open any of the boxes, in fear of losing that scent, or losing herself to it.

Steeling herself, she avoids Darla's neatly stacked boxes on one side of the room, and checks the labels of the others until she finds the one from her real estate career. She roots through it and pulls out a leather camera case. Inside, firmly strapped against the plush red lining, her old 35mm and accessories wait as orderly as she had left them. Film canisters line the mesh side pockets. She removes the camera, and checks the film and batteries. They're still fine. The old Pentax is out-of-date technology, but she has always liked the quality of the photographs it produced. It feels like an old friend in her hands and she surprises herself with a smile as she snaps the lens cover back on. Just the idea of having a plan, having something creative to do, feels good somehow. She imagines Darla saying *it's about time*, but knows it's only her own inner voice trying too hard.

Hanging the camera strap over her shoulder, she goes back downstairs and pulls on her hiking boots. Outside, she avoids the pastures at this end of the lake, in case the moose is still hanging around, and heads to the north road. She will start by taking shots of the ranch house from the far end of the lake. She hasn't hiked this way since meeting their tenant in the garden last month. Today the fear of the moose outweighs her fear of running into Virgil Blue. The Clydesdales are no longer in the corral, so he's probably out working on his wood-lot anyway.

Nearing the turnoff to his cabin she slows her pace. She peers down his driveway, but can make out nothing more than the fir and mountain ash trees encroaching on either side of the narrow road. Confused by a pang of disappointment she wonders what it was she expected to see? Or hear? The woods are quiet; no strains of violin music seep through the trees. Feeling a little ridiculous she resumes her speed walking. After a while her laboured breathing and the blood pounding in her ears gives way to the everyday hum and buzz of the forest: the staccato chattering of a squirrel scurrying down a tree trunk; the familiar cry of chickadees; the hollow thumping of grouse wings in the distance; and the raspy cries of crows winging through the branches above.

Crows. It seems to Julie that wherever she goes lately, there are crows.

Were they always there, or had she only begun to take notice of them on the day of Darla's funeral as she stood staring out of their family-room window while hushed voices droned on behind her?

I'm so sorry.

Is there anything I can do?

I'll just put this platter of egg salad sandwiches on the coffee table here.

Oh, please don't let me intrude.

I'm so, so, sorry.

Unless it was her sister speaking, she pretended not to hear.

Wishing everyone silenced, gone, she had concentrated on the ebony bird sitting like a lone sentry on the back porch railing. No cocking of his head back and forth, no fluffing of feathers, his bottomless black eyes stared into the window as if trying to connect with her soul.

She noticed the dark visitors daily after that. Others joined it, perching in the trees behind Julie's golf course home. In the morning she could hear the scratching of their feet on the shake roof, as if chiding her for lying in bed, nagging her to get up, get up and get on with life. They became her constant companions, even showing up out here. She began to think, to hope in a small secret place in her heart, that it was Darla trying to communicate with her. Then she remembered Darla telling her once that the crow was Levi's totem, his spirit guide, and she recalled seeing him place his crow pendant around Darla's neck that night.

Now, whenever she encounters the birds, she is overcome with aversion to them, can only think of them in their mythical role as harbingers of death. *You're too late*, she thinks angrily as two swoop down from the sky. Their barking cries trail behind as they glide above her with liquid strokes and disappear around the bend. An unexpected shiver passes through her despite the warmth of the day. The road winds on, leading closer to the lakeshore, then wandering away again as it cuts through the forest. The crows' raspy voices grow louder as she approaches a fork in the road. To her right a narrow logging trail leads up to the timbered hillside. She stays on the lower road, and on the next turn comes upon the reason for the cacophonous cries. A few yards ahead, on the side of the road is the limp body of a dead bird. She recalls reading somewhere that finding a dead crow is good luck. *Good luck for whom*, she thinks wryly. Certainly not the crow, or his companions who are gathered around their fallen brother. Except for in old black-and-white movies she has never seen so many gathered together in one place, hadn't even realized that there were flocks this size in the area. Some hop about on the ground near the lifeless pile of ebony feathers. Others blacken the branches of the fir tree above, their raucous 'caws' filling the air as if they can will the dead bird to take wing. Julie approaches slowly. No elbow wing of feather lifts in threatened flight as she stands before them. Despite her aversion, something about the scene, the connection between these animals, their concern for their comrade, brings the pressure of tears to her eyes. She blinks them back, and slowly slides the strap from her shoulder. Picking up the camera she removes the leather cover with a gentle, soundless touch and lifts it, closing one eye to focus on the gathering of mourners. At the first shutter click, a few birds lift in flight. Julie's finger continues pressing, *click... click... click*. The cries become more urgent, and a flurry of wings lift in unison. She continues to shoot as they rise up, capturing images of the black wave swimming into the blue sky.

As she lowers the camera, her refocusing eyes catch a movement in the shadows beyond the abandoned tree. At first her brain refuses to make sense of the hulking dark form. A wavering black stump? A large dog? Without thinking she raises the camera and zooms in on the apparition. The automatic focus turns the blur into the form of a black bear. Julie's shaking finger involuntarily presses down. *Click.* The huge head lifts, then in one smooth movement the animal stands upright on its hind legs. Towering over the underbrush, its menacing clawed paws held up in front of its eerily human form, the bear sniffs the air.

Her heart pounding in her ears Julie takes a tentative step backwards. The animal turns toward the sound. Everything she has read scrambles in her head as she freezes in its stare. Is she supposed to meet his gaze, or avoid it? Unable to look away, she tries frantically to recall the instructions for a bear encounter. *Back away slowly; wave your arms to identify yourself as human. Speak calmly.*

She cannot find her voice. She lifts her suddenly heavy arms and takes a tentative step back, panic rising in her throat.

Bears want to avoid you as much as you want to avoid them. If a bear gets too close... The bear spray! The camera drops to the ground as she grabs blindly at her belt. Still standing upright the bear swings his head from side to side, and lets out a loud grunt. Julie's fumbling fingers find the leather case, snap it open and free the can of bear spray. With trembling hands she raises it up, pointing it like a gun in front of her. The bear drops to all fours.

Activate spray if the animal comes to within fifteen feet.

She can't possibly wait until he is within fifteen feet. She turns and bolts into the bush on the other side of the road. Dodging between the trees, branches snapping around her, she crashes through the undergrowth, stumbling as her foot slips on a moss-covered boulder. Unable to keep her balance she pitches forward, arms flailing. She hits the ground with such force that the wind is knocked out of her and the spray can flies from her grasp. Her crash landing is punctuated by what sounds like the blast of a horn. Deafened by a ringing in her ears she thrusts herself up on all fours, frantically trying to scramble away. Rose bush thorns and brambles claw at her clothes, holding her back and she steals a frantic glance over her shoulder. A few yards behind, in the flickering shadows, a dark blur is closing in on her.

She slumps to the ground. Throwing her arms over the back of her head, she forces her body to remain still. *If all else fails play dead.*

The commotion behind her abruptly ends. After a silence that seems to last forever, she lifts an arm to peek back, and finds, standing behind her, their tenant Virgil Blue.

She rolls over onto her back, her heart still racing, and pushes herself up on her elbows. "The... bear?"

Virgil holds up a red-and-white can. An air horn. The kind she has seen at hockey games. An involuntary nervous laugh rises and she slumps back to the ground. Taking a moment to catch her breath, she studies her rescuer. Instead of a cowboy hat, a sweat-stained black cotton skullcap—the sort bikers wear under their helmets—covers his head. The slanted sunlight exposes his face and the calm concern there.

After a moment Julie sits up. Tugging away barbed twigs and branches from her clothes, she looks back up at him and says, "I'm fine, thank you." Only after the words are out does it occur to her that he hasn't asked. But the question is clear in his dark eyes, and in the arm he is holding out, offering her a hand up. The hand she had refused to accept last month. Swallowing her pride, and her shame, she grabs his forearm and lets him pull her to her feet, stumbling against him as she rises. His plaid flannel shirt smells of freshly cut wood, and horsehide. The warmth of his skin against hers, the shock of touching another person—when was the last time she had actually touched anyone?—leaves her unsettled, confused, and she steps back quickly.

She hurries to stay close behind him on the way back to the road, glancing around at every step for any sign of the bear. There is none, just the two massive Clydesdales standing on the road, their hides twitching beneath leather harnesses while they wait patiently for their driver.

"You were working," Julie says kneeling down to retrieve her camera.

Without responding to her, Virgil lets out a long whistle. Seconds later, his dog, which Julie has only seen from a distance, comes streaking through the underbrush where the bear had stood. Close up, the grey-and-black dog is much larger than Julie had thought. If she had encountered him alone she might easily have mistaken him for a wolf. As it is, she's relieved that Virgil is between them as the dog approaches. But then, belying his menacing appearance, he lopes over with his tongue lolling out and sits panting at his master's side, happily accepting the rewarding scratches to the back of his ears.

As Julie stumbles to find the right words to thank him, Virgil nods curtly and turns away. Stunned at his rebuke she stands watching him walk back to his team of horses. *Well, okay, I guess I deserved that.* Returning her camera to its case she notices with a twinge of disappointment that the lens has shattered.

After stroking the horses' necks and withers, Virgil reclaims the reins from where they lay on the ground behind the animals massive haunches. Their tails switching flies away, the Clydesdales swing their heads around to watch him.

"Wait, I, uh, I," Julie hesitates then rushes forward. "Please. I need to talk with you." Virgil holds up a hand to still her. As he does so she notices the odd angles of his left thumb and forefinger, and for a moment wonders how such a deformed hand could be responsible for such beautiful music.

While she watches from the side of the road, with the lightest of touch on the leather straps, Virgil signals the horses to alertness. Using only the language of a clicking tongue and pursing lips he manoeuvres them around on the narrow road. Julie hops out of the way until the team is facing the other direction.

Frustrated, she hurries to keep up as they head home. This man and his dog have just saved her life. She at least owes him a better attempt at making peace with him. "Mr Blue," she says, when she reaches his side, "I'd like to apologize for my behaviour the other day."

With no visible prompt, the horses stop in their tracks and stand motionless, each with one hind leg resting. Virgil turns to face Julie. Taking both reins in one hand he touches his lips with the other, a mime's gesture, then tugging at the red bandanna on his neck he pulls it down to expose the laryngeal scar in the V hollow of his breast bone. It's the same scar her father wore after his throat cancer surgery.

"Oh, I'm sorry," she says. "I didn't know."

He replaces the scarf. One click of his tongue and the horses plod forward again. During the silent walk home, Julie wonders why in the world Ian has neglected to mention that Virgil is mute. Even odder yet is the glimmer of warmth she feels over having made peace with this man. A feeling, which at one time she would have defined as happiness.

14

Virgil's story

Happiness. The word has a world of different meaning to different folks. To him, it brought to mind a memory, an image hidden away in the darkened corridors of time. A young boy sitting in a dimly lit kitchen.

The year 1959. The place Tulsa, Oklahoma, where the distance between the paved tree-lined streets of town, and the dirt roads of the country, was an easy walk, and a hard world away. On the darkened road of a mobile home park, in front of an aluminum-sided house trailer, a patch of crabgrass encroached on the gravel path leading to the porch. Marigolds struggled to bloom on either side of the wooden steps. Inside, the edges of a yellow gingham curtain lifted in the evening breeze, letting in the scratchy light from a distant yard lamp. A fringed swag lamp hung over a rescued chrome kitchen table. One man's trash; another family's treasure. The boy sat with his family, the dinner dishes cleared. The air still carried the waxy aroma from the seven, blown-out make-a-wish, birthday candles lying in the chocolate crumbs on the cake platter. On the tabletop next to it, covering the remnants of other families' stains and scratches, sat a gaily wrapped long rectangular box, reused ribbon trailed from a blue bow, tied by his mother's hands. He met her dark eyes across the table, proud eyes that reflected his ancestral heritage—tired eyes. Eyes that today betray how anxious she is for him to love her gift. He will, he promised himself; her desire to please him was enough, more than enough, because whatever was inside the box, whatever she had purchased, he knew was with her sweat and by no one else's generosity.

His stepfather—absent since his sister, Melody, was born four years ago—had fled under the pressure of another mouth to feed. His fifteen-year-old twin brothers did what they could to help their mother, who worked two jobs to carry them. They were already chomping-at-the-bit to enlist in the army, to earn their way. Even now they teased their mother at the table that all *they* want for their birthdays when they turn seventeen, is her signature allowing them to join up. They could send money home every month, they promised. *Give you army rifles for your birthday? Eh?* She shook her head, clucking her tongue and ignored their pleas.

The boy thought it wasn't such a bad idea. Perhaps then she could quit her night job and start living on more than four hours of sleep. Maybe if they had enough money, their mother would give in to the letters from the north, asking her to return home to her people in the Chilcotin country of Canada—a country and a people that the boy only knew of from old photographs and his mother's sparse stories.

He looked down at the box. He didn't want to open it. Given his mother's distaste for anything to do with guns he knew he would not find the white straw hat, fringed chaps, holster and pistols he has coveted to play out his solitary cowboy fantasies. If he could, he would leave the box unopened. He would keep it on the shelf above his bed beside the photograph of his father and just look at it. It would save him from being disappointed by some plastic water-launcher from Kresge's, or perhaps a brand new pair of trousers and a shirt, instead of the church-bazaar discards he wore every day. Better to leave it unopened and hang onto the dream of being a cowboy—like the father he never knew.

But she, they, would not let him ignore the gift. His little sister clapped her hands. *Hurry, open it, open it.* His brothers, Jackson and Jerome, flashed white-toothed grins. *C'mon lil' brother.* His mother smiled quietly, she would not betray her anticipation. But he knew. It was greater than his own.

His hands moved slowly. Long thin fingers untied the trailing ribbon and carefully removed it, along with the bow, with painful precision. He sorted them, rolled them all up into a tiny blue ball to be used once again and placed it on the table beside the box. He removed the squares of Scotch tape from the folds at each end, turned the box over and ran a finger along the joined edges. Lifting the paper with great care, he removed it and smoothed it out then folded it into a neat square, while his impatient brothers rolled their eyes. Placing the wrapping paper next to the ribbon, he turned the cardboard box right side up. Avoiding his mother's eyes, not wanting her to witness the disappointment in his at the moment of discovery, he concentrated on sliding his thumbnail over the tape running down the join in the middle. He lifted the cardboard flaps, at the same time squeezing his eyelids shut. After a moment he slowly opened them—and looked down to discover the impossible. The gift was so unexpected, and so precious to her, that he had never allowed himself to wish for it. Inside the box, lying on a layer of tissue, its gleaming wood smelling of his mother's furniture polish, was pure joy—happiness—in the shape of his father's violin.

15

Ian returns from his office in town after midnight. On the cusp of sleep Julie considers getting up to talk to him but decides against it. She is still confused by her encounter with Virgil Blue earlier today.

They had walked home together, accompanied by the creaking of the horses' harnesses and the clanking of chains dragging on the gravel road. Julie had wanted to expand on her apology, or attempt to account for her rude behaviour on the day they first met, but sensed an explanation was unwanted. All the way back she stole glances at the reins resting lightly in Virgil's palms, noting the evidence of healed scars on both hands, the deformed fingers of his left and wondering once again how those fingers could possibly play the violin. Perhaps she had imagined it after all.

When they reached the yard, he gave a quick nod goodbye without meeting her eyes before he and his team veered toward the barn. Inside the house Julie had stood at the den window watching as he, with a deftness that belied his gnarled hands, unharnessed the horses and rubbed them down.

In the morning, Ian is already at his desk, hunched over the computer, when Julie comes downstairs. She heads to the kitchen to make coffee, but curiosity gets the better of her and she goes instead to his office and stands in the doorway. Sitting at his desk, his back to her, a new banker's box at his feet, Ian is so focused on his work that he's unaware of her presence.

"Why didn't you mention that Virgil is mute?" she asks.

Startled, Ian swivels around his chair to face her. "Mute?" His eyebrows furrow in the preoccupied manner they do when he is concentrating on something.

"I ran into him yesterday."

"Yeah?" he says, bending over the banker's box on the floor. "And how did *that* go?"

"It would have gone a lot better if I had known." Julie leans against the door jamb and crosses her arms. Trying hard to keep an accusatory note out of her voice, she says, "I just don't understand how you could neglect to mention something like that."

Ian retrieves a handful of files from the box. "I don't know. It never occurred to me at first, I guess," he says, sitting back up. "Then after you met him that day, I just assumed you knew."

"Well, I didn't."

Ian pushes his glasses up onto his forehead. Squeezing his eyes shut he pinches the middle of his nose, a habit he has whenever he is tired or thinking. "I'm sorry," he says when he finally looks up at her. "I didn't think." The sincerity in his expression matches his words.

Julie shrugs. "You spend so much time with him. How do the two of you communicate?"

Ian pauses for moment, then says, "He's a good listener," as if telling himself something he has just realized. "When he has something to say, which isn't often, he writes it down. He does have one of those voice gadgets like your father had, but I've never heard him use it. Guess he hates the mechanical sound of it as much as your dad did."

Julie had witnessed her father use his Electrolarynx only once, and that was to tell her mother, in a robotic-sounding voice, to stop fussing over him. The surgery that stole her father's voice had stopped his throat cancer from spreading. For a while.

Julie studies her husband. Something about the way he holds him-self now reminds her of her workaholic father. Like him, Ian looks consumed by his profession. Even now he has lowered his glasses and turned his attention back to the stack of files in his hands. There's no reason for him to work this hard, or to work at all for that matter. They are financially secure. It's a point of fact that he had used to convince her to move out here—they have enough money to last the rest of their lives. *More than enough. No need for that college fund; no need for the bundle stashed away for an only daughter's lavish wedding.*

Yet, here Ian is, putting in more hours than he ever did when they lived in town. His way of coping, she guesses, burying himself in work. Running away, after all, hasn't been enough.

Not ready to give up the conversation, but wanting to change the subject, Julie lets her gaze stray outside to the lake. "We should have a dock," she muses, half to herself.

"A dock?"

"Or not."

"No... I mean, yes. Of course we can have a dock. A great idea." Ian places the files on the desk and turns back to her. "I'm just surprised. Dare I ask what brought this on?"

Aware that this is the first time since they moved out here that she has suggested a change, Julie senses his pleasure in her taking any kind of ownership in their new home.

"It occurred to me the other night when I went for a moonlight swim."

"A swim?" If Ian is startled he hides it well. "Must have been chilly."

"Not bad. Probably the wine kept me warm." Why is she doing this, baiting him? Is she looking for a confrontation?

To Ian's credit, instead of the expected lecture on the foolishness of swimming in the dark, under the influence, he smiles and shakes his head.

"I wonder why the Woells, who seemed to have thought of everything out here, never had a dock built," Julie continues. "Even Virgil has one."

"Speaking of our tenant, where did you run into him?"

She opens her mouth to tell him about the bear encounter, but on second thought decides against sharing that right now. She can't stand the idea of an 'I told you so.'

Instead she tells him, "On the north road. He was with his team—working somewhere up on the hillside, I guess. I didn't realize his woodlot was so close."

"It's not. He's doing some logging for us."

"Oh." Julie unfolds her arms and asks, "Cutting down the beetle-kill?"

"Yes, and doing some selective logging."

She raises her eyebrow, the previous owner's reluctance to cut trees coming to mind.

As if reading her thought, Ian says, "If we don't prune the forest, Mother Nature will do it for us, one way or the other. Fires, insect infestation. Selective logging makes the forest stronger, not weaker."

"Let me guess. Virgil Blue's idea?"

"Yes, and no. He lent me a report from the Cariboo Horse Loggers' Association. After I read it we decided to do some timber thinning at the same time that he removes the bug-killed pine. We'll share any profits."

She imagines the two of them sitting over their coffee mugs at Virgil's table, their heads together over notes and plans. Virgil writing, Ian nodding agreement. The vision reminds her of the 'talking trees' supporting each other in the forest.

At one time it would have been her with whom Ian talked things through, her he leaned on. No more. His making decisions about the ranch without discussing them with her proved that. Still, it was good that he had Virgil. She wondered for a brief moment if he ever spoke to him about Darla. If he had ever said her name out loud in the neutral territory of a stranger's cabin.

"Well that's good then," she says. "I'm glad."

Ian's expression suddenly changes. He nods at the other office chair beside his desk.

For a moment Julie doesn't move. Then she slowly settles on the edge of the indicated chair with the same apprehension she reads in Ian's face.

Perhaps this is it then. Perhaps Ian has had enough of this non-marriage, and is not willing to give it any more time. Divorce is common after the death of a child. It was something she learned at a Compassion Group meeting for parents who had lost a child. Her doctor had recommended the group. Ian flatly refused to go. Although he gave no reason, she knew why. He couldn't share his feelings with her, how could he share them with strangers? Julie went alone, but unable to stand the collective pain, she herself had quit after only a few sessions.

At the last meeting a young mother, whose son had drowned, confessed to an uncontrollable anger at everyone, an inability to talk with anyone close, especially her husband, without lashing out. In a quiet voice, neither laced with sympathy nor judgement, the psychologist-facilitator had asked her to try stopping for a moment before speaking with a loved one. 'Take the time to remind yourself that the only objective, the only outcome that's important, is to finish the conversation still feeling good about the other person, and yourself.' 'Compassionate understanding,' he called it.

Perhaps now is the time to practise this advice. No matter where this conversation leads, Julie promises herself, she will hold onto that objective.

Tentatively she places her hands on her lap. "All right."

"There was a telephone message at the office yesterday," Ian says slowly. "From Levi Johnny's mother."

Julie stiffens. Her resolve extinguished by his unexpected words, she blurts, "They didn't give her our new number, did they?"

Ian shakes his head. "But I thought about calling her back."

"Why? Why would you do that?"

"I don't know. Curious? I wonder what she could have to say," he watches her reaction. "The word in town is that Levi Johnny is in a bad way. That he's left school, gone back out to NaNeetza, given up hockey."

"Darla gave up her life," Julie whispers.

At the sound of their daughter's name Ian's shoulders sag. "Don't," he says.

He lowers his head, but Julie cannot stop herself.

"And he got a fine. A fine. God! Driving with undue care and attention? What's that? A slap on the wrist. He got off lightly."

Ian looks up. "I'm not so sure."

"What does that mean? You said yourself he reeked of booze."

"His alcohol level was less than .002. That's nothing. Maybe..." He stops mid-sentence and holds up his hand—as if to stop his thought, or her objection. "Anyway. I wondered if we should talk to her."

"No!" A flood of panic washes through her. "Oh God! Do they know where we live?"

"This is the Chilcotin, Julie. It may be spread out over thousands of square miles, but it's still a small community. Everyone knows what everyone else is doing. The minute the Woells sold to two greenhorns from town, I'm sure it was all over the grapevine. We're probably old news by now."

The sound of a car horn outside punctuates his words. They both turn to the window just as a car pulls into the yard. "Just what we need right now," Ian growls. "Another bloody tourist who doesn't know how to read."

It's been a good month since anyone has missed, or deliberately ignored, the Private Property sign at the top of the hill. In the beginning, exploring tourists in SUVs, campers, and bus-sized motor homes would appear in the ranch yard at least twice a week. Many drove back up the winding road in a huff, as if insulted to discover that the huge log home wasn't a lodge ready to serve them. Ian had a larger sign made and posted it at the first turnoff. If that doesn't work, he swears that he will have a locked gate installed. It hasn't come to that, partially because the number of accidental tourists decreased and partially because Ian is worried what kind of impression a locked gate would give to the locals.

"What's the matter with these people," Julie asks, jumping to her feet. "Are they blind?" Feeling a pressure cooker valve of relief at finding a safe place to vent her anger she rushes from the room. Whoever it is, they have chosen the wrong moment to come down their road. She'll give the intruders a piece of her mind they won't soon forget. Storming through the house to intercept them, she decides she might be ready for that gate.

She throws the mudroom door open just as the car—a Cadillac so new that the gold paint still glistens beneath a layer of road dirt—comes to a stop in a dust-filled cloud.

Striding across the back porch Julie feels Ian's hand touch her shoulder. "I'll take care of this," he says.

They both stop short as the driver's window rolls down and reveals the Cheshire-smile on the face of the person behind the wheel.

Ian is the first to recover. Stepping off the porch he calls out, "Hello Doreen," to Julie's mother.

16

Trust Gram to blindside them like that. Really, though, it's Mom's own fault. She's turned her back on the world and now it's snuck up to bite her on the butt. If she bothered to check her email more than once a week, if she had answered the phone when Dad was in town, or even checked the messages, she would have got the warning. Aunt Jessie, who knew that Gram had suddenly decided to make a surprise visit, tried to give Mom a heads-up.

You have to hand it to Gram; she's feisty for sixty-eight years old. But her timing isn't the greatest. I get it though, why she didn't bother to ask Mom if it was a convenient time for a visit. She knew the answer. It would never be convenient. So believing it better to just show up, yesterday she packed up her new car and drove as far as Waverley Creek. Early this morning—because Aunt Jessie, who refused to be part of her plan, wouldn't give her directions to the ranch—she used her GPS to locate Spring Bottom Lake.

The expressions on my parents' faces when that window rolled down would have been freakin' funny if I didn't know what was behind them. I could feel their silent groans. And as much as I love Gram, like them I was sorry she had picked that moment to show up. It was too bad she had interrupted Mom and Dad the first time they were trying to have a real conversation. And they were talking about Levi. They need to talk about him.

The rumours Dad heard in town are true. Levi is broken. He tried to talk to Mom after the accident. He needs to, for her, for himself, for everyone, including me.

He made his first quiet attempt at the funeral, but Mom just looked right through him as if he wasn't there. It was pretty brave of him to show up and face all the accusing stares, the whispers: 'Judge let him off because he's a big shot hockey star.'

'Point zero, zero two alcohol level? That's enough—he's an Indian.'

Worse yet, is knowing that those thoughts crossed my mother's mind. She refused to return his phone calls, pounding the erase button on the answering machine the moment she heard Levi's voice. I guess like Gram he could have just arrived at their door when they still lived in town, but that's not his style. He would never impose his presence on anyone. After my parents moved away Levi gave up. Now he sits out at his mother's house in NaNeetza Valley watching television and sleeping. Once in a while, childhood friends who never left the reserve come to visit, bringing whiskey or six-packs of beer. So far Levi has endured their good-natured teasing about his abstinence, but his mother is frightened for him. That's why she tried to get a hold of my parents. She knows that the suffering won't stop for any of them until it stops for all of them. She's a smart woman. My mom is too, but right now she is wearing her grief wrapped around her like a cloak and it's choking out all the things she knows to be true. A part of her, the loving, tolerant part, has been dampened down, smothered under her need to blame. Turning her back on Levi is so unlike who she used to be that it's making her sick, and she doesn't see it.

Sometimes, though, when she looks into the mirror, even she doesn't recognize herself. It's more than the physical change, more than the weight loss, the stringy unkempt hair—man, Gram's going to have a field day with that one—more than the not caring about what she wears anymore. There's a permanent hard expression on Mom's face that keeps everyone at a distance.

I've seen that scary expression before. Ironically enough the first time I noticed it was on the face of a First Nations woman in town. I was ten years old the day Mom and I pulled up behind a little red car at the traffic light outside the mall. When she reached around to grab something from the back seat, Mom's foot must have pressed on the gas pedal and our car jerked forward to rear end the vehicle in front of us. While the woman driver climbed out of her car to inspect the damage, Mom grabbed her insurance papers and joined her. The wrinkle in the bumper was totally her fault, Mom admitted. She apologized over and over again, promising to have it fixed, while the woman stood there in stony silence. I shrank back at the expression in her dark eyes. Even then I recognized that it was about more than her car. It was about hate. It was not something Mom could break through, yet she tried, with a constant chatter as she copied out her insurance information. Without a word, the woman snatched the paper, jumped into her car, slammed the door and drove away.

"Wow. Did you see how she looked at you?" I said when Mom was back in the car. "She hated you, just because you're white."

"Try putting yourself in her shoes," Mom said. "Imagine encountering that look every day?"

Mom used to be like that. Everything I came to believe about not having an 'us' and 'them' attitude toward anyone, I learned from her, without lectures, but just by watching her. But lately a new expression, an expression of intolerance, has hardened her face, something I never believed I would see.

Even now it flashes across her eyes as the heavy car door opens and Gram steps out of the Cadillac. Wearing her attempt at Western clothes, embroidered designer jeans, and a cream silk shirt under a brushed suede jacket, she chirps, "Surprise!" She lifts her arms up and swivels her hips, "Ta-da!"

Sometimes Gram rocks. She says nothing about my mother's neglected hair, which I am sure took a lot since she always has an opinion on Mom's appearance. On the way into the house everyone hides behind polite chatter, holding back what they truly want to say. Gram wants to ask if they are bloody wacko to move all the way out here. Dad wants to ask how long she's staying. And Mom wants to ask what the hell she's doing here.

Mom needs to remember what she always told me. People show up in your life for a reason.

17

Why is it that whenever her mother's around Julie always ends up feeling like a child again? This time it starts the moment she pastes on a smile and walks down from the deck into her mother's embrace.

As they share a stiff hug, Julie reverts to the little girl who used to sit out on the veranda steps of their Point Grey home, waiting for her parents to return from one of her father's sales trips.

Sometimes she sat there all day, wearing her best dress with ribbons tied in her hair by one of the procession of housekeepers who marked her childhood. The moment the green Oldsmobile that her father called 'the boat,' turned into the driveway, the passenger door would fly open and her mother would bounce out. Leaving the door wide open, she would rush over and throw her arms around Julie. Smelling of cigarettes and her latest perfume, she would cover Julie's face in lipstick kisses, then rub the red smudges in with her thumbs—checking to assure that both cheeks had an equal amount of 'blush'—all the while professing how much she missed her sweet girl. Yet over time, Julie began to wonder why her mother couldn't stay home like the mothers of her friends did.

Only after Jessie was born, and it became clear that even a new baby could not keep her from accompanying their father on his monthly business trips, did Julie stop thinking it was her fault. She stopped waiting on the steps whenever her parents were due home. If her mother noticed at all, it was only to remark what a good big sister she was to spend all her time with baby Jessie.

Now, inside the ranch house, her mother marches straight through the mudroom into the living room. Behind her Julie says to Ian, "Why don't you take Mom's suitcases up to the guest room while I show her the house?"

Ian's eyes ask the question, *Where?* Both know that the guest room is full of unpacked boxes.

Julie mouths silently, *My room.*

He raises his eyebrows, then shrugs *Okay*. The deception has begun. Later she can find some excuse to rush upstairs, change the linen and move some of her clothes and personal items into the master suite. She'll do anything rather than let her mother know the state of her and Ian's marriage, including sleeping with him. It has been ten months since they've shared a bed, but surely they can manage in a king-sized one for a few days. God, she hopes it's only a few days, but by the girth of those bulging suitcases, who knows? Despite all her travelling with Julie's father, her mother has never learned to pack light.

Julie tours her through the first floor in realtor mode, pointing out features, while her mother gives the appropriate oohs and ahhs.

"I have to admit that I'm impressed," she says following Julie into the den. "I don't know exactly what I expected, but except for the nasty drive out here, you have a lovely home."

"Isn't that just the quaintest picture?" she adds gazing out the window above the computer desk in the den. Julie takes in the scene of the pasture beyond the barn, the four cow ponies and the two Clydesdales standing like statues against a backdrop of green willows down by the creek. Until that moment, she has never truly taken in this view. Suddenly it's another thing she would like to capture on film. Ironic that it took seeing it through her mother's eyes to appreciate it.

"But I must say the house is way too large," Doreen continues, "for two people to rattle around in. And this is all certainly too isolated for my taste." There it is. She can't resist. Balancing a positive with a negative—stroke a little, jab a little—it's long been her mother's style. Although this jab is a lot softer than normal. At least she hasn't given an all-out personal critique of Julie's clothes or appearance, which at the moment is probably the worst her mother has ever seen her. She's mentioned nothing about her weight, her lack of communication—yet. The visit's just begun.

"Your office looks cozy," she says studying the uncluttered desktop, the blank computer screen, the empty bookshelves lining the walls. "Although, it's certainly much smaller that Ian's, isn't it?"

"This is the den. Ian needs a larger space. He still works."

"You've given up your career completely then?"

"Yes, Mother," Julie says. "A little hard to sell real estate from here."

"What do you do all day, then?"

Julie shakes her head. "Come to the kitchen," she says. "I'll make you a snack. You must be hungry after your drive."

Ian already has the tea steeping when they enter. Doreen takes the seat at the head of the table as he brings over three mugs.

"Oh, no," she says pushing hers away as if it's tainted. "A proper china cup and saucer for me, please."

Julie meets Ian's eye and a well-at-least-she-said-please look passes between them.

Taking a container of carrot muffins from the counter, Julie says, "This is what I do," in answer to her mother's earlier question. "I bake—," *muffins and cookies that go stale in the pantry, cakes that never get cut*. Shaking away the nagging inner voice, which sounds a lot like her mother, she concentrates on placing the muffins onto the plate. "I cook, clean. I even garden a little. You know, all those things that homemakers used to do." She waits for her mother's reaction, but she appears to have missed the sarcasm.

"I do a lot of hiking," Julie adds turning to face her. "And I'm thinking of—"

"Hiking? Surely not alone out here! What about wild animals?"

"It's fine." Julie places the platter on the table. "As I was just saying, I'm thinking of taking up photography."

Ian's eyebrows rise at her words, but he says nothing.

Julie opens the refrigerator door and takes out cheese and grapes. "I was planning on going to town soon to buy a better camera," she says, giving voice to a thought that has only just now occurred to her. "So perhaps, when you leave, I'll follow you in and pick one up."

Doreen holds up her teacup and, ignoring Ian as he pours, says, "Well that was about as subtle as a sledgehammer. I just got in the door and you're already fishing for my departure date. Is there a rush?"

Caught, like a kid with her hand in the cookie jar, Julie feels a blush rise to her cheeks. "No, no, of course not," she says looking helplessly at Ian, who's grinning. If she didn't know better, she'd think that he's enjoying this. She cuts the cheese, arranges it on a glass plate with the grapes. Placing it on the table, she says, "You two have a bite while I run upstairs and get your room ready."

"Oh, don't fuss, Dear. I'm fine with anything."

"Not without linen," Julie throws over her shoulder. "Give me ten minutes." She glances back quickly and gives Ian a silent apology for leaving him stranded with her mother. Chalk and cheese. Oil and water. She'll have to risk the two of them being alone together.

Twenty minutes later she comes back down to the sound of her mother's laughter. In the kitchen, Ian is sitting with his elbows on the table, his mug cupped in his hands. "Doreen was just telling me about your childhood experience with horses," he says with a smile. "I didn't know you used to ride."

Of course he knows. There is nothing about her he doesn't know. During the good years of their marriage they had shared everything. She clearly remembers telling him about the English riding lessons her mother insisted she take when she was a child. In the beginning, unable to master the up and down rhythm of 'posting' she had slid off her pony again and again, until the instructor threatened to pad her with pillows. Ian hasn't forgotten the story. His expression asks for her indulgence. He's learning to feed her mother's ego.

"Do you ride any of those horses I saw out in the field?" her mother asks. "Surely that would be safer than hiking by yourself."

"I've never really considered it. It's been so long since I've been on a horse," Julie says taking her seat. "At any rate I don't have a saddle."

Ian rises and goes over to the counter to retrieve the teapot. "Actually there's a couple of saddles in the tack room in the barn."

"I'm sure they must be Western. I only learned English riding."

"And not too well," her mother says into her cup.

"As I recall, I got quite good at it."

"You should try it again." Ian says as he fills Julie's cup. "How different can it be?"

"I might just do that," she replies with a shrug. Up until now she has had no desire to ride any of the saddle horses, which, like the Clydesdales, she has always considered as belonging to their tenant anyway, but her mother's barb has found its mark.

"Good," Ian replies. "I'll ask Virgil about those saddles."

"No! Don't bother—"

"Virgil?" Doreen asks.

"Our tenant in the old trapper's cabin just down the road," Ian explains. "He does odd jobs around the ranch. No, that's not true," he corrects himself. "Virgil runs the place. He's been here forever. We inherited him, I guess you could say."

"So, you're not all alone out in the wilderness after all," Doreen says studying Julie's face.

18

Exhausted from a day of maintaining the illusion that her life is okay, Julie bids her mother goodnight and heads down the hall. In the master bedroom Ian is already in bed. With the duvet turned down, he sits with his back against the oak headboard, wearing a t-shirt and plaid pyjama bottoms. He lowers the book he is reading when she comes into the room. She closes the double doors, then feeling his eyes following her, she goes into the ensuite.

She takes her time brushing her teeth and changing into her nightgown. When she returns to the bedroom, Ian is lying on his back, his eyes closed, his bedside lamp turned off. She slips into her side of the bed and switches off her night-light.

"Goodnight," Ian says quietly.

"Goodnight." Settling onto her side, Julie's foot accidentally brushes up against his calf. She jerks it away, mumbling, "Sorry," and moves closer to the edge.

After a few moments Ian whispers, "Julie?"

"Hmm?"

"Do you think we'll ever find our way back to each other?"

She swallows, afraid to answer right away, and then says quietly, "I don't know."

"Well, I guess that's one step above a no," Ian says as he turns over.

Back to back, they lay still in the darkness. Julie can sense his body heat across the bed. It's been so long since she's felt a warm body next to hers in the night. Such a simple pleasure she once took for granted. Ian is one of only two people in her entire life that she has ever shared a bed with. The other was Darla.

Within minutes Ian's breathing is shallow and even. It's unlike him to fall asleep so quickly. He must have taken a sleeping pill. She rolls over onto her back, certain she's destined to lie there all night staring into the darkness.

Sometime later, she emerges from a dreamless slumber, her sleep-filled ears trying to locate the strange sound that awoke her. Beside her Ian shudders. It takes a few moments before she realizes what's happening. He is weeping, stifling his tears in his pillow. She recognizes the pain. She knows all about waking up in the middle of the night hanging onto a dream of Darla that is so real, so vivid, that she believes her daughter is still alive, only to have that feeling snatched away. And then having to face the unbearable truth all over again. Until now, it has never occurred to her that she isn't the only one this happens to.

She wants to reach out for him, to comfort him, but they are too far beyond that. His inability to share his grief, to even speak their daughter's name, stops her. His sorrow is private. She swallows a rising sob. Remaining still, she wills her breathing to a slow and even rhythm, feigning sleep. After Ian's shudders quell, she moves slowly, as if settling her body in sleep and lets one leg stray over and furl around his warm calf.

Ian's side of the bed is empty when Julie rises the next morning. Sorting through the clothes that she had moved into the walk-in closet yesterday, instead of her usual baggy pants and a sweatshirt, she chooses a pair of freshly ironed jeans with a tailored shirt. She puts on her pearl earrings, brushes her hair and attempts to arrange it in some sort of style with a hair clip. "Who are you trying to kid?" she asks her mirrored image as she applies lipstick and rouge.

Downstairs Ian is already ensconced in his office, the bevelled glass door closed for the first time. Julie brews a fresh pot of coffee, finishing just as her mother enters the kitchen. "Is Ian hiding from me?" she asks.

"Good morning to you too," Julie says from the other side of the central island. "No, he still works every day."

Taking in her mother's taupe pantsuit, heavy gold earrings and matching necklace—an outfit more appropriate for high tea at Victoria's Empress Hotel—she smiles and asks, "What can I make you for breakfast?"

"Toast, and some of that coffee I smell would be wonderful." Doreen sits down at the table, waiting to be served. "So, you really don't miss working?"

Right to it then? This is one question Julie doesn't have to give any thought to. "No, not at all," she answers. It's the truth. At one time the passion for all aspects of her career had been second only to her family. Now, it means less than nothing to her. Not one thing about her old job calls her back, not the buyers, sellers, bankers, lawyers, the co-workers, nor the long hours.

"I'll bet your clients miss you."

"I doubt that. I'm probably 'Julie Who?' by now." She pours a cup of coffee and places it in front of her mother.

"It just seems to me that you would want to work more, not less, now... now that... well you know."

The teaspoon drops from Julie's hand and falls onto the table with a clatter. "What? Now that *what?*"

"Oh Julie, don't be like that," her mother sniffs.

Be like what? She's always wondered what her mother means when she says those words. Julie takes a deep breath, and counts to ten.

"I'm sorry I didn't wait for an invitation if that's what this is all about," her mother continues. "But I was afraid that would never happen. I just wanted to spend some time with you." She concentrates on stirring sugar into her coffee. "It can't be easy, living way out here, in this big house and no... no..."

"Darla. You can say her name, Mom. Darla!"

"Yes, Darla," her mother says, her voice catching. "I'm sorry. I didn't come all the way up here to upset you."

Then exactly why did you come?

Five days into her mother's visit Julie still hasn't figured that out. Wrapping a shawl around her shoulders, she takes her early morning coffee out to the back patio. She needs this time before her mother rises to fortify herself for another day of avoiding verbal pot-shots and holding her tongue. Here she is, a forty-four-year-old woman, and she still can't stand up to her mother. Like Ian, her mother tiptoes around the most important connection between them. But it isn't just Darla she never talks about, Julie notices; it's Jessie's girls, Emily and Amanda, as well. Not boasting about her granddaughters is so unusual for her mother that the absence is glaring.

Julie lowers her coffee mug, cupping it in her lap as it strikes her that, whenever she talks to her sister on the phone, Jessie never says anything about her girls anymore either. When was the last time she emailed photographs of them? Is everyone afraid that the subject of her sister's children is too painful for her now? Are they right?

Just then the harnessed Clydesdales emerge from the shadows behind the barn and plod out into the orange glow of the morning sun. Virgil follows behind. Julie swallows her last few mouthfuls of coffee, combs her fingers through her hair and stands up. Pulling her shawl tighter she walks over to the railing. "Good morning," she calls out, as the team clatters across the yard. "Beautiful day, isn't it?" Then she feels herself blush, because, of course, he can't answer.

He glances her way with an acknowledging nod. She lifts her hand to wave back, then lowers it self-consciously when she sees that he has already turned away.

"Virgil Blue?" Her mother's voice startles her.

She spins around to find her standing in the mudroom doorway. How long has she been there? "Yes, that's our tenant," Julie says.

Her mother comes over and joins her at the railing. "Interesting name," she says watching the team plod down the road. "Strange that you've never mentioned him before my visit."

"Why would I?"

"So, when do I get to meet this wild cowboy?"

"That's not likely. He's a bit of a hermit," Julie says retrieving her coffee mug. "And he particularly steers clear of women, so I'm told."

"Too bad. He's a rather handsome devil, isn't he? Quite an intriguing-looking black man."

Startled, Julie stares down the road. "He's not *African-American*," she says. "He's First Nations."

"He may be part Indian," her mother replies, ignoring the correction in Julie's voice. "But my dear, I know a black man when I see one."

19

Julie moans in her sleep. A growing warmth radiates from her core. In her fading dream she lays spooned in the arms of a faceless lover, feels his breath on the back of her neck. The forgotten desire, the lustful passion, is independent of her being as long as she can hang onto a shred of sleep. And in the trying, she loses it. She is suddenly aware of Ian, moving with her, moaning with her. She tries to recapture the abandon, the freedom of surrender. In her last wisps of slumber she lets him continue, sensing that he too is just rousing from sleep, his morning erection pulsing against her back, his expert hands searching. He has always been such a generous lover, so tender, so giving, taking his time, her pleasure as important as his. She has never known any other.

He kisses the nape of her neck and whispers her name. And the moment turns too real, the feeling nothing more than carnal lust, the satisfying of an itch. Sensing the change in her, or coming fully awake himself, Ian suddenly pulls away. Julie climbs from the bed leaving him lying on his back, one arm covering his face.

Later when she hears Ian come downstairs and go straight to his office, she prepares a breakfast tray of toast, eggs and coffee. Rapping lightly on the glass she opens his office door and enters before he can wave her away. She sets the tray down on the end of the desk, takes the mug of coffee and places it in front of him. He stops whatever he is working on and places one hand on hers. "I'm sorry," he says quietly. "I thought you wanted it, too." When she doesn't respond he removes his hand. "It won't happen again." He turns his attention back to the computer screen.

"I'm sorry, too," Julie whispers, closing the door softly behind her.

She glances up to see her mother slipping into the kitchen. Even in this big house it seems she's always there at the most inopportune times. If she came here to console Julie, there is very little evidence of it.

During the last few days they have established a kind of routine. In the afternoon, while her mother watches her daily soaps, Julie goes out for her walk. Since her encounter with the bear she keeps to the open fields, within view of the house. Ian works in his office with the door closed most of the day. After the evening news he normally heads upstairs to his room for the night. Her mother—unimpressed with the reality shows that Julie has become hooked on since moving out here—usually retires early as well. Last night, however, they had all gathered in the den after dinner to watch the conclusion of the Democratic convention.

They had sat in silence, each lost in their own thoughts, Ian on the recliner, Julie on one end of the couch, and her mother on the other. Watching Barack Obama's acceptance speech, Julie thought about Darla's schoolgirl crush on the handsome senator. *How Darla would have loved to see this day.* She had wanted to say it out loud, to share the flood of bittersweet memories—Darla's excitement over the historical election, the family discussions it caused. Stealing glances at her husband and mother, she had wondered if watching the newscast was triggering their own memories of Darla. Were they thinking of her, missing her as well? But like Julie, for the entire evening neither of them said a word.

Now Julie straightens her shoulders and follows her mother into the kitchen. "I hope you have something a little more casual to wear," she says retrieving the coffee pot from the stove. "You and I are going for a walk after breakfast."

Fully expecting an argument, Julie's relieved to hear the "Okay, Dear" response.

A walk together will do them both good. Her mother loved Darla, too, and Julie is determined to find a way that they can share memories of her.

In the mudroom Julie takes the leather case down from the shelf above the washing machine.

"What's that?" her mother asks.

"Bear spray," Julie says strapping it around her waist. "Bears, cougars. You never know around here." She has to hide her smile at her mother's horrified expression. Opening the door, she adds, "Don't worry, we'll stick to the open fields, so it's unlikely."

Searching her daughter's face, Doreen hesitates. Then walking past her, she mumbles, "You're just messing with me now, aren't you?"

Outside she glances into the pasture. "Your man must not be working today."

Julie follows her gaze down to the creek where the horses stand in the shade of the willow trees. "Probably gone to town," she says, as they cross the ranch yard. "And he's not 'our man.' He doesn't have to work to anyone's schedule, but his own." Ignoring her mother's raised eyebrows she opens the corral gate. If Virgil has gone to town he must have left very early because Julie hasn't heard his truck pass the house this morning. The moment the thought enters her mind, so does the realization that she is becoming attuned to his comings and goings.

"So, how often do *you* get into town?" her mother asks while Julie closes the gate behind them.

"Not often. Ian picks up whatever we need when he goes into the office every few weeks." She doesn't mention that she avoids going because she fears that she will see Darla in every young dark-haired girl on the city streets, or at the mall. And the even worse fear, that she won't.

"You let him do that?"

"Do what?"

"Go to town alone?"

Turning away, Julie rolls her eyes. They enter the empty field in silence and make their way along the snaking fenceline. The dried stubble crunches beneath their hiking boots and Julie finds herself surprised by her mother's pace. Although it isn't the speed walking that Julie is used to, it's more than a leisurely stroll.

"So, exactly how long do you intend to bury yourself out here?" her mother asks.

Unsurprised at her directness, Julie slows down while she contemplates the question. Finally she answers, "I don't know. I think Ian plans to stay forever."

"Does he do any real ranching? I haven't seen him working outside since I got here."

"There isn't much to do, now that haying is over. The cattle are out on the range until the fall. And Virgil looks after the horses."

"And what if this Virgil leaves?"

Walking side by side now, Julie looks over at her mother and shrugs. "I suppose we could always lease out the land to another rancher. Ian never intended to make money at this anyway. It's really just the space, the privacy, he wanted."

"And you?"

Julie stops and breaks off a long stalk of yellow grass by the fence. "I don't hate it, if that's what you're asking," she says. Then with a grin she puts the grass stem in her mouth and chews on the end of it, fully aware that the clichéd move, the corniness of it, will irritate her mother. And sure enough, her mother clucks her tongue and mutters, "You better watch out that you don't get 'bushed.'"

They continue toward the far end of the field, the sun on their faces, a breeze at their backs. Above them the wind gathers speed and whistles through the treetops on the other side of the fence. From somewhere in the forest, comes a familiar creaking moan. Doreen freezes and grabs Julie's arm. "What was that?"

"Oh, that's just the talking trees."

Her mother's hand falls away and she mutters, "Oh, for heaven's sake, Julie, you really are turning native."

Julie stops in her tracks and holds her arms wide in a gesture of surrender. "What is it, Mom? What do you want from me?"

"I just want you to be happy."

"Happy. What's that?" she snorts and continues walking.

At the far end of the field, the remnants of an ancient Russell fence runs parallel to the newer snake fence. On the sloping hillsides beyond, naked branches and thin tree trunks form a grey mesh forest.

"Lodge pole pine," Doreen says, studying the stand of trees. "Your father used to call them pecker poles." She walks over to the tripod corner of the old fence and places a hand on a weathered rail. With her back to Julie, she says quietly, "I know you don't think I was much of a mother when you were growing up."

Startled, Julie remains motionless behind her.

"And perhaps you're right. I was away far too much, travelling with your father. But everyone mothers in a different way." She turns around slowly. "Did you really believe that I liked living out of a suitcase for a good part of every month?" Without waiting for an answer she turns back to the fence and, as if talking to herself, her eyes focused somewhere in the distance, says, "Your father was a travelling salesman when I met him. By the time you were born he owned the company. We had no worries about money, but he still insisted on being on the road. It was in his blood."

Wondering where this is all going, and not quite sure she wants to hear it, Julie touches her arm, "Mom, you don't need to—"

"Yes, I do. Just listen. I want you to know. It's no secret that your father was a ladies' man. No secret how he treated women."

Certainly her father had been a flirt. Julie remembers the twinkle in his eyes when he affectingly addressed every female as 'Darling' or 'Sweetheart.' She remembers how he would hang mistletoe in their front entry every Christmas, and then sweep every woman who walked through their door into his arms for the required kiss, while her mother stood by watching with pursed lips. But that was just how he was. Surely it was all innocent teasing.

"I'm not going to tell you the details of our marriage," her mother says, "but I want you to understand that my travelling with him all those years was my way of protecting my family. Things were very different then. I didn't want to be a single mother, and even more, I didn't want my girls to lose their father to some silly temptation. You and Jessie worshipped him, and you still should. He was a good man. I may not have been the perfect mother, Julie, but I did what I had to do. And I am, and always was, *your* mother, just like you will always be Darla's. That part never goes away." Her voice catches. "Even if your children do."

Julie swallows. This is her opening to a conversation about Darla, to a beginning of sharing their memories of her. She moves closer and places an arm around her mother's shoulders.

But when her mother turns to her, the vulnerability that Julie expected to see in her eyes is missing. "Why I'm telling you this," her mother says stepping back and looking away, "is that it's different for you now. There's no reason for you to put up with any of this any-more. I had no choice. You do. You don't have to stay out here. You can always come back to the city. You always have a home with me."

Disappointed, Julie drops her arm and says, "Let's go back to the house."

On the silent walk home, as much as she resents her mother's infer-ence that there's no reason to stay in her marriage, it also makes Julie aware of how obvious the rift between her and Ian is. How long before he has had enough of this non-marriage? How long before she has? Until now she hasn't considered where she will go, where she will live, if it never heals. And how can it if they can't talk about the only thing that connects them, their daughter? It isn't all Ian. She is as frightened as he is to face the enormous truth that hangs between them. She sees it in his eyes. He doesn't have to say it out loud. If she hadn't let Darla off the hook so easily that night, if she had enforced her 'grounding,' their daughter would still be with them.

She doesn't want to think about it. And she doesn't want her mother's presence forcing her to. As they approach the ranch yard she takes her hand. "Mom, I love you," she says. "Now go home."

Her mother misses a step, then nods and continues walking. At the back porch she says, "Julie, I love you. Now cut your hair."

20

Mr Emerson is starting to fade around the edges. He says that I'm gradually letting go of my earthbound thinking, because, even if Mom can't see it, I understand why Gram showed up.

I still have a way to go, he says. But it's all good. Almost no one gets it right away. At least I've stopped asking him all the silly questions I did at first, like, can I go back as a bird, or a cat? Or, what will happen when I pass through the white light? Because the only answer I ever get is, 'you already know' or 'you will remember.'

It's not just Mom and Dad who are holding me back, he says. It's me as well, because even though I'm heading in the right direction, hanging onto earthly fears and attachments keeps me from getting to knowing.

I can't let go of my fear for Levi, though. Less than two hundred kilometres southwest of the valley where my parents struggle with their demons, Levi struggles with his. I watch him sink lower and lower into himself. And although time means nothing here it certainly does for him. His coach drove out to visit him. He tried to talk past that invisible wall Levi has put up around himself, but it didn't work. Even his threat that if Levi doesn't snap out of it, if he doesn't return to the team by the end of this year, he will lose his shot at the 'big time,' brought only a shrug. The thoughts that buzzed around in Levi's mind as his coach spoke had less to do with playing hockey and more to do with a promise. A promise he failed to keep. He gave no one his word that he would be a hockey player, and it means little to him right now. But he made a promise to my mother to bring me home safely that night.

She's the only person who can help him now. It's not forgiveness he wants from her, or to explain himself and offer up excuses. He's too honourable to shift the blame. No, he believes there is still a way to keep his promise. The slowly fading Mr Emerson says Levi remembers something most people forget.

21

In town, on the way to a parting lunch with her mother, Julie catches herself checking out her new haircut in the rear-view mirror. Her attempt at appeasement backfiring, she had found herself sitting like a brooding adolescent while the hairdresser styled her hair according to her hovering mother's directions. During lunch, she keeps reminding herself that 'in less than an hour this will be over,' the same technique she uses at the dentist. As soon as they are finished her mother will be on her way home to Vancouver.

"You should consider what I said, before too long," Doreen says, putting down her fork after her last bite of Caesar salad. "I can't imagine how you must be dreading winter, let alone the drive all the way back out to that place today."

Julie bites her tongue. *Fifteen minutes.*

"Just think, you could go back into real estate, or accounting, even return to university if you wanted," her mother says, watching Julie over the rim of her coffee cup. "There's nothing to stop you now."

Julie believes there is no real intention of being cruel, but she sometimes wonders if she can hear herself. She's about to ask, then decides it isn't worth the effort.

In the parking lot she waves her mother off with relief. Then, fully aware that she is still in childish mode, she goes on a spending spree.

By the time she's finished, her purchases fill the back seat. Among them is a professional digital camera and accessories, photography books, and a backpack with a built-in iPod and speakers.

Before heading home she makes a hurried trip to the grocery store, the danger zone in a small town, where you're more than likely to run into someone you know. She dreads the change in expression when someone recognizes her: their panicked look of not knowing what to say; the averting of eyes in pretence that they hadn't seen her; the flooding of sympathy when they do. And worse yet, is that look of fear she often encounters, as if tragedy is contagious.

She rushes through her shopping with the sad realization that she has become less afraid of meeting wild animals in the bush than she is of running into old acquaintances.

She almost makes it, but in the fresh produce department she hears someone call her name. Turning slowly she finds, standing behind her with a grocery basket on her arm, Valerie Ladner. The last time Julie saw her was as a blur at Darla's funeral.

Before Julie can respond she feels Valerie brush her cheek with a kiss. She lets herself be hugged, the awkwardness of the embrace double-sided.

"I never had the chance to tell you how sorry I am," Valerie whispers.

As she pulls away Julie senses that the woman's apprehension is about more than sympathy.

"I've always felt bad about that night," Valerie tells her. "Perhaps if I hadn't taken up Ian's time..." her voice cracks on the words and her eyes cloud over.

Julie hardens herself; she could not abide to see this woman's tears. Yet in Valerie's tortured expression Julie reads the need for redemption, the need to purge herself of guilt. Julie is about to snap, *You give yourself too much importance*, but something stops her. She reaches, pats Valerie's hand in a forgiving gesture and turns and walks away. Pushing her cart toward the checkout tills, Julie feels an unexpected lifting of her spirits.

On the way out of the store she glances across the street just as Virgil Blue comes out of the medical clinic. She holds back and watches him walk slowly to his pickup truck. His dog, waiting patiently with his head hanging out of the driver's window, jumps over to the passenger seat as his master climbs in. Julie waits until Virgil has driven away before heading out to her own car.

22

During the night an early frost settles on the valley leaving notice that autumn is close behind. In the morning the brittle grass sparkles with hoarfrost, a crystalline carpet spreading down to the shore. Out on the lake, one by one, loons appear like apparitions in the fog-like grey mist hanging over the still water. From her kitchen window Julie counts six of the water birds who, as certain as the coming of winter, are gathering to fly south. She wonders how soon they will leave. Used to their concerts of tremulous calls, she can't imagine not hearing them before she goes to sleep each night. A melancholy sadness floods through her at the thought of their departure. How empty the lake will be without them. Like the curious emptiness in the house this morning.

She turns her attention back to the breakfast dishes thinking how ironic it is that, as relieved as she was to see her mother leave, in a strange way she now feels her absence. Perhaps it's because during her visit she had served as a kind of buffer. Now that her mother is no longer in the house, the space between her and Ian seems expanded, a gulf impossible to breach. They eat breakfast in silence, neither attempting to resume their interrupted conversation from the day her mother arrived. Whatever his reasons for avoiding it—anger at her for returning to the guest bedroom?—Julie feels relieved. She doesn't want to revisit the conversation about Levi Johnny, or about talking to his mother.

In the living room Ian opens the fireplace doors to throw another log in. The sound of crackling wood fills the house. Early this morning he had started the first fires of the season in both the kitchen stove and the central fireplace. Unlike the draughty gas-fired heat of their furnace in town, the wood heat fills every corner of the house like a comforting hug.

While Ian goes back to work behind the closed door of his office Julie finishes up her housework. She spends the rest of the morning reading the instruction booklets for her new camera, and downloading music to her new iPod backpack. Later, when she steps outside, leaving the cocoon of warmth behind, she feels the bite of the crisp morning air. She pulls the collar up on her Gore-Tex windbreaker, and adjusts her backpack before starting out. This time, instead of hiking in the open fields she heads up the north road. She can't avoid it forever. How likely is it that she will run into the bear again anyway? Silence was her mistake then. This time she's prepared. The backpack is like a portable boom box. She might miss out on some of the sounds of nature, but any wild animals will have fair warning of her approach. The moment she can no longer see the house, she uses the remote control in her jacket pocket to switch on the iPod. Suddenly the strains of a Vivaldi concerto blast from the speakers on the sides of the backpack. She quickly adjusts the volume until it's loud enough to carry a distance without being completely overwhelming. When she originally thought of this idea she had wondered if it would interfere with the quiet solitude, which she has become used to on her hikes. But as she walks, the music of Joshua Bell's Stradivarius violin blends with the sounds of the forest as naturally as the wind. She tells herself that her choice of this particular artist has nothing to do with Virgil, other than the fact that their tenant's nocturnal playing has served to remind her how much she loves the music of this virtuoso violinist.

Passing the logging trail leading up to the woodlot, she notices hoofprints in the freshly churned earth, evidence that Virgil and his team have passed this way.

She approaches the next bend in the road with trepidation. At the spot where she encountered the bear, there is no sign of the dead bird on the roadside, or the flock of crows that had blackened the tree branches above where it lay. Still her heart quickens, pounding in her ears along with the music. As she hurries by, she checks over her shoulder, peering deep into the forest on either side. Half an hour later, other than squirrels skittering up and down tree trunks—too busy gathering winter provisions to be concerned with the mobile concert—she sees no sign of any animals. She slows her pace, beginning to wonder, what is she doing here? Tempting fate? The idea of taking photographs seems somewhat less exciting now. Still, she continues on until she arrives at the northern end of the lake. Spotting a better vantage point at the water's edge, she leaves the road and heads toward the marshes along the shore. She picks her way gingerly through the bulrushes and sun-bleached deadfalls, which reach up like bony fingers from the spongy bog. The wind has stopped and the scent of peat moss underfoot and the faint aroma of distant chimney smoke fills the air. Near the water's edge, she finds a firm foothold on a grassy hummock and stops to stare down the lake. All along its shore, yellowing poplar and birch leaves, evidence of Jack Frost's overnight touch, dot the green landscape like random brush strokes. The mirrored image of a ragged treeline cutting into a washed blue sky reflects from the lake's glass-like surface.

She turns off the music and in the sudden silence hears the distant honking of Canada geese in flight. She scans the sky but there is no sign of the birds. Shrugging off her backpack she takes out her new camera, removes it from its case and focuses on the scene before her. As she takes her first photographs the call of the wild geese becomes louder. She glances up and quickly changes the camera's angle to capture the image of the vee formation flying so low that she can hear the whooshing of air beneath their wings. She clicks continually as they pass directly overhead and then skim down the lake, heading south. *Going home.*

She lowers the camera watching the birds become dots above the ranch house roof, and wonders if the log house on the distant shore will ever feel like home to her. Will anywhere without Darla?

Back on the road, with the music blaring once again from her back, she considers exploring the logging area above the lake. But nearing the fork in the road, she changes her mind. Glancing up the trail she sees something moving in the flickering shadows. Her heart leaps into her throat leaving the blood pounding in her ears even after she realizes that it isn't a wild animal but Virgil Blue emerging in the afternoon light. He stands silhouetted on the ridge of the hill for only a moment before turning away.

Julie switches off the iPod, and heads up the logging trail. By the time she reaches the spot where Virgil had stood, he's nowhere in sight. Pine and fir needles crunch under her hiking boots as she skirts around a log pile. In the clearing beyond, scraps of bark, boughs and branches carpet the ground. The air is sharp with the scent of pitch and freshly cut timber. At the far end of the landing, behind his team of horses, Virgil is bent over a felled tree securing a chain to the butt end. If he notices Julie when he straightens up to take the reins, he gives no sign. She scrambles up a bank and watches as the horses lean into their harness. With mouths working their bits, and sweat lathering beneath leather collars, they strain forward at Virgil's silent command. Before long the massive tree trunk jerks forward, and then skids easily behind the team as they cross the landing. Only after it comes to rest alongside the log pile, does Virgil glance Julie's way. His dark eyes and unchanged expression give no indication of his reaction to her presence, other than to acknowledge it. She lifts her hand in a quick wave, and then holds up her camera with a gesture that asks for permission to use it. Feeling foolish at the realized error—*he's mute, not deaf*—she hollers a little louder than necessary, "Do you mind if I take some photographs?"

Virgil's nod is so brief, and he resumes his chore so quickly, that she wonders if she has imagined his consent. Still, she focuses her camera and takes a few test shots of him unhooking the skidding chains. When she gets no sign of protest she climbs down the bank and removes her backpack. Placing it on the ground on top of her jacket she readies her camera again. When Virgil straightens up he points down at her backpack. Confused Julie looks from him to the ground, and asks, "Is it in the way?"

He shakes his head, and then taps his ear, the meaning clear. For the rest of the afternoon, while Julie follows at a distance taking photographs of Virgil and the horses at work, the music of Joshua Bell fills the forest.

Later that night Julie rises from her bed. Finding her way downstairs in the dark she removes the shawl blanket from the back of the couch and wraps it around her shoulders. Out on the front deck she stands in the moonlight, smiling. It hadn't been her imagination after all. From across the water, just like the violin music that had played out from her backpack today, comes the sorrow-filled strains of the Vivaldi concerto.

23

Virgil's story

Sorrow. No one makes it through life without experiencing it. He was born to it—its presence replacing the father he had never known. A father lost to the Korean War, one week before the ceasefire was signed, one month after his youngest son's birth. The boy kept a picture of him tacked to the panelled wall in his room. In the old sepia photograph, not a soldier, but a cowboy, wearing sheepskin chaps leans against a corral fence, a lariat coiled in his right hand. A wide-brimmed Stetson pushed back on his forehead reveals a flashing white-toothed smile shining from his father's handsome face. Every time his mother gazed at the photograph the boy sensed her silent mourning for a lost husband, and he believed there could be no greater heartache.

Until his fourteenth birthday.

Despite the money the twins sent home each month, the mobile home grew steadily sadder-looking. After his brothers joined the army on their eighteenth birthdays their mother went through the motions of carrying on life as normal. But once they shipped out to Vietnam, she gave up all pretence. The crabgrass lawn was gone, replaced by dust and bits and pieces of windblown trash. The wilted marigolds shed ignored yellow and orange petals onto the weed-covered path. The porch sagged with neglect.

Pedalling as hard as the worn-out wheels of his second-hand bike would allow, the boy hurried home from his Saturday music lesson. Taking the skidding turn into the trailer court, he thought about how he could do more to help his mother. Perhaps he could fix the front porch. All it would take is a few boards, a hammer and some nails. He cringed at the thought of using a hammer. He secretly feared hitting his fingers with it. But today he turns fourteen and it's time to become a man. And he would. He would have to find time between schoolwork, his newspaper routes, violin lessons and practice. He would start tomorrow, after the surprise horseback ride his mother has arranged for his birthday gift. For an entire week he has tried to rein in his excitement so that she doesn't find out that his little sister, Melody, has spilled the beans. Birthdays mean so much to his mother that he would have no trouble acting surprised when she presented him with this gift. He had long outgrown his desire for toy guns, but still dreamt of being a cowboy, like his father. He had learned very early though to be guarded about who he shared this information with. When he was eight years old he had made the mistake of taking the photograph to school.

A nigger cowboy! No friggin way! Even worse was the laughter.

After recess, Margie Smith, who sat in the desk behind him, had leaned forward and whispered not to listen to them, that she thought it was neat that his father was a cowboy. On the way home from school the blonde, blue-eyed girl asked to see the picture again. He stopped and took it slowly from his pocket. He handed it to her, wondering what he would do if she too mocked it, or even worse, tore the picture up. He stood nervously while she studied the photograph, then handed it back saying, *Neat!*

If it was true, as his sister told him, that for his birthday, his mother has paid for him and a friend to go riding at the stables on the outskirts of town tomorrow, Margie was the one he would invite.

On the corner to his street, their neighbour, Mr Fowler, stepped out onto his covered porch. Lifting the black violin case from the handle bars, the boy held it up to let his old teacher know he had been practising. The old man nodded from his trailer porch. Since the boy's seventh birthday, in exchange for a few dollars and some yard work, Mr Fowler gave him lessons once a week. Then last year, their neighbour announced that he had gone as far as he could. *I ain't good enough for anything more'n list'nen to the boy practise now,* he told his mother. *He needs a real teacher.* He gave her the name of an instructor in town.

She had bartered with the boy though, extracting a promise in exchange for professional lessons, which would be paid for from the money his brothers sent home. She made the offer only once. And he had given his oath that he would not follow in his brothers' footsteps when he grew up, that he would not go to war. Now, every Saturday, he rode his bike into town for lessons.

But it was a boy's promise, made with fingers mentally crossed behind his back. Surely by the time he was old enough to join his brothers she would understand if he retracted it. He would face that when the time came.

His wheels wobbled as he hung the violin case on the handlebars again. He gained control, waved back at Mr Fowler and turned onto their road. The smell of cabbage boiling for Saturday dinner filled the air. But it was not coming from their trailer. They would not eat corned-beef and cabbage tonight. His mouth watered at the thought of the chocolate cake and ice cream waiting at home. He smiled wider yet knowing that in a few moments he would see his mother happy, or pretending that she was happy, for a few hours.

A taxi was parked in front of their house. His heart leapt into this throat. His brothers home for his birthday?

He skidded into the yard, kicking up dust in his wake and letting his bike drop to the ground. Sprinting across the dirt, he almost stumbled before he leapt onto the porch. Throwing open the door in excitement, he pushed inside to find two army officers, who were not his brothers, in the entryway. With hats tucked under their arms they stood, as if rooted, a few feet from his mother. In the living room, his little sister sat on the couch, her cream-coloured skin ashen. His birthday cake waited on the side buffet. Above it, his brothers' stern faces stared out from matching frames.

He looked from his brothers' army photographs to his mother, who was listening with a stony expression to one of the officers murmuring that he hoped she would 'find comfort in the fact that your sons were together when they gave the ultimate sacrifice for their country.'

When the words stopped, when there was no air, no sound, left in the room, his mother reached between the officers and opened the door. The two men nodded as they filed past her and walked out into a world that would never be the same. The door closed. The ticking of the kitchen clock sounded loud until the taxi motor roared to life. On the couch his sister Melody hiccupped, pulled her hand away from her mouth and buried her head in the sofa cushion and wailed. His mother stepped over to the sideboard, removed her sons' photographs from the wall and shuffled, an old woman making her way down the hallway to her bedroom. The sound of her door opening and closing startled the boy. He moved over to the couch, slumped down and wrapped his arms around his sister. He rocked her trembling body while the animal-like keening seeped out from beneath the door at the end of the hall.

24

The next day Julie uploads the digital photographs onto her computer in the den. Sorting through the ones that she took at the north end of the lake, she is disappointed in their amateurish quality. Obviously there's a great deal more to learn, much more to photography than simply taking a snapshot of an interesting landscape. She spends some time testing her new software, playing with colours and hues, cropping and enlarging, in an attempt to recapture whatever excitement she had experienced at the original thought of this new hobby. But the spark of passion has fizzled. Feeling inertia threaten, she moves on to the images of Virgil working with his horses. Like the others, the shots are technically unskilled as well, shadows and light, settings and distances, she sees now, are all wrong. Still, in these images there is something that she hadn't noticed from behind the camera. She goes back through them slowly, glancing over her shoulder every now and then to check that Ian is still in his office. She studies each shot: Virgil watering the Clydesdales; guiding them through a narrow path, the green of the forest all around; one of the horses nibbling an unknown treat from Virgil's open palm; leather reins hanging loose over chestnut backsides while giant heads are turned toward their master. Looking at the images now, Julie realizes that they are more than photographs of a man and his horses. Each one told a story. A story of trust, connection and undoubted love.

Over the next few days, whenever Julie hears the distant drone of a chainsaw in the forest, she feels the urge to return to the landing. But she can't find a good excuse to do so.

Throughout the following nights Ian keeps a fire going in the central fireplace. Before dawn on Friday morning Julie comes downstairs while he is stoking it up. The reflection of the flames glow orange on his face as he closes the fireplace doors. He glances up at her. "That should keep it going for another six hours or so," he says straightening up. "Just throw another log on around noon." He brushes his hands on his pants. "Did you make a list of what you want in town?"

She goes into the kitchen and returns with the list. "Oh, and some red wine," she adds.

"Yeah, I've noticed we're getting low," he says accepting the list from her.

Julie feels herself flush. Before she can reply, the jarring screech of Jake brakes and the roar of a truck engine sound outside.

"That'll be the logging truck," Ian says standing up. "They're picking up a load of logs this morning." A flash of headlights sweeps through the office.

Julie leaves him peering out the window and goes back to the kitchen.

A few minutes later Ian comes out of his office carrying a box of files. "I don't know how late I'll have to work," he says crossing the living room. Then as if it's an afterthought he adds, "I might stay in town overnight."

Julie's coffee mug stops on the way to her lips. Staring at him over the rim, she shrugs.

Ian stops at the kitchen entryway. "What? What does that look mean?" He drops the box to his feet. "Why don't you just say it, Julie?"

"There's nothing to say," she answers placing her mug on the counter with measured care.

"Look, the roads can be treacherous at night now; there are deer every few miles. I don't want to drive in the dark if I'm tired. But, if that's a problem..."

"No, of course not," Julie says. "Really. Give me a call if you have to stay. It's okay."

Ian studies her for a moment as if contemplating her sincerity. They both know what they are not talking about.

She considers telling him about running into Valerie Ladner the other day at the grocery store. Considers letting him know how she had extended the hand of forgiveness to her. But that would require talking about the night that Darla died. A forbidden subject with Ian. And it would require Julie to explain to herself why she had found it so easy to let Valerie off the hook, while a part of her still hangs onto her anger at Ian. *Would I be this unforgiving over a single, thoughtless kiss, if Darla hadn't died?* The unbidden thought takes her by surprise, as does the answering one. *If Darla hadn't died, would it have ended at one kiss?*

An hour after Ian has left for town, Julie hears the rumble of an engine. She makes it out to the back patio in time to see the fully loaded logging truck head up the hill, Virgil's pickup following behind in the early morning light.

Listless after her conversation with Ian she tries to study her photography book, but finds she can't concentrate. The coffee isn't cutting it this morning. She considers going for a hike but can't summon up the energy. If it wasn't so early she'd pour herself a glass of wine. *Well, why not?* She uncorks a bottle of Merlot. She hadn't missed Ian's remark about the wine supply. It's true that she's having a glass or two more often in the evenings than she used to. It helps her sleep. Ian has his sleeping pills, she has her wine. She pours a glass, and takes a long sip, thinking that wine has replaced the women friends with whom she once shared the petty complaints of life. Women who listened to each other with the unspoken understanding that it only meant something while they dumped whatever they needed to dump, and then promptly forgot it. The only sounding board she has now is her own mind. And that is better when she doesn't listen to it. She takes her glass and the bottle, along with her book into the living room.

She wakes to the sun glaring in her eyes. The sudden roar of a low-flying airplane startles her to a sitting position. Shielding her eyes, she rises from the couch, makes it to the front window just as a float plane screams over the house, flying so low that she can see the watermarks on the bottom of the pontoons. It races down the lake then circles over the treetops at the north end and heads back. The engine cuts, and for a moment the plane seems to hang on the wind before dropping in altitude. Sunlight glints on the wing tips as it skims over the water and touches down; a rooster-tail spray follows behind as the plane heads toward Virgil's bay.

Julie has no idea whether Virgil has returned while she was napping. But something tells her he hasn't. She goes upstairs and from the balcony off the master bedroom watches the float plane taxi through the water to its destination. It drifts to a stop, the door pushes open and the pilot climbs out to jump onto Virgil's dock. He ties the aircraft down then begins to unload cargo. When there's still no sign of their tenant, Julie combs her hands through her hair. She'll have to go over and let the visitor know that Virgil is away.

By the time she reaches the front of the cabin, the pilot, who has replaced the headphones with a battered straw cowboy hat, is kneeling in front of a large animal crate.

"Virgil's not home," Julie calls out from shore.

The pilot stands. "Well, that's too bad. I was hoping to have a visit with him."

Julie hesitates for only a second before stepping onto the dock. From a distance, judging by size, the denim jacket and blue jeans, it

136

was easy to assume that the pilot was a man. But to Julie's amazement, according to the well-endowed bustline of the person grinning down at her, it's a woman. Trying to hide her surprise, Julie takes the huge work-worn hand being offered to her.

"Well, you're just a little bit of a thing, aren't you," the pilot says pumping her hand as firmly as any man. "Terri Champion."

"Julie O'Dale," Julie answers wondering briefly if her breath smells of alcohol, then decides it's impossible for the Amazon pilot to smell it from that height. "Virgil's not home," she repeats. "I don't know when he'll be back."

"Oh, that's okay. This delivery's for you anyway." A yelp comes from the animal crate.

Julie skirts around an old willow-switch chair on the dock and kneels down to peer into the kennel. A black nose presses against the wire grate. "Oh, no," she says straightening up quickly. "No. This is some mistake."

"Nope. No mistake. This little fellow is bought and paid for."

"By whom?"

"Can't say who paid, but Virgil ordered him. He's from the same line as his own—a mixture of Australian sheepdog and German shepherd. If there's a little wolf in there, no one's saying," she gives Julie a wink, which might have been comical under other circumstances. "But you won't find a dog better suited to this country," she continues, "I should know. I breed 'em."

The puppy flops down inside his crate, placing his grey-and-black head on his paws.

"He's a little traumatized by the flight. But he did pretty good." The pilot leans over. "Didn't you, fella? What a good boy you are." The crooning words sound odd coming from such a mountain of a woman.

"He's six months old. Housebroke. Trained him myself, so of course he's bonded with me." She looks up at Julie and grins while the dog licks her fingers through the grate. "He'll bond with you in no time. A few days? A few weeks? Depends."

"Not me," Julie says. "I'm sorry. Look I don't care if it was Virgil, or my husband, who's responsible for this, but I never asked for a dog. And I don't want one."

"Well, he's not going back with me. So you can either let him sit out here on the dock and argue it out with Virgil when he comes home, or you can help me take him over to your place."

25

Fifteen minutes later, in spite of Julie's futile objections, Terri-the-Pilot carries the dog kennel onto the back porch of the ranch house. Julie follows behind with the puppy tugging at the leash.

"You should bring his crate inside for the first few nights," Terri says, setting it down. "It's his safe place. After he adjusts to his new home you can decide if he's an inside or outside dog."

"Virgil can decide," Julie corrects her. "I'm not keeping him."

"Right." Terri straightens up. "He needs lots of walking. Take him out into the fields for the first while, where he can see the house. And keep him on the leash until he transfers his loyalty to you. It won't take long. You'll know when."

Julie shakes her head. There isn't any point arguing—the woman just doesn't listen. Perhaps if she stalls long enough Virgil will return and then he can deal with her. "Would you like to come in for a cup of coffee, or tea?" she asks.

"Thought you'd never ask," Terri grins. "Tea's great. I'll just go back and get the pup's food while you make it." She gestures to the dog and says, "Stay, Pup." Then striding across the porch, calls back over her shoulder, "And I like my tea strong… none of that chintzy waving a bag through the water."

The dog whimpers but remains at Julie's side, the leash hanging loose between them.

Inside he sits on the kitchen floor, his black eyes following Julie as she fills the kettle then puts muffins on a plate. At the same moment the kettle starts its high-pitched whistle, the mudroom door opens without a warning knock and Terri calls out, "Hello this place."

"In here," Julie calls, pouring the boiling water into the teapot.

"Wow," Terri whistles, coming through the living room. "Fancy digs. Looks different from when the Woells lived here."

"It's the stuffed animals," Julie says placing two mugs onto the table. "They're gone."

"Ahh, well to each his own." Terri plunks herself down at the table. She picks up the pottery mug. "I don't mean to be picky, Gal, but have you got any china teacups in that fancy hutch of yours. Tea tastes so much better in real china don't you think? Something like wine in crystal," she adds glancing at the wine bottle and glass on the living-room coffee table.

Trying to hide her surprise, and her embarrassment, Julie removes the mugs from the table. She returns with the teacup, and sets it in front of her guest.

Terri sits back after Julie settles in her chair. "Look," she says looking directly at her, "I heard about your daughter. Darla, right?" Her voice, like her face has softened. " I just want to say right off, that I'm darn sorry. I don't have any kids of my own so can only imagine how hard that was, is, for you."

The directness of her words has a grace that erases the awkwardness of the moment. This rough-around-the-edges woman has just cut through the inevitable getting-to-know-you questions that Julie has come to dread. Especially those about '...any children?' How do you answer that one? Worse yet, are those encounters with friends who don't know what to say so avoid mentioning Darla at all, as if she'd never existed. Instead of being startled to hear a stranger say her daughter's name, Julie finds a measure of comfort in it.

"Thank you," she says quietly. She picks up the teapot and pours a little into Terri's teacup. "Dark enough?"

"Good enough. Fill 'er up."

After Julie pours, her guest cups the teacup in her huge palms, her fingers surrounding the rim, and asks, "So how are you doing out here in the wilds, Gal?"

Julie shrugs. "I'm fine." Then she meets Terri's eyes. The genuine concern she sees there, and the candour in her voice deserve more than a dismissive answer. She leans back. "I'm getting used to it, I guess. But it's different. Hard, in many ways. It's beautiful here, yes. But there are certainly things about living in town I miss. Mostly our home. But I suspect that it's the memories of our daughter there that I miss, more than the actual house. There are no memories of her here." She looks down at her cup, surprised at what has come out of her mouth. She has said more to this stranger than she has to anyone in the last year. "It's lonely here," she continues in spite of herself. "Lonely in ways that have nothing to do with isolation." She shrugs. "But then I suppose right now I'd be lonely no matter where I was."

"I expect so," Terri answers quietly. "Well, anytime you feel like company I'm just over the ridge."

Julie meets her eyes again and smiles. "So what about you?" she asks pushing the muffin platter to her. "What brought you to the Chilcotin?"

"The short story is that I came from Montana in the late fifties," she says accepting the offering. "On a holiday with my folks, met my future husband, Sam Champion, and stayed. Been ranching ever since, even after my Sammy died—God rest his soul—I kept the place going. We're just northwest of here. I could have driven over, or come on my ATV through the bush, but I like to fly any chance I get, especially before the ice starts to form on the lakes." She breaks her muffin in half and slathers it with butter. "I was hoping to get a visit with Virgil, too," she says taking a bite.

"He went out with the logging truck this morning. I've no idea when he'll be back."

"Sorry I missed him. Virgil used to wrangle for me. He was my lead hand, 'til about twenty years ago. He moved over here, when my spread went from a working ranch to a 'dude' ranch. Likes his privacy, as you may have noticed."

"Elke Woell told us that he doesn't have much use for women, so I'm surprised to hear he worked for one."

Terri lets out a barking laugh. "He probably never even took notice that I was a woman. No, *Frau* Woell was a blondie. That's probably it. He steers clear of fair-haired women." She studies Julie's hair. "Your hair isn't really blonde, or brown, is it? It's somewhere in-between. Me, I used to be auburn, but now I'm just grey." She lifts her hat to reveal her close-cropped silver hair.

"Besides, Virgil and I have something in common." She reaches for another muffin. "We're both Yanks. He showed up at the ranch looking to cowboy for us back in 1971."

Julie picks at the corner of her own muffin. "Was he one of the Vietnam War resisters?"

"Nah. He'd never have been accepted even if he had been drafted. Have you seen his hands?"

Julie nods. "How did that happen?"

Terri chews the last bite of muffin and washes it down with a long swallow of tea. Her teacup rattles into the saucer. "Can't say," she says wiping her mouth with the back of her hand. "That's Virgil's story to tell, not mine."

"Well, that's hardly likely, is it." Julie picks up the teapot and refills Terri's empty cup. "When did he lose his voice?"

"Oh 'bout four years ago. But he didn't talk all that much before that, anyway."

By the time the pilot leaves, Virgil still hasn't returned. Julie stands on the dock watching the float plane lift off the water and skim over the treetops at the north end of the lake. She is surprised to find that she's sorry to see it go. She glances at the piece of paper that Terri wrote her telephone number on, 'just in case,' folds it and places it in her pocket.

After the plane is out of sight, she looks down at the dog whimpering at her side. "Well, now what am I supposed to do with you?" she asks. The puppy looks up. He tilts his head as if contemplating her question, and Julie finds herself scratching his ears.

"Okay, let's get you some dinner." She tugs lightly on the leash and the dog follows her off the dock without resistance. On the shore Julie stops to study the front of Virgil's cabin. Today is the first time she has seen the front side of his home. On the covered veranda, a second willow chair, which matches the weathered one down on the dock, sits in the corner beside a wooden planter barrel, spilling over with marigolds—the hardy yellow and orange flowers an unexpected sight on a bachelor's porch. For a brief moment Julie is tempted to climb the few steps and peek in the front window. Her conscience gets the better of her curiosity, and she heads home, passing under the mountain ash flanking the driveway. Earlier, before closing the cockpit door, Terri had pointed out the trees, their branches laden with orange-red berry clusters. "Brace yourself for winter, Gal," she'd warned. "That heavy berry crop is a sure sign of a harsh one coming."

Julie shivers. She doesn't need Terri, or the mountain ash, to tell her. This will be a hard winter no matter what the temperature.

26

Every season, every month, every day, looms before Mom with torturous memories of 'what was'—what I did then, and will never do again.

As long as she keeps looking at the world through eyes of 'before' nothing will change, and she will remain stuck, unable to move on. And so will I. I don't need Mr Emerson to explain that. I wish I could tell her though. Not for myself, I'm okay, but for her sake, for Dad's, for Levi's. I wish that I could stop her from sinking deeper and deeper in the sludge of 'what used to be'—a nowhere place. She lives in past tense now—the future too empty to consider—marking time by the day of my death.

Last Christmas, their first without me, was torture for them both. They hid from it. Dad at his office downtown, Mom in the wine she drank while she sat all alone in front of the TV in our family room. No lights, no Christmas decorations, no tree, no gifts, no turkey. But the harder they tried to pretend it was just another day, the worse it became. Now she dreads next month, October 26th, the one-year anniversary of 'The Day.' Instead of celebrating my living, she wallows in the circumstances of my dying. And although I can wait forever—forever meaning something entirely different from where I am now—Levi can't.

Even the Elders, who come to talk to 'their warrior on ice,' leave shaking their heads. It's Mom who Levi needs to speak to. If she would just meet with him, if she could see what was happening to him, she would have to listen to what he has to say. She wouldn't turn her back on someone who needs her. Would she? Mr Emerson says these are not the questions I should be asking.

Hanging onto earthbound worries will not lead to understanding and remembering.

I'm not sure anymore if these are his thoughts or mine. It's getting harder and harder to tell. There is an elusive memory about the white light that teases me. Like wisps of smoke, remembrance floats within my grasp, if only I could let go of my attachment to earth and reach for it.

But I can't. I can't let go or stop worrying. About Mom and Dad and Levi. Especially Levi. My father, and even my mother, could find a way to heal, a way to go on with their lives, given enough time. But Levi doesn't have time. Like Mr Emerson, he's fading away. His face is so hollow now; the dimples I once loved to see appear no longer mark his cheeks, even if he could remember how to smile.

His sole plan right now is to do a sweat—a vision quest to the spirit world—on the anniversary of my death. If Mom had only answered his call, he was going to invite her to join him in the sweat, or to participate in a healing circle. At one time I know she would have seen this as an honour. I'm not so sure now.

With the arrival of this puppy though, I see a tiny chink in the armour of her grief. It's freakin' funny watching the cute little guy follow Mom around the house. He shadows her every move, while she does her best to ignore him. In the kitchen, she fills his dish and places it on the floor. The dog remains sitting on his haunches, looking from her to the dish and back to her, as if waiting for permission. "Okay, go get it, Pup," she says. She doesn't know what to call him, hadn't thought to ask Terri. Watching him gobble down his dinner, she catches herself mulling over names, then shakes her head. She starts to turn away, muttering to herself that she will do nothing more than the necessary for the dog before she delivers him to Virgil. She stops short, and looks down at the puppy pushing the dish forward with his nose trying to get at the last dregs of his food. "Now you have me talking to myself," she tells him before heading into the den. The dog looks up and follows her, his huge paws padding across the kitchen tiles. He plops down in the doorway and lies with his head between his paws, his tail swishing across the floor, while his black eyes watch her, watching television. The moment she glances over at him, he lifts his head, and his ears stand at attention. She lets out an involuntary chuckle, the first genuine laughter I have heard from her since, well, since 'The Day.'

"Oh, no, you don't," she scolds him. "You're not worming your way into my heart." After a while she glances down during a commercial and is startled to find the puppy's mottled grey head resting on her lap, his eyes closed while her hand unconsciously scratches behind his ears.

She jumps up and switches off the television then goes out to the back porch to bring in his kennel for the night. The puppy watches her drag it into the mudroom. He enters it without coaxing, but remains standing behind the wire grate, his eyes following her as she leaves the room. On her way upstairs Mom tries to ignore his whimpering. But I know she'll give in. She was always a soft touch. Sure enough, before long she's back in the mudroom, letting the dog out, telling him that it's only because she can't stand listening to all his whining. She wrestles the crate up to her bedroom, bumping and banging the walls, while he follows at her heels. The minute the kennel is in place next to her bed he enters and settles down.

"Don't get any ideas," Mom says climbing into bed, "this is only for one night."

Hah! Yeah right!

27

"What's this?" Ian asks coming into the mudroom early the next morning.

"I thought you could tell me," Julie says, glancing up from the stool where she is hastily pulling on her runners. At her side the puppy lets out a low growl. "It's okay," she assures him, then stands up, grabbing her jacket from the hook by the door. The dog rises as well, keeping himself between her and Ian.

"Where did *you* come from?" Ian asks kneeling down to eye level with the black puppy, who pushes his body against Julie's legs.

"Apparently from Virgil. Did you ask him to get us a dog?"

"No, of course not. I wouldn't..." He stops mid-sentence. "Oh Jeez. I might have nodded when he suggested it in one of his notes, way back. I never gave it any more thought. Maybe I gave the impression that I had agreed to it."

"Yeah. Maybe. Because here *it* is." She leans over to snap on the leash, and then opens the door. "And *it* needs to go right now."

Ian rises and follows her out. "He certainly seems protective of you already. Maybe a dog's not such a bad idea, Julie."

"No!" she replies, without looking back. "No!"

After the puppy relieves himself, he heads straight for the north road, dragging Julie like a pull-toy on the leash behind him. Nearing

Virgil's driveway, his straining becomes more urgent. She allows him to turn down the road, struggling to keep up with him.

Virgil's pickup truck is once again parked at the back of the cabin. *Well, now is as good a time as any.*

Suddenly the leash is yanked from her hand and the dog bolts. Julie chases after him, then realizing where he is headed, she slows to a walk, watching the puppy streak past the cabin and down to the lake—the last place he'd seen Terri. He leaps onto the dock and paces back and forth, yelping out over the water as if he can summon her back. Julie smiles sadly at the sight, then joins him on the dock. After a few half-hearted whimpers, he comes over and stands at her side, his attention still on the lake. He looks so forlorn that Julie can't resist stroking his neck. "I'm sorry, Pup."

After a while she turns and looks up at the cabin, then back to the dog. "Well, what do you think?" she asks.

He tilts his head. "You decide," Julie says making her way off the dock. Walking up to the cabin she peers over her shoulder just as the dog stands up and pads over to the ramp, the leash dragging free on the wooden boards behind him. The moment he is on shore he starts toward the road then stops and glances at her impatiently, as if asking whether she is coming or not.

Julie holds her hand up in the 'stay' gesture she saw Terri use, then climbs the porch steps. Even before she reaches the door she senses the cabin is empty. She knocks anyway, listens for any signs of life then knocks harder. Hearing nothing inside, she goes over to the window. Unable to detect any movement in the darkened interior, she makes a peephole with her hands against the glass to block out the light and tries to peer past a dreamcatcher hanging on the other side of the glass. She jumps at the sudden touch on her hip, and looks down to find the puppy pushing up against her.

"Caught me," she laughs nervously. She bends over to retrieve the dragging leash. "Looks like we don't really need this. But, just in case," she says, leading him off the porch. "Wouldn't want to lose you before we can hand you over to Virgil."

With the leash hanging loose between them they walk away from the cabin, Julie feeling a twinge of disappointment, mixed with an equal amount of relief, that Virgil isn't there.

Only when she is taking off her runners in the mudroom back at the ranch house, does it occur to her that she had slept through the entire night last night—without hearing either Virgil's truck or Ian return home—that in fact last night was the best sleep she'd had in almost a full year.

Later over breakfast, with the dog fed and curled up at her feet, she tells Ian about Terri Champion's visit. Like her sleep last night, the conversation is the easiest she and Ian have had in a long while. She finds herself laughing while she relates Terri's request for a china teacup, and compares it to her mother's preference.

"Sounds like an interesting character," Ian says taking the last bite of his omelette.

"Yes, she is. I like her."

Ian bends over and looks under the table. "And what about you?" he asks.

"*He* is going back to Virgil."

Ian straightens up. "Are you sure?"

"Yes."

"That's too bad."

"I already tried to return him," Julie says, ignoring Ian's words, "but either Virgil's not home, or he's a very sound sleeper. We were just over there."

Ian raises his eyebrows but quickly recovers. Julie wonders briefly if his reaction is to the unlikelihood of her remark about Virgil sleeping in, or to the fact that she had gone over to his cabin.

"He's probably logging." Ian takes a sip of coffee, then adds, "If you want, I'll take the dog back to him later."

149

"That's okay." Julie reaches for his empty plate and stacks it on top of hers. "I'll do it myself."

Once again an expression of surprise flickers across Ian's face, but he says nothing as Julie clears the table.

28

By the time Julie finishes puttering in the kitchen, changes her clothes, puts on her backpack and hiking boots and goes back outside, the sun is directly overhead. How quickly the landscape has changed overnight. Earlier this morning, preoccupied with chasing after the dog, she had missed the brilliant display of fall colours. Now, in no rush, the puppy at her heel, she takes it all in.

Unlike the reds and orange of the coastal autumns of her youth, the Chilcotin fall blooms golden. Across the lake, poplar, cottonwood and aspen groves burst yellow among dark hues of evergreen. All along the north road, sunlight slants through the forest, giving the deciduous trees a fluorescent glow, and accenting the rust undergrowth. A sudden gust of wind creates a tiny dust devil on the road in front of them, lifting up a whirlwind of golden leaves. Like snowflakes, they swirl and rise on the updraft, before fluttering back to the ground to litter the dirt road. Excited by their flickering movement, straining at the end of his leash, the puppy pounces and snaps at one, then another.

Julie laughs out loud at his antics. She catches herself and shakes her head, mentally relisting all the reasons why she does not want a dog.

It's too long a commitment. Years.

I don't have the energy to train him. He's already trained.

Pets tie you down. Where is she going anyway?

They're messy. No, that's her mother's reason, not hers. At any rate she's not keeping him and that's that. She doesn't have the space in her head, or her heart.

Still, as they approach the turnoff up to the landing she catches herself slowing down, delaying, just as she had dragged her heels leaving the house after breakfast.

Without the music blaring from her backpack—*chalk up one advantage to having a dog*—she can hear the distant whine of a chainsaw. She gives the leash a gentle tug and starts up the rutted trail. At the same moment Virgil's dog suddenly appears at the top of the hill. He stands motionless, his tail curled into a question mark, the hair on the ridge of his back standing up. "It's okay," Julie calls out. She has no idea what the dog's name is and can only hope he remembers her. On guard, he watches them approach. The puppy yips and leaps forward tugging at the leash, wanting nothing more than to play. The older dog starts moving stealthily toward them, looking for all the world like a wolf ready to spring. Julie stops and pulls the pup to her side. Suddenly a whistle sounds from above and Virgil's dog stops in his tracks. He remains where he is as his master joins him.

"Thanks," Julie calls out continuing up the hill, "I wasn't sure what his reaction would be to us."

As if expecting them and there's no need for acknowledgement, Virgil points to her hand and then at the puppy's collar.

Julie stops and looks down at the leash. "Really?" she asks. "Let him go?"

Virgil nods.

"Okay," she says slowly. Fighting her reluctance, and she realizes, her protectiveness, she does as he asks.

The moment the pup is free, he crouches down, submissive, allowing the older dog to check him out with his nose. Virgil watches for a few moments, then turns back up the hill. Finished sniffing and apparently satisfied, his dog follows. The puppy bounds after them. Julie rolls up the leash and shoves it in her pocket. All the way up to the landing the older dog struts beside his master ignoring, or tolerating—Julie is not sure which—the exuberant puppy.

When they enter the clearing, the Clydesdales, more concerned with their noon meal, don't bother to lift their massive heads from their feed bucket. Julie follows Virgil to the far side of the landing, where the remnants of his lunch sit on a stump. As they approach, a crow lifts from a chair-high log bolt next to the stump and wings clumsily away, a bread crust clasped firmly in its ebony beak.

Motioning Julie to the log bolt, Virgil sits on the edge of the stump and removes a Thermos and a blue tin cup from his lunch bucket. While she shrugs the backpack from her shoulders and takes a seat, he fills the cup and the Thermos lid with coffee. With neither offer, nor acceptance, the tin cup passes from his gnarled fingers to hers.

She wonders if he would like to hear the music again—is about to ask when he rests his elbows on his knees, and with steam rising from the Thermos lid cupped in his hands, he watches the puppy. At his side his dog sits at attention, also keeping an eye on the pup, who has tired of trying to entice him to play and has now turned his attention to the horses.

The pup circles them cautiously, snapping and retreating with a yelp when a hind leg suddenly kicks out the moment he gets too close. Julie restrains the impulse to call out a warning. If Virgil is unconcerned, why should she be?

She settles back and sips her coffee, while the lulling sounds of autumn surround her: dried aspen leaves clicking in the breeze; the *chick-a-dee-dee-dee* call of the tiny migrating birds flittering through the branches; pine cones thudding to the ground nearby. Lazy autumn insects add a background drone to the music of the forest. Finally the puppy tires of being ignored by the horses and scurries around investigating his surroundings.

Beside her, Virgil takes a final gulp of his coffee, rises and throws the dregs in an arc across the ground. From the top branches of a nearby spruce tree a crow barks impatient orders. Virgil packs his Thermos away, and fishes out an unfinished sandwich. Tearing it apart he tosses pieces into the air and the demanding bird swoops down to claim his due. As if waiting in the wings, a squirrel races across the landing for his share.

Without ceremony, Virgil pulls on his work gloves and walks away, leaving Julie sitting on the stump as he returns to his horses. Without wasted movement, he removes their feed buckets, adjusts leather harnesses and collars, then takes up the reins and turns the team around. Dismembered boughs and branches crunch and snap beneath their hooves, filling the air with a renewed evergreen scent. Feeling dismissed, Julie watches Virgil drive the team toward a logging trail on the north end of the landing. A moment later the puppy plunks his head onto her lap.

She jumps up and hollers, "Wait!"

Without breaking stride, Virgil glances back over his shoulder.

Pulling the leash from her pocket, Julie rushes forward, waving it in the air. Halfway across the landing, with a will of its own, her arm drops to her side. She stops. The pup halts beside her. She hesitates for a moment, and glances down at it. When she looks up again Virgil has turned his attention back to his horses.

She shoves the leash back into her jacket pocket. "Thanks for the dog," she says to his retreating back.

29

Within days there's no longer any need for the leash. During their walks, the puppy bounds here and there, giving fruitless chase to teasing squirrels and chipmunks, flushing out flared-neck willow grouse. Yet the moment she calls him, he always stops mid-bound and races back to her for his ear-scratching reward.

Ian accepts his presence without questions or an I-told-you-so, for which Julie is grateful.

They both laugh out loud the first time they catch themselves speaking to each other through the animal.

"You need to tell Julie she's feeding you too much, Pup."

"Tell him that's because that's just what you are, a growing puppy."

And yet, even in their awareness, before long, this using the dog as a conduit between them becomes habit.

"What do you think, Pup? Should you and Ian fill the woodbox?"

"We'll go do that little thing for her right after lunch then, eh, Pup."

Pup. Unoriginal at best, but she can come up with no other name that seems fitting. And so Pup it is.

His exuberant company adds a dimension to her daily hikes that is comforting, reassuring. He's an excuse to talk out loud, to raise her voice in hopes of warning any larger animals that may be nearby. She turns the iPod backpack speakers on less and less.

Each morning arrives a little darker, a little cooler, yet by afternoon the temperature can often rise to a summer high. Stiff winds come out of nowhere—patiently undressing the leaf-bearing trees—and then disappear just as quickly. Hoping to record the beauty of this Chilcotin autumn before the aspen, cottonwoods and willows are naked skeletons, Julie brings along her camera whenever she's outside. Snapping pictures wildly during her hikes, she returns home and downloads them every evening, only to be disappointed not to have captured the true colours of the day. Still, she tries again and again, hoping to find the right light, the perfect shot, before those golden hues are stripped away.

And, at the end of each hike, before heading home, it is now her daily ritual to visit the landing.

If the clearing is empty, and often it is so, she climbs up on the knoll above and waits while Pup plays below. The moment he lets out an excited yelp and takes off onto one of the many logging trails leading into the landing, she knows it won't be long before he and Virgil's dog—who has accepted Pup's right to be there and even sometimes lowers himself to play with him—come racing back together. And close behind will be the team of Clydesdales, their harnesses rattling and leather creaking as they drag newly felled timber to the landing.

Sometimes she turns the music on before they arrive, welcoming Virgil into the clearing with the strains of a Vivaldi or Mozart violin concerto. Each day, his body language portrays nothing more than the rote movement of his chores, as he unchains the logs and loosens harnesses. Yet, each day he brings his Thermos and joins her on the knoll. Often, now, she brings muffins with her in her backpack or other baked goodies to share with their coffee. A silent ritual, for even she does not speak during these encounters, as if speaking would somehow diminish the moment. She is not certain if Virgil's unacknowledged acceptance of her presence is shyness, or politeness, on his part, and does not want to know. It is enough to be here.

Then one afternoon in early October no lunch bucket sits on the stump at the edge of the clearing, and she knows without question that Virgil is not working that day. On the way home she sees that his pickup truck is not parked at the back of his cabin. The next morning it's the same.

A dusting of snow covers the ground on Friday, the third day of his absence. Wrapping herself up to take the dog for a quick walk in the early morning darkness, Julie follows Ian outside to his idling truck.

"You look after Julie while I'm in town, Pup," Ian says, opening the door.

She glances down at the anxiously waiting dog. "Who's looking after whom, eh?" she asks, shivering in the cold. She's still not ready to let him go off alone for his morning constitution, wonders if she ever will be. Pulling her jacket tighter she turns her attention back to Ian, who is still standing by the open truck door, staring at somewhere beyond her.

"What's this?" he asks. "Another gift from Virgil?"

Julie follows his gaze back to the house until she sees what he's referring to—a tall, narrow cardboard box leaning against the siding near the back door with a life-sized picture of a camera tripod visible on the front.

"Strange," Ian says. "What makes him think we need one of those?"

"He must have noticed me taking photographs."

"Must have," Ian agrees, but he doesn't sound convinced. He studies her face, then shrugs, and climbs into the truck. She waves goodbye, hoping he hasn't noticed the flush she feels rise to her cheeks. She is surprised by her own reaction—relief that Virgil is back.

Beside her Pup whines at the truck driving away in a whirl of dry snow. "Okay, let's go," Julie tells him, and he runs ahead of her searching for a spot to relieve himself. Once he's completed his business, he begins to examine the changed landscape, pushing his snout and blowing in the fresh snow, growling at every new suspect shape under the thin blanket of white. Only as they head back to the house does it occur to Julie that there's no other tracks, except their own—no evidence that Virgil or the horses have passed this way. Perhaps he went to work much earlier, before the morning snowfall. But later, when she and the dog go for their daily hike, the snow lays clean, undisturbed on Virgil's driveway, even though the pickup truck is parked behind the cabin. On the logging trail, and up on the landing, the carpet of snow is unmarked. Virgil is not here. The following day he does not show either. Neither is he there the next day, nor the next.

30

Virgil's story

It snowed the night they came and smashed his hands. Weightless flakes fell in hushed silence into the footprints leading across the campus grounds. No roommate or neighbours—all either hiding behind dormitory doors or conveniently out late on that distant night—warned of their coming.

Jarred awake by his door exploding inward, he saw the first surge of bodies lodged in the doorway, momentarily stuck, struggling against each other in their haste to get at him, before bursting through. He knew right away that this was not some sophomoric prank, not some rite-of-passage ritual. Naked, except for jockey shorts, he leapt out of bed, his first thought only to protect his violin from the ball-peen hammer gripped in one of the intruder's hands. On any given day he could have taken any one of them, perhaps two, but there were too many. They, with their muscled necks and wrestler's shoulders, overpowered him before he took a single step. They body-slammed him onto the floor; a tooth cut into the inside of his cheek as his face ground into the linoleum. Two football players—he recognized the popular line-backers, who had never made an attempt to hide their animosity toward him whenever their paths crossed on campus—yarded his arms above his head then pinned them to the floor with their knees. Another three heavyweights sat on his back and legs. No hoods or masks hid their faces, so certain were they of their righteous indignation, so blinded with a rage fuelled by alcohol. He fought, knowing it was futile, yet refused to beg for mercy.

Out of one eye he saw the violin snatched from the stand on his desk. The instrument slowly turned over in menacing hands. A voice crooned, "Daddy's fiddle, hmmm?"

His struggling stopped, and a moan rose in his throat. *Fiddle*. He had called it a fiddle.

"What do you think of your music scholarship now, boy?"

"This is what we do to niggers around here who mess with our girls."

Even before the violin came slamming down on his splayed fingers, like a dull axe blade, again and again, even before the hammer gave the parting blow, he knew it was over—less than a year and his university days were done. And he knew why. The badly mended bones would forever-after remind him of his foolish infatuation and his even more foolish giving in to it.

She had looked so much like Margie Smith. The Margie of his childhood who had never become anything more than a friend. He liked to believe that was because he, unwilling to jeopardize that friendship, had remained silent about his feelings. After high school, Margie had headed north to university, and he, east on a musical scholarship.

Alice Edwards, who even dressed like Margie, in her leather-fringed vests, miniskirts and knee-high leather boots, had caught his eye during his first lonely week on campus, and never let go until she had satisfied her curiosity. Blinded by the blonde hair hanging straight and silky to her shoulders, the blue eyes, inviting him into her world, he had entered without caution.

But, unlike the girl she no longer reminded him of, every thought that popped into not-Margie's head, popped out of her mouth, uncensored and unedited, a trait that had become tiresome even before they made scratching, clawing, animal love, for the first, and last, time on his dorm room cot.

Once the deed was done it was clear that they had both been looking for something other than each other. He had been looking for Margie in the scent of her skin, in the secret creases of her body, the sweet juices of sexual abandon, and because he had never known these intimacies with Margie, had not found it with her either. And she—by her own admission as she lay naked and glistening with sweat on the twisted sheets afterward—had simply been looking for a 'notch on her belt'; he was, in fact, her token 'coloured.'

Six weeks later she reappeared at his dorm-room door casually demanding three hundred dollars to get rid of the results of their one-night stand. Sitting down on the edge of the cot to absorb the news, he heard himself offer to marry her, but was shamefully relieved when she snorted, "What? Are you crazy?" She walked casually over to the desk muttering, "Me have a black baby—Christ!" She took the violin from its stand. "You could sell this fiddle for the money."

He jumped up. "It's a violin," he said removing it from her hands. "It was my father's."

"Is that him?" she asked pointing at the photograph pinned alongside those of the rest of his family on the bulletin board above his desk. When he nodded, she laughed. "A negra cowboy, now if that don't beat all."

"I'll get the money."

And he did, dipping into the fund that he and his mother had so carefully budgeted to last.

He would just have to work longer hours at the restaurant where he bussed on the weekends to replace the funds. He never got the chance. One day, a week after delivering the money, he ran into Alice on campus—the captain of the football team at her side—looking no different than she had when he last saw her.

They came that night.

Before they left him curled up on his dorm-room floor, his unfeeling hands cupped and protected—too late—against his bleeding and battered body, they took the ball-peen hammer to the violin. On top of its splintered remains, they tossed the torn photograph of his father. And he knew; only she could have told them.

In the morning the snow was melted, the footprints across the campus grounds were gone. And so was he.

31

For three days, a relentless rainstorm drenches the Chilcotin country-side. This morning, slanted rain splatters against Ian's office windows and beats a soft rhythm upon the roof.

Delivering a steaming cup of coffee to his desk, Julie glances outside. The valley lies socked in under a blackened dome of low-hanging clouds. Whitecaps foam on the windswept lake. In the ranch yard runnels of water meander in every direction, creating lacy patterns on the mud-slick surface. Through the mist, Julie can make out a tendril of smoke rising from Virgil's chimney, visible now through the leafless branches, which intertwine through the evergreen canopy above the cabin.

Last week, before the heavy rains started, Ian had gone to the cabin to collect the October rent. Curious to know if he would find their tenant at home, Julie had stood at the office window watching as a flock of migrating finches lifted from branches of the mountain ash along Virgil's driveway, heralding Ian's arrival and then his departure, an hour later.

She envied him that visit, had wanted to go with—no instead of—him. The idea of visiting Virgil in his home has played on her mind for days, yet she can find no good excuse to do so. She wonders if the two men sit in silence, during their time together. If Virgil ever uses his Electrolarynx to speak? How strange and impossible that seems, yet a secret part of her laments the thought that she will never hear this man's voice.

Still staring out of Ian's window, Julie asks, "So what's our tenant up to these days?"

She turns to see Ian glance up from his computer screen, his hands poised motionless over the keyboard. "Virgil? He's over in the barn this morning. Why?"

"Just wondering if he's still logging."

"Hmm? Yeah. Far as I know." He returns his attention to the computer, frowning as he searches for where he left off.

"I haven't heard him working up on the north slope lately," Julie says hoping her voice sounds casual. "Is he cutting in another area?"

"I don't think so." Ian pauses, then pushes his glasses up onto his forehead and pinches the bridge of his nose. "What's this sudden interest in Virgil anyway?" he asks.

"Oh, nothing. Just curious why I haven't noticed any smoke from his chimney lately."

Ian leans back in his chair. "He went to town for a few days, but he's back now." He places his hands behind his head with his fingers knit together, and contemplates her. "When this rain lets up he's going to start rounding up the cattle and bring them down from the summer range. If you were really serious about trying out the saddle horses one day, why don't you ride along with him?"

Julie shrugs. "I just might do that," she says walking out of the room.

As she enters the barn, Virgil doesn't bother to glance up from the first stall, where he is bent over at the waist behind one of the saddle horses, a hind hoof held firmly between his leather-clad thighs. He must know that she is there, his dog having warned him long before she slid open the heavy overhead door, just wide enough to step inside, yet neither he nor the bay mare he is working on give any indication they are aware of her presence. She pushes back the hood of her macintosh, and wipes the rain from her face.

While she waits for Virgil to finish, she turns and slides the barn door closed then stands in front of the stall letting her eyes adjust to the dim light. Except for the day when they came out with the realtor—and, she has to admit, she wasn't paying attention to much more than Ian's reaction then—this is the first time she has been inside the barn. She is impressed by the unexpected neatness, the orderly storing of equipment and tools on walls and work counters. The ranch odours are intensified in here. Once again she finds the mingled earthy and animal scents of fragrant hay, horsehide and manure comfortingly pleasant.

Above her, the rain beats a staccato dance on the tin roof. The other horses shift in their stalls as Virgil's hammer taps nails into the mare's new shoe. He takes the last nail from between his pursed lips, taps it home, and then releases the newly shod hoof. He straightens up and pats the horse's rump as she swings her head around to him.

"She looks like she's enjoying her pedicure," Julie says.

Virgil nods at the sound of her voice, acknowledging her presence without meeting her eyes. He shifts over to the mare's other hind leg, which she has lifted without prompting.

Julie takes a few steps closer to the stall. "Ian says you're going to bring the cattle down from the summer range," she says. "I, uh, well I wondered, if it wouldn't be too much of a problem. I mean—if I wasn't in the way, that is—if I could ride along with you?"

Overhead a barn owl lifts his wings and hoots his proverbial question as Virgil straightens up. Before he can deny her, Julie adds, "I do know how to ride. Well, a little. I took English riding lessons when I was a child. My mother would tell you I wasn't great at it, but Western saddles look a lot easier, and I just thought…"

Realizing with a start that she is rambling, Julie gives a nervous laugh. "You never know, I might be a help."

It seems an eternity until he finally gives a brief nod. Before he turns his attention back to the mare, he holds up one finger, followed by a sunburst gesture of both crooked hands.

"Right," she acknowledges, "the first sunny day."

She leaves the barn knowing the truth; Virgil has agreed to this against his will.

32

She doesn't have long to wait. The clouds break that afternoon, exposing promising patches of blue before nightfall. The following morning, stars twinkle in the predawn sky through the window above Julie's bed. She rises in the darkness and slips into her housecoat.

Downstairs in the mudroom—and in these last few days Julie has truly come to appreciate why it's called a mudroom—she lets the dog out, closing the door quickly against the morning cold. They have only just begun to allow Pup outside on his own. Julie has reluctantly given in to Ian's argument that there's no good reason why either of them should stand around in the pouring rain while a dog, who never seems to want to stray too far from his mistress anyway, does his business. So far there has been no reason for concern. Still, she watches him through the mudroom window. Over at the barn, light spills from the open doorway, revealing the familiar silhouette of Virgil's dog sitting guard.

She goes back up to her room and quickly dresses, layering her clothes for the unpredictability she has come to expect of the Chilcotin weather. Back downstairs she tosses her woollen ski cap and mittens on the top of the washing machine, retrieves her camera from the closet and hangs it around her neck.

"You're going out early," Ian says, coming through the doorway.

She glances quickly over her shoulder. "Yep," she replies pulling on her cap. "Today I'm the assistant wrangler."

A blast of cold hits her the moment she opens the door to call the dog.

Beside her Ian shivers. "It's bloody freezing this morning. Are you certain you want to do this today?" he asks for the second time. If it hadn't been his suggestion in the first place, Julie might wonder if he's as nervous as she is.

"I'm dressed for it," she says, letting the dog in. Agreeing with Ian that it's best to leave Pup home, she slips outside before he can follow. As she hurries across the yard, the first rays of sunlight break over the eastern ridge exposing the edge of an azure sky. Two horses, the bay mare and the black gelding, are saddled and waiting in the shadows beside the barn, their reins tied loosely to the top rung of the corral fence.

Julie bids good morning to Virgil, who is laying a coiled lasso over the gelding's saddle horn. Certain that the bay mare is meant for her, she walks toward her, giving her hind end a wide berth. The mare sidesteps nervously and Virgil comes over. Before Julie can protest, he removes the camera from around her neck. As he retreats into the barn with it she wonders if this is his way of letting her know that this day is meant to be about work and not pleasure, or an indication that the ride is going to be a little rougher than she has anticipated.

Determined to mount her horse before he returns, she steels herself. *Okay, here goes.* Reaching up she grabs the back rim of the saddle with one hand and the horn with the other, but placing her left foot into the stirrup proves to be a little more difficult. "Either this horse is too tall or I'm too short," she mutters. Suddenly Virgil is beside her, bending over with his crooked fingers knit together for her to step into. The moment she complies he boosts her in one swift motion onto the saddle, which shifts slightly sideways with her weight. Beneath her, the horse's flanks expand with a heaving breath and Julie's heartbeat pumps madly into her throat. Still she forces her shaking hands to grip the saddle horn while Virgil adjusts her stirrups. Once he is satisfied that they are short enough, he unties the reins and leads both horses through the gate and out into the south field. He passes Julie her reins and mounts his own horse. As if sensing Julie's nervousness, the mare fights the bit, tossing her head, antsy at having an unskilled rider on her back. Virgil circles his horse and comes alongside. Their thighs rubbing together, he reaches over and loosens the leather reins in Julie's hands, then trots ahead. The mare follows, her nose almost touching the gelding's tail, her rider bouncing along feeling like a child at some country fair.

They ride through the empty field in the morning light, Virgil's dog bringing up the rear. Mist rising from the winding creek rolls across the stubble pasture and between the horses' plodding feet. When they reach the far fenceline, Virgil leans from his saddle to lift the wooden latch of a gate that Julie wasn't even aware existed. After the horses step through, and Virgil closes the gate, the mare once again falls in behind the black gelding. They enter the trees, the incline rising with each plodding step through the unfamiliar terrain. Julie turns to look back at the forest closing in behind them, thinking how easily one could get turned around, lost—how quickly she herself has become disoriented, without the lake, logging roads and fences as landmarks to guide her.

She's glad Virgil knows where he's going as the horses make their sure-footed way through scrub brush, dry-washes and narrow animal trails. At times Julie has to scrunch right down over the mare's withers to avoid low branches. And all the while she is trying to find the sweet spot she is certain must be somewhere on the saddle to stop herself from bouncing about so wildly. *What idiot ever said a Western saddle was like riding a big old rocking chair?*

At first her body instinctually tries posting, as she had done on the English saddles of her childhood, but finds she only creates more airspace between herself and the saddle with each bounce.

She watches Virgil riding ahead, tries to emulate his posture. Unlike her, his shoulders and torso rise and fall in an easy rhythm, while from the waist down he moves as if he is one with the animal between his legs. He holds the reins loose in one buckskin-gloved hand, the other hand rests on his thigh. After a while, Julie's trial and error imitating of his erect upper body posture, the surrendering movements of his hips, the angle of his boots resting in his stirrups, starts to pay off. With the weight off her trembling knees, the bouncing ride gradually becomes, if not exactly comfortable, at least somewhat less jarring.

Breathing in the crisp morning air, heavy with the rain-freshened scent of wet earth, decomposing leaves, and dry pine needles, she finds herself relaxing into a swaying rhythm with her saddle. As the horses weave expertly through the heavy terrain, Julie concentrates on the back of Virgil's head. She finds herself staring at the only part of his body that is not covered, the area between the bottom of his cowboy hat and the collar of his canvas jacket. As if aware of her scrutiny, Virgil reins the black gelding to an abrupt stop. Lifting a heavy fir branch that blocks the path, he pulls it back, sidesteps his horse to the edge of the path, and ushers Julie by. Once she is through, he spurs the gelding on up the bank then down again to retake the lead.

As he does so a cow bawls somewhere in the bush above. Virgil's dog bolts up the mountainside and his horse swings around in one swift movement to strain forward in an uphill trot. Without warning Julie's mare follows suit, and she can do no more than grip the saddle horn with both hands to keep from sliding off. Just when she is certain she can't hold on a moment longer, the dog flushes out a heifer and young steer from the thicket. Using the coiled lariat to usher them along, Virgil drives them through a clump of low-lying juniper and back onto the trail.

After what seems like hours, they break out onto an alpine clearing where a group of Hereford cows, some lying in the sun, others grazing, turn their massive white heads to greet them.

Before long, twenty range cattle are bunched up in front of Virgil's horse for the trek back down to the valley. Brushing the rumps of the ones who fall behind with his lariat, he keeps the herd moving forward, while his dog nips at the heels of any strays.

The procession winds steadily downhill. Soreness creeping into muscles she has never given thought to, Julie is reluctant to spur the mare into a trot, so she allows the gap between them and Virgil to increase but never so far that she cannot see the tail end of his horse. She recognizes nothing in the landscape and is certain this is not the route they took on the way up. Left on her own, she doubts if she could find her way home.

Typical of Chilcotin extremes the temperature rises with the late morning sun. Beneath layers of clothing, sweat trickles down Julie's spine, and between her breasts. Virgil removes his canvas jacket, rolls it up and attaches it to his saddle. Julie juggles the reins from one hand to the other and struggles out of her own outer jacket. Tying it down while on the move proves a little more difficult. She locates the leather toggles and then, confident the mare will continue to follow Virgil's horse, she wraps the reins around the saddle horn. She quickly lays her scrunched-up jacket across the front of the saddle, and fumbles with the ties on one side.

Without warning, the mare dances sideways, her ears lying flat, her nostrils snorting. Thrown off balance, Julie's left foot slips out of the stirrup and she grabs for the saddle horn. The panicked mare throws her head downward, her arching neck tugging at the reins, which unravel and snake to the ground. Lunging forward to grab them just as the horse rears up on her hind legs, Julie slides, rather than falls, from the back of the saddle and across the mare's rump. She hits the ground with a thud, the wind knocked out of her, as the horse bolts away. Too numb to know if there is anything hurting, besides her already aching muscles, not to mention her pride, Julie slowly pushes herself up.

And as she does she catches a glimpse of a dark form moving in the forest above. Scrambling to her feet she screams, "Bear!" and runs toward Virgil, who is trotting back on the trail.

He reins his horse in beside Julie. "A bear," she says breathlessly, pointing up the hill. "Did you see it?"

Beneath his cowboy hat Virgil's forehead knits together, as he scans the hillside. But there is nothing to see except the dappled sunlight streaming through the trees. Had she imagined the hulking beast? Without confirming or denying the bear sighting, Virgil shifts in his saddle. Leaning over he offers her his arm. Without hesitation, as if she has done this every day of her life, she reaches up and grasps his forearm, and in one quick movement is pulled up onto the back of the horse.

Feeling awkward and not knowing what to hang onto, she grabs the back rim of the saddle. But when the gelding suddenly begins to move, Julie jerks forward, and with a will of their own her arms wrap around Virgil's waist. They remain there even after they catch up to the herd.

As they make their slow descent she is forced closer. Her cheek presses against his flannel shirt, and she breathes in his musky scent of sweat and a spicy soap she cannot identify. Even through his clothing she is aware of his body warmth, and the tight muscles of his abdomen working with every movement. She feels herself blush at the intimacy of her thighs pressed against his hips and is glad he cannot see her face.

By the time they reach the valley floor she has relaxed into the rhythm of Virgil's body swaying with the animal beneath them. Once they drive the cows into the south field, they leave the herd and head down the field toward home. Over Virgil's shoulder, Julie spots the bay mare—her jacket dangling loose from the saddle—standing by the corral fence. Holding her reins and watching them approach is Ian.

Julie is uncertain if the clouded look of concern on his face is due to the fact that her horse has arrived home without her, or because she has just now thought to remove her arms from around Virgil's waist.

33

Sometimes in the brief space between sleeping and waking my mother thinks she feels my presence. She's right. I'm there, trying to find a way into her dreams. For a fleeting moment she almost grasps my message but there is never enough time in that in-between place.

Mr Emerson says that I am taking a risk. At least I think it's Mr Emerson. It's getting more and more difficult to tell where these thoughts come from. 'Thoughts' is probably the wrong word. It is more like knowing a truth, and I'm not certain if this 'knowing' is my own, Mr Emerson's, or even, as I am beginning to suspect, coming from some larger consciousness. God? I don't know. I'm still working on that.

Anyway there will be no such ephemeral—now there's a cool word, definitely Mr Emerson's influence—moment for Mom this morning. Even in her sleep her all too human body grounds her to reality. She rolls over gingerly, waking slowly, with every sore muscle and stiff joint reminding her that she is a forty-four-year-old woman who spent four hours on a horse yesterday. Even her fingers ache. There wasn't a chance that she would sense me trying, once again, to fill her dreams with his face, his name. Levi.

I just want her to talk to him. The first anniversary of my death is almost here. Mom's trying to pretend it isn't coming by filling her mind with distractions. Levi is planning to do a 'sweat,' a vision quest, on that day, and this morning he started to fast in preparation. It's dangerous enough to attempt to enter what he calls 'the spirit world' but his body is not as strong as it used to be, and I am afraid for him.

He wouldn't have to do this if Mom had only answered his calls; if she would only agree to meet with him, hear what he needs to say. There was a time when she would have been more than happy to, a time when, of all my friends, Levi was one of her favourites.

He was Kajul's friend first. Well, not hers exactly, but her older brother, Kuldeep's. Levi moved into the school dorms in town when he was in grade seven. Kuldeep Sandhu was a hockey jock as well, the only Indo-Canadian player on the team. Levi was the only First Nations. Maybe because of that, or because they were both quiet and not the party-hardy type, the two ended up hanging together. Mom was always saying how fortunate we were to live in such a racially diverse town. But if she could have seen our school cafeteria at lunch hour she might have had a different view. Every clique and ethnic division was obvious by where you sat. Kuldeep and Levi avoided it. They usually walked over to the Sandhus' house for lunch. Because it was so close to the school, Kajul and I often did, too. Of course neither Levi nor Kuldeep paid much attention to us girls then. Still we went to every one of their hockey games to cheer them on. Then, when Kajul's brother went to live with his uncle at the coast so he could play for the Surrey Juniors, Levi just fell into hanging with us whenever he wasn't practising or playing hockey. It was neat. Kajul and I both had a bit of a crush on him from the start. I was secretly glad though when she said she could never act on it, because, no matter how progressive her parents were, there wasn't a chance they would ever understand anything more than a friendship between her and Levi. East is east and west is west and all that old stuff.

Mom once said that Levi, with his quiet handsomeness and unassuming ways, was going to grow up to be the kind of man that everyone fell a little bit in love with. When I was in grade nine, even though he was a grade ahead of me, we both ended up in Mr Emerson's English literature class. I think I fell more than a 'little bit' in love with him the day we had to read out loud our first class assignment, which was to write a short story in the form of a myth or legend. Of course we all expected that he would write about some fictional hockey player.

Although he was something of a legend himself, at least with the hockey fans, when he stood at the front of the class, he appeared neither proud nor, like many of us, nervous. Without looking up from his paper he introduced his story, "The Legend of Crow." I had to lean forward to hear his slow, but unfaltering, words.

"In the beginning," he read, "Crow was a wise and magical bird with pearl white feathers and a beautiful singing voice. Crow was friend to all of the other birds. They would gather in the trees to hear him sing and to listen to his words of wisdom. The lonely Eagle, also a friend of Crow's, became jealous of all the adulation being heaped upon Crow. But Crow was so enjoying all the attention of those gathered around him, he forgot to watch for signs of danger. And so Crow did not see the resentment growing in the eyes of his old friend Eagle.

"One day, as the birds of the world met once again to hear Crow's wondrous voice, Eagle watched from high above. Enraged, he flew up to the Sun and stole a glowing ember of fire. Then he flew back to the forest with the ember held tightly in his talons, intending to set fire to the very trees on whose branches the admirers of Crow sat perched. Above the forest Eagle let the ember drop. As the fire fell from the sky, the frightened birds scattered in panic. Only Crow flew toward the glow. Since Crow had no strong talons with which to carry the burning ember, he caught it in his beak. As he flew away from the earth, the black smoke streamed across his feathers and the heat scorched his throat. Still, Crow flew on and on, to the other side of darkness. By the time the fire had gone out, he had reached the Spirit World. There, Crow was honoured as a brave and loyal bird. Since he was the first bird to find the path to the Spirit World, he was allowed to return to earth, where, with his forever blackened feathers and raspy voice, Crow became the messenger between the two worlds."

It was the most words I had ever heard, or ever would hear, Levi say all in one go. He ended his story by telling the class that the crow was his spirit guide, and showed us the carved pendant he wore around his neck. Then he added with a shy smile, that his mother often teased him when he was a child that the crow was his spirit guide, because, just like the bird, he couldn't sing. He never shared the essay he wrote for the class assignment with her. Neither she, nor the Elders, would have been too impressed with him messing with ancient legends.

Remembering his story, I think he takes this spirit guide thing way too seriously now. But, hey, what do I know? I'm just a dead white girl.

34

Hanging onto the railing and wincing with each measured step, Julie makes her way downstairs in the glare of the late morning sun.

"Virgil's long gone if you were thinking of going to round up cows with him again," Ian calls from the living room. Throwing a log onto the fire he pushes it into place with the poker, shuts the fireplace door then straightens up and brushes his hands together. "Uh oh," he says watching her take the last few steps. "Saddle-sore?"

She grimaces. Saddle-sore is too mild a term for the way her body aches. "More like I've been trampled by a herd of horses, rather than just jostled around on one."

"Bet you wish you had a little extra padding on your behind now."

Ian's comment is the first time he has made any sort of reference to her weight loss. The skin rubbed raw to the bone in the most inconvenient place is testament to the truth of his observation.

"Very funny," she says heading into the kitchen. "The only thing I'm wishing for right now is a cup of coffee."

"It's made," he says, following her. "So did you at least enjoy…"

His words are interrupted by a sudden commotion outside. They both turn to the sound of the dog's frantic barking, and the cause of his concern, the increasing roar of an approaching ATV.

"Another bloody quad," Ian snarls and heads into the mudroom.

Julie groans. Only last week one of these obnoxious-sounding all-terrain vehicles had appeared on the west side of the back field. Ian had stormed out of his office and across the front lawn, arms waving. Although Julie hadn't heard what was said when he met the trespassing hunter at the head of the creek, she did see the vehicle spin around, black mud spitting up from beneath the balloon tires and splattering Ian, before it roared away.

Intent on intervening in an altercation with another hunter this morning, she rushes after him as quickly as her punished muscles will allow.

Pulling on his boots in the mudroom he mutters, "Jesus. They just roar across our land as if they own it." Without lacing up his boots he throws the door open and bolts out. Julie follows in her stocking feet.

Out on the road an excited Pup is running alongside the approaching ATV, yipping and leaping at the driver.

"It's all right," Julie yells over the engine noise. "It's Terri."

The vehicle pulls up, the knocking engine throttling to a shaking stop. The sudden silence fills the late morning air like relief.

Wearing a heavy camouflage jacket, which matches her vehicle—and makes her appear even more imposing than Julie remembers—Terri-the-Pilot leans back and grins at them. "Hello, girlfriend," she calls out, pulling the black watch cap off her head and wiping her brow with the back of her hand.

Still in her stocking feet, Julie smiles at her from the bottom step. "Hello there yourself," she says, surprised by how glad she is to see this woman again.

Terri climbs out of the four-wheeler and kneels down to greet the dog. "Just thought I'd stop by and see how you're making out with the pup." She nuzzles her face into his neck. "And I see just fine. Eh, fella?"

Taking in the gun attached to a rack behind the seat, Julie asks, "Out hunting?"

"Nah, not really," Terri says scratching behind Pup's ears. "Picked up a few grouse on my way over. That shotgun's mostly to warn any bears or hunters that I'm in the area—not that this noisy contraption ain't enough." Standing up she strides forward wiping her huge hand on her jeans before offering it to Ian. "Terri Champion," she says, as he grasps it.

"Oh," Julie interjects, quickly. "My husband, Ian."

"Kinda figured that," Terri grins. "Glad to meet ya," she says to Ian who appears at a loss for words. She turns her attention to Julie and instead of taking her outstretched hand, enfolds her in a hug. "Great to see you again, Gal."

Releasing the startled Julie she returns to her vehicle. "Like I said I bagged some grouse this morning. Got way too many for myself." She reaches into the back of the ATV and retrieves a fistful of birds, holding them upside down by their legs. "These fool-hens are just too stupid to run away. Half of them I took down with rocks. Much better sport than shooting 'em. Anyway, they're good eating. Thought I'd drop a few off with you folks, if you're so inclined."

"I've never had grouse," Julie says. "I'd love to try it."

"Well great, I'll just clean these up for you and then take a few over to Virgil."

"Sorry, but you've missed him again," Julie tells her. "He's out rounding up the cattle."

"Well, darn, I was hoping he'd offer an old friend a cup of coffee," Terri says raising her eyebrows innocently.

Julie opens her mouth to offer the expected invitation, but Ian, who has found his voice, beats her to it.

Before going inside, Terri retrieves a plastic bucket from the back of the ATV. Hanging onto the dog, Julie watches in fascination as the woman plucks off the bird's tiny heads as easily as separating flowers from stems. Then placing the headless carcasses upside down, she steps on either wing and in one swift motion yanks up until only a thick mound of glistening pink meat is in her hands. It's over in moments, and she places the cleaned breasts in the pail and hands it to a stunned Ian. "Give Virgil a couple of those," she says, cleaning up the feathers and remains from the ground. "Keep the rest for yourselves. They're right easy to cook. Just throw them in some tinfoil with a little salt and pepper, garlic, onion and a dab of butter. Bake 'em in the oven, along with some potatoes. Mmmm!" She grins and winks at Julie. "You can thank me next time you see me."

Inside, they sit around the table with their coffee, Ian quizzing Terri about the overland journey from her ranch to theirs. "Takes me not much more than an hour," she tells him. "I could have come in the float-plane, the lakes are still wide open, but it's grouse season so thought I'd take advantage of that," she says downing the last of her coffee.

Julie pushes away from the table and slowly stands up.

Terri watches her retrieve the coffee pot. "Can't help but notice you look a mite tender, Girl," she says holding up her cup for a refill. "Something happen to you?"

"She went after cattle yesterday," Ian says into his mug. "I'm not certain if she is sore from the four hours on horseback or from falling off her horse and having to ride home double with Virgil." He glances up and meets Julie's eyes.

Ignoring his implied question she replaces the coffee pot on the stove.

"Whew," Terri whistles. "Four hours. That would do it. Didn't anyone mention that you have to ease yourself into horseback riding?"

"I know now, 'she said *easing* herself into her chair.'" She chuckles at her own joke but winces as she sits down.

"That must have been a first for Virgil, riding range with a woman. Excepting myself, of course." In the silence that follows Terri glances from Ian to Julie. "Ah, well, so did you at least enjoy the ride?"

"As a matter of fact, I did. I intend to try it again as soon as my muscles and joints stop rebelling."

"Really?" Ian says, studying the bottom of his cup. "That's great. I just might ride along as well."

35

Pup cocks his head and whimpers when Terri climbs onto the ATV, but he remains sitting between Ian and Julie after the quad roars away. Watching the tail lights disappear down the road, Julie experiences her own tug of regret at seeing Terri leave. *Darn, I wish I'd thought to take her photograph.*

"She's quite the character, isn't she?" Ian says. "I rather like her."

"Yeah. Me too," Julie says more to herself than to Ian, who has turned to go back into the house.

Hugging her sweater around her she calls out, "I'm going to get my camera."

The pungent fragrance of sweetened hay and horsehide surrounds Julie as she enters the barn. She stands inside taking in the now familiar aroma, an aroma that, like the barn, the horses, even the hay stored in a mountain of bales outside, belongs to Virgil. She and Ian are the intruders here.

Her camera is still hanging where Virgil left it just inside the door. She unhooks it and leaves, disappointed to find the barn empty. On the way back to the house she thinks about Ian's declaration that he might come along riding next time she goes and is uncertain how she feels about that. No, not uncertain, confused, because a large part of her hopes it was just talk. It makes no difference, anyway; it will be a few days before her aching body is in any shape to mount a horse again. Walking seems to help though. She decides that later she will hike over to Virgil's and deliver the grouse meat.

She cleans the kitchen, and separates the bird breasts into freezer bags while Ian works in his office. When she is certain he is immersed in his files, she takes one of the bags and, leaving the dog in the mudroom, steps outside. Hurrying across the yard she glances over at the corral but sees no sign of either Virgil or the black gelding.

Along his driveway flocks of spotted thrushes rise from the mountain ash trees, dropping red berries to the ground as they scatter. Now that most of the leaves have fallen, Julie is struck by how different the forest surrounding the cabin looks, how raked and park-like the ground between the trees appears. For the first time she notices the colourful little birdhouses decorating many of the poplar and birch trees.

Behind the cabin, Vigil's pickup truck is parked in its regular spot. The cabin windows are dark and Julie senses before she steps onto the front porch that it's empty. Still she knocks on the door. Hearing no movement inside, she steps over to the front window and peers in, past the dreamcatcher hanging on the other side of the glass.

Confirming her belief that Virgil is not home, she goes back to the door and tries the knob. It turns easily. She hesitates for a moment, then decides that there's no harm in taking the grouse inside and leaving them in the sink for him.

A musk-filled scent fills her nostrils the moment she pushes the door open, the same unique masculine fragrance of spicy sweat and woodsmoke she had breathed in while riding behind Virgil yesterday.

She steps inside and, closing the door, slowly surveys the interior.

A hulking wood cookstove takes up most of the wall near the door, its cast-iron top still radiating warmth. An old copper boiler, filled with split kindling and wood, rests next to it. In the kitchen area to her right, afternoon sunlight streams in through the window above the sink. It spills across the counter, casting a yellow light on the chrome table and chairs. An antique oak roll-top desk fits snugly between the end of the cabinets and the built-in bookshelves that line the wall all the way to the far corner. In the shadows a brown leather couch, its overstuffed armrests shiny with wear, faces a cabinet television that looks too ancient to work. A braided area rug covers the plank board floor. Through an open door at the other end of the room, an iron bed, made up with a patchwork quilt tucked military tight at the corners, is visible.

Impressed with the unexpected orderliness of this bachelor home, Julie smiles. She goes over to the sink and turns on the cold water. While she waits for it to fill, she surveys the spotless counters, the clean dishes stacked in orderly fashion in the open overhead cabinets.

Even the glass window above the sink is streak-free. Her attention suddenly focuses on the dreamcatcher hanging there. Abruptly she shuts off the tap and tosses the plastic bag of grouse meat into the cold water. She leans forward to take a closer look, and a shiver runs down her spine. The woven spider-web-like circle looks like—no it is identical to—the one that used to hang over Darla's bed. The one that was supposed to keep her from harm. The one that Julie had tossed into the trash the day of her funeral.

36

Levi gave it to me. It was to catch any evil spirits that tried to enter my dreams while I slept. At the same time he told me that my totem, my spirit guide, was the bear, 'the healer' in his culture. I thought that was pretty cool. And even though I saw no reason to believe that the childhood legends Levi grew up with were any more realistic than those in my Big Book of Children's Bible Stories, which Gram, who really knew how to put a downer on a kid's sixth birthday, gave me, I liked the idea that he wanted to protect me.

He gave one to Kajul Sandhu too, so it really wasn't any big deal, except he told her that her spirit guide was the deer. I have to admit that I was a little jealous of the idea that he saw her as a beautiful deer and me as a burly old bear. But then, it was me who he kissed in the end.

Levi was not the first boy I ever kissed. Hey, I was sixteen years old, what does anyone expect? Mom was the blindest one of all about that kind of stuff. Because she was so late taking an interest in the opposite sex, she just assumed I was like her. I guess compared to some girls I was, but still I was curious far sooner than she was. I was twelve when I started to wonder what it would feel like to have a boy's lips touch mine. I decided to find out that summer when I went to visit Gram in Vancouver. But she was way more suspicious than Mom ever was. When I started spending more time with the boy who lived at the end of her street, Larry Young, a freckled-faced redhead who was the same age, and just as curious as I was, she made sure we were never alone together. Instead of allowing me to go to the beach on the bus with him and his friends she insisted on driving us. She said it was because she hardly ever got to do things like that with my mom when she was young, so she was going to get all the time in with me she could. But she wasn't fooling anyone. While we swam and sunned ourselves on the beaches of English Bay, she would sit on a nearby log, or on a folding chair, wearing her floppy hat and caftan, pretending to read a book while keeping watch from behind her frog-eye sunglasses.

Sooner or later, though, she had to go to the bathroom. The first chance we had we pulled the blanket over our heads and fumbled around in the tented light until we found each other's mouths. I still remember how startled I was by the metallic taste of Larry's wet lips and tongue. I wasn't quite sure I liked it. Before I had a chance to try it again, the blanket was torn away, swirling sand up in our faces as it flew off.

Gram never made a big deal about it, I'll say that for her, it was almost as if she expected it, and that was why she came back so quickly. She said nothing to Mom. I didn't know why. At the time I suspected it was so she could have something on me. But after that, whenever anyone mentioned the beach, or blankets, or anything that would remind us of that day, she would flash me a wink. And then when I shaved one side of my head, while Mom was trying so hard not to say anything, Gram told me I looked perfectly lovely. I realized then that somehow she enjoyed sharing our little secrets, having our little alliance that excluded Mom. I thought it was just a silly game, but now I see that it was more than that. I see how much her relationship with Mom hurt her, and how determined she was to not let that happen with me.

They are so hard on each other, Mom and Gram. It's as if some dream-catcher-like web in their minds filters out their spirit of love for each other. They don't know how to talk to each other anymore. If they did, maybe Gram would tell Mom the same thing she told me after that day at the beach. A little kiss is no big hairy deal.

37

The blood pounds in Julie's ears as she examines the dreamcatcher hanging in the window. Her imagination must be playing tricks on her. It cannot be. But it is. The rawhide-wrapped circle is identical to the one that had hung above Darla's bed—with the same burgundy beads woven into the same spider-web pattern. And, just like the one Levi Johnny gave to her daughter, black crow feathers dangle from the bottom of the circle.

She turns away, the questions buzzing through her head. How likely is it that there are two so similar? Had someone rescued the one she had discarded? If so, how had it found its way here, into Virgil's window? She shakes her head. *This is just crazy thinking.* She grabs a dishtowel from the counter. While she dries her hands she lets her gaze search the room again, for what she doesn't know.

Focusing on the wall above the roll-top desk, she replaces the towel then goes over to examine the display of photographs hanging there. She is drawn to one in which two soldiers, obviously twins with identical expressions of mock seriousness, are standing in front of an old house trailer. Each has an arm around the shoulders of the teenage boy standing between them holding a violin and bow. *Virgil?* She looks closer, checking the boy's hands but sees no sign of deformity.

She compares the three young faces in the picture to the man's in the small sepia snapshot next to it. The yellowed hues are faded and a map of criss-cross wrinkles mar the old photograph, giving evidence that it has been pieced and glued back together, but anyone can see that the African-American cowboy leaning against a corral fence is related to, probably father to, the twin soldiers. And the cowboy's sparkling grin reaching across the years is identical to the young boy's.

She turns her attention to a larger photograph, a studio portrait in which a middle-aged First Nations woman and a teenage girl are sitting on a bench. Standing behind them, with a hand on each of their shoulders, is a younger version of Virgil Blue. Although Virgil's copper skin is a shade darker, he has the same handsome face, the same high cheekbones, aquiline nose and wide-set amber eyes as the woman. The young girl does not.

The startling combination of blue eyes, fair skin and dark hair reminds Julie so much of Darla that it takes her breath away for a moment.

Replacing the photograph Julie glances down at the open roll-top desk. Like the rest of the cabin, the oak desk is neatly organized. Envelopes, rolls of stamps, pens and pencils, are stored in the small cubbyholes. Neat stacks of yellow-lined notepads fill the top ledge. Nothing unnecessary litters the dust-free desktop, except for an envelope lying on top of a handwritten letter. Curious, Julie allows herself a glimpse of the exposed salutation,

With Love,

Melody.

Feeling like the intruder that she is, she hesitates for only a moment before picking up the envelope to uncover the rest of the page.

... I hope you are paying attention to the presidential campaign. Do you remember what you said the night you left? I do, word for word. You swore that you 'would not return until the day a man of colour was elected president of these United States.'

189

In our mother's memory, I intend to hold you to that oath, my brother. And when that day comes, as I am certain it will, you and I will visit her resting-place together.

An odd sense of relief rushes through Julie with the realization that the letter writer, Melody, is Virgil's sister. She shakes her head. *God, what has gotten into me? Stop. Enough of this.*

A sudden commotion outside causes her to drop the envelope. She swings around at the sound of Pup scratching and whining at the door. A heartbeat later a shadow flits across the window and familiar footsteps pound across the porch.

38

Ian doesn't bother to hide his irritation when Julie opens the cabin door.

"What's going on?" he demands, grabbing at Pup's collar.

"Nothing. I just brought the grouse over." She slips outside, closing the door behind her.

"I had no idea you'd left." Ian says, letting go of the straining dog as Julie bends down to calm him. "He was going crazy in the mudroom; when I opened the door he bolted down the road." He straightens up and looks past her. "Is he home?"

"Virgil? No."

"And you went inside. Julie, that's not right. It's the man's home. Neither you, nor I, have the right to go in when he isn't here."

The impatience in his voice startles her. She stops petting the dog and looks up at him. For an entire year now, his patience with her, their patience with each other, has bordered on indulgent and a part of her is almost relieved to see him lose his.

"Yes of course," she says, standing up. "You're right. I shouldn't have."

Ian opens his mouth, then whatever he was about to say is lost as he closes it, turns and walks away.

"Come, Pup," Julie says and follows, anxious now to get away before Virgil returns and finds them there. Once she catches up to Ian at the end of the driveway she has to hurry to keep up with his long stride. As they near the ranch house she asks, "Have you ever noticed the dreamcatcher in his cabin window?"

"What?"

"The dreamcatcher hanging above Virgil's kitchen sink. It's identical to the one Levi gave Darla."

Ian misses a step, then staring straight ahead, continues walking, the muscles in his jaw working.

"Really," she continues, breathlessly. "It's exactly the same, right down to the black feathers hanging from the bottom."

"So what? They must make thousands of those things to sell to tourists in town. They're everywhere."

"Yes, but what are the odds that there are two so similar... I even thought for a moment that it was Darla's—"

Ian halts in his tracks. "Don't." The word is a low growl in his throat.

"Don't what?" Julie stops short, takes a quick step back and looks up at his determined profile. "Don't say our daughter's name out loud?"

He turns to her, his face a mask of sorrow. "Don't do this. Don't make everything about..." frustrated he holds up a hand. "Just stop. We have to put it behind us. Jesus Christ, Julie, you have to find some closure. Find a way to let go."

She opens her mouth in protest, but nothing comes out. Let go? If she hears that line, or the word *closure,* one more time she will scream. What does it mean anyway? Closure? Let go? Of what? A wound that will never heal? Watching his retreating back she whispers, "I can't."

Over the next few days the returning cattle fill the south pasture. Most mornings and evenings Ian helps Virgil spread hay bales in the field for the gathering herd. Julie spends most of her time looking at the world through the eye of her camera, taking photographs at every opportunity, then photoshopping any promising ones and emailing them to her sister. And even the odd one to her mother. She is certain though—and she has to admit that perhaps it is deliberate—that the ones she chooses to send to her mother will do nothing to improve her opinion of life in the 'wild': an opaque layer of ice forming along the shoreline; the glint of sunlight captured in the icicles hanging from the willow branches; a bruised sky above the north ridge, dark with the promise of snow.

Thursday morning she sets up the new tripod on the front porch and takes random shots of the cows out in the pasture, docile and complacent in their captivity, milling about with fresh snow dusting their backsides like powdered icing sugar. Later, while playing with the settings on her camera in the den, through the back window she catches sight of a horse and rider at the end of the field. She pulls on a sweater, rushes back out to the porch and re-attaches the camera to the tripod. Focusing and refocusing she clicks over and over while the silhouetted image grows larger in her viewfinder. And as it does she decides that, regardless of how her aching body feels, tomorrow she will go out on the mare to help round up the cattle again. Back at her computer she uploads the images, labels each one and attaches them to a brief email to Jessie. *"Thought Emily and Amanda might like to see what the real 'wild west' looks like."* Then, for the first time in far too long she realizes, she ends the message with, *"My love to the girls."*

Before pressing the 'send' key, she takes one last look at the photograph labelled 'Bringing in the strays.' And once again she is taken by the perfection of the image of Virgil Blue astride the high-stepping black gelding, looking for all the world as if he is one with the animal.

39

Virgil's story

The Chilcotin seeped into his pores. From the moment he returned to his mother's birthplace, and his father's adopted home, he took on the land like a lover, ignoring her unpredictable mood swings and rejections.

His mother's family, what was left of them, her brother and his family in NaNeetza Valley, welcomed him. It was all he could hope for. Acceptance would have to be earned. At first he moved from ranch to ranch learning his father's trade; between jobs he went horse logging with his uncle.

It was from his uncle that he learned the reason his parents had taken his twin brothers and left the Chilcotin to return to the United States before he was born.

"Your father, that man, he don't wan' see his children herded up like cattle and taken away to Indian Residential School," his uncle told him one night, while he sat staring into a campfire.

His own children hadn't escaped the forced removal from their people and their culture. After their return, one by one, his three sons had scattered to the four winds. One became lost to the mean streets of East Vancouver; one was somewhere in Alberta; and the eldest perished in a hotel fire in Waverley Creek.

The youngest child, a daughter, Marilyn, returned to her family at age twelve. She was there in body, but whenever Virgil visited, she sat in a kitchen corner like an old woman, a mute testament to the Catholic-run school's mandate to 'kill the Indian in the child.'

"But that Indian, her not dead," his uncle told him. "Her spirit just sleeping. Hibernating, like the bear."

Often, whenever he stayed at his uncle's home, just as he had done for his little sister, he made things for his young cousin in an attempt to coax a smile. He hollowed out birch logs to make birdhouses, which he placed in the trees outside her window. He carved tiny wooden animals from deer horns and made her a necklace. He wove a dream-catcher in a circle of willow and hung it over her bed to catch the good dreams and keep out the nightmares. But still the nightmares came.

Then, one warm summer day, he climbed out of his pickup truck carrying a battered violin case. He sat down on the discarded car seat outside of his uncle's home and opened the case to remove the second-hand instrument he had found in the Swap Shop in town. Placing the violin under his chin, he picked up the bow, and for the first time since the bones had healed, he willed his gnarled fingers to play. Before long the door opened, and his cousin, her hair tangled and matted, her feet bare, stepped outside and stood before him. When the song was finished, he lowered the bow and looked up to meet her dark eyes.

Placing her hand on his cheek, she said, "You make my heart come glad." From that day on, his young cousin and his uncle's family became the touchstone for him as he reclaimed his mother's heritage.

As ancestral memories of these vast mountains and valleys, forests and plateaus, lakes and rivers awakened in his blood, the self-pity and anger that he had embraced that snowy night on a faraway campus slowly seeped away.

He took to cowboy life as if born to it, the solitude suiting him just fine. Finding work was easy in those days. Every spread could use an extra ranch hand, especially one with so few needs, a warm place to hole up, three squares, enough wages to cover tobacco, a beer now and then, gas for his pickup truck, and a good book to replace the last one. Fortunately there were no shortages of dog-eared paperbacks in the bunkhouses.

He had long ago lost track of the Western novel in which he had found his adopted name. But he never forgot the feeling of familiarity when he first came across it, the feeling that this name belonged to him. In that very moment he replaced his birth name—the slave name of a dead president—with Virgil Blue. Now he cannot remember being anyone else.

Five years after arriving in the Chilcotin he became lead hand on the Champion Ranch, and because that job came with a cabin of his own he stayed on. He might be there still if it hadn't turned into a dude ranch. He moved on to the Spring Bottom Ranch and has been there ever since. He's seen two owners come and go, and wonders if he can stay with the latest.

For many years he hoped that his mother, too, would return to her homeland. But his sister Melody had been born in a world too far removed. Their mother could not take her daughter away from the only life she knew, from her school, her friends. His sister finished high school, university and then married. And still his mother never came. When she became a grandmother, he knew that she never would. And now this letter from his sister reminding him of a long ago promise. But it's too late.

40

Persistent stars still sprinkle the early morning sky as Julie pulls on the silk-thin Merino wool leggings. She has learned her lesson about riding in blue jeans. The New Zealand long underwear will keep her warm today, as well as buffering her from the skin-chafing denim seams rubbing against the saddle.

Downstairs, the cold rolls in on clouds of crystallized vapour, as she opens the mudroom door to let the dog out.

In the kitchen, Ian glances from the open fridge door when she comes into the room. His eyes travel up and down her body, taking in her outfit. "Good morning," he says, then returns to studying the inside of the fridge. "Going hiking?"

"Uh, no." She walks over to the stove and feels the coffee pot. "I thought I'd help Virgil with the cows. Would you like an omelette?"

"No, I'm good, thanks." He closes the fridge door, and leans against the counter. "Virgil's done though," he says, concentrating on peeling the orange in his hand.

Julie feels a quickening of her pulse. "Done?"

"He's finished the roundup. Except for a few stragglers," he says, glancing up to meet her eyes, "which, he says either will or won't find their way back; the cattle are all in."

Catching the telltale tic at the corners of Ian's mouth, the thought crosses Julie's mind that in some strange way he is relishing this particular piece of news. Then as quickly as the nervous twitch appears, it is gone.

"Why don't you come to town with me today?" he says, popping an orange section into his mouth. "Maybe we could get a motel for the night, catch a movie."

Doesn't he realize what day tomorrow is? She studies his face, looking for any sign, one way or the other, but sees nothing there. Nothing to indicate that he is aware. How can he not be? Or perhaps he is, and like the rest of the year, this is his way of handling it. Ignoring it. How she wishes she could.

Still, if she is being entirely honest with herself, she has to admit she had intended to as well; going out to round up cattle again today and tomorrow was to be her escape.

But go in to town? "No," she says, knowing he will not protest. He won't mention, neither of them will mention, nor bring up the fact that tomorrow is the anniversary of the day that is always there on the edge of their lives. She has no idea if, like herself, Ian tortures himself with all the 'should haves,' and 'could haves,' of Darla's last day. She only knows they are unable to share their grief, here, or in town. She retreats to the den with a cup of coffee, closing the door behind her.

She checks her email, deleting all but her sister's. Jessie, dear Jessie, her simple message thanking her for the photos, then asking if she wants to talk. Perhaps she will have a glass of wine and call her later. Listening to Ian preparing to leave for town, she mentally counts the full bottles in their cabinet. Seven bottles of red, Chianti, Pinot Noir, and Merlot, and seven bottles of white in the cooler—who cares what kind? She realizes with a start that she is constantly aware of every ounce of wine in the house. Just like an alcoholic. *If you're not careful you'll become the horrid cliché of a wino housewife.* The little voice in her head sounds too much like her mother's.

After she hears Ian's vehicle drive away, she sits and stares out of the den window. In the growing light of dawn, she watches Virgil spread hay in the pasture, and then return to the barn. Before long the barn door opens, and he comes out with his dog and heads back to his cabin.

A blush stings Julie's cheeks when he opens the cabin door. "I, uh, I brought you some potatoes," she says holding up the paper sack. "We'll never eat half..."

She lowers the bag. "Really, I came to apologize for going inside your home the other day—with the grouse from Terri Champion. I'm sorry, I should never have, I—"

The stuttered apology dies on her lips as Virgil, appearing unsurprised at seeing her there, nods a greeting. Still wearing his jacket and hat, he steps back and ushers her inside. Relieved, she enters without hesitating, passing by so close that she can smell the earthy aroma that fills the warm air between them.

She stands waiting in the kitchen area while he closes the door, removes his jacket and hat and hangs them on metal hooks. In no hurry, he lifts the stove lid and pokes at the embers inside, as if he has forgotten her presence in his home.

"I'm sorry," Julie repeats. "I really had no business being in here the—"

Virgil dismisses her concern with a wave of his hand, and then gestures to one of the kitchen chairs. Without waiting for her to sit down he leans over and grabs a handful of kindling from the wood box.

"I'm sorry I bothered you. I should go," Julie says, but even to her own ears her words carry no conviction.

Virgil straightens up and meets her eyes. She reads the silent plea there and lowers herself slowly onto the indicated chair.

She places her hands in her lap, and watches him rekindle the fire. Before long a flame flickers up between the sticks of wood. He adds larger pieces and closes the lid. By the time he slides the coffee pot from the back of the stove to the front, the fire is crackling beneath the cast-iron surface.

Without warning, he disappears into the bedroom door at the back of the cabin. A moment later the sound of a door closing is followed by the metallic whine of a bathroom tap being turned on.

While she waits for Virgil to wash up, Julie slips out of her jacket and hangs it on the back of her chair. From outside comes the playful growling of the two dogs wrestling on the porch.

No longer feeling like an intruder, Julie takes a closer look at her surroundings. She checks the top of the roll-top desk, empty now of any sign of the letter that was there a few days ago. Had Virgil detected anything amiss with it?

At the far end of the room, a black violin case, which she hadn't noticed last time, leans in the corner. The thought of asking Virgil to play for her comes to mind, but she knows she will not. Not yet anyway. She will have coffee, she assumes that is what he meant by asking her to stay. For the moment she is glad to be here, relieved that Virgil was not affronted at finding her at his door, and she is willing to drink warmed-over morning dregs if that is what it takes to pass part of this day in his silent company.

She is reminded of the peaceful moments sharing coffee with him up on the landing; her mind races ahead to future visits with Virgil in the warmth of this cabin, and at that thought she is filled with a comfort that if asked to, she could not define.

The changing morning light pools on the kitchen counter and her attention is drawn to the window above the sink. Still disturbed by the dreamcatcher hanging there, she forces herself to look past it, to concentrate on the sun lighting up the western ridge, the wind skittering down the lake's surface like a shiver. And she is struck by how different her life is now, how strange, and sad, and heartbreaking, the road that has led her to this moment, sitting in this ancient cabin, in the depths of the Chilcotin, listening to the water run in another room while she waits, with calm anticipation, for the occupant to return.

She's glad Ian is in town, that there's no likelihood that he will show up looking for her today. For some reason she doesn't want to share this time, this space, with him. She suspects he feels the same way about his visits with Virgil. She tries to imagine him sitting here on those days he comes to collect Virgil's rent. Does he notice the things she does? The violin in the corner? The grand collection of books? Does he ever wonder about the photographs on the wall, about Virgil's life, his family? And had he ever noticed the dream-catcher in the window before she mentioned it? No, she thinks, he wouldn't have, or if he had he would never admit, even to himself, that it was like the one that hung over their daughter's bed. Something in her believes, that like her, Ian wants this place to remain separate, free of reminders of their other life, a place of refuge from memory. Perhaps that's why the sight of the talisman hanging above Virgil's sink bothers her so. She tells herself she is being silly. Ian is right, why wouldn't there be other dreamcatchers like it, many perhaps. Still she wishes it was not there.

She turns to the sound of the door opening at the back of the cabin. Virgil emerges from the bedroom and comes into the kitchen wearing a fresh shirt and smelling of Irish Spring. His close-cropped hair glistens with dampness, emphasizing the pewter-grey at his temples.

He smiles slightly at the sight of her, as if relieved to find her still there, then looks quickly away and concentrates on checking the fire. When he is satisfied, he goes over to the cupboard, takes out a mug—*one mug, not two?*—and places it on the table along with a bowl of sugar and a teaspoon.

Pleased that he remembers how she takes her coffee, and grateful for something to do with her hands, Julie cups the empty mug while she waits for him to pour. After he does so he fills a glass of water for himself and joins her at the table. The water surprises her, given how evident it was that he enjoyed his coffee on the landing, bringing two Thermoses with him each day.

The warmed-over coffee is as strong as she expected. She reaches for the sugar bowl again. At the same moment, anticipating her reaction, Virgil slides the bowl closer and their hands touch. At the feel of his flesh, she stops and stares down at his fingers. Without thought, she gently brushes his deformed knuckles with the tip of her fingers. He pulls away slowly, leaving her hand hovering in mid-air over the table, picks up his glass and studies the bottom of it.

Astounded at her lapse of judgement, Julie stands and walks over to the roll-top desk. Keeping her back to Virgil, she concentrates on the portraits. She will leave, she tells herself, the moment she has recovered from this faux pas, she will leave.

After a while she clears her throat. "Family?" she asks, indicating the large studio photograph of his younger self, then glancing over her shoulder.

He nods.

She points to the woman sitting in front of him in the portrait. "Your mother?"

A nod.

"And sister?"

Another nod.

"They're lovely," she murmurs, studying the display once again. Minutes pass with the only sound in the room the growing fire.

"Is this your father?" she asks touching the small sepia snapshot.

Glancing back for his response, she catches him—his glass held motionless mid-way to his mouth—watching her. Has she trespassed that badly? But he nods once again.

"A handsome man," she says looking away. She wants to ask him about the people in the other photographs, but wonders if perhaps she has pressed too far. And yet a part of her senses that he has something on his mind. Is it her imagination? Does he have something he wants to say to her? Or does he feel she is pushing the boundaries and only indulging her because he is a tenant on their land? She decides to keep the one-sided conversation going and chance one more question. She leans closer to a photograph of an older First Nations couple and a younger woman with a smiling toddler on her hip. "And these people?"she asks.

Behind her Virgil's chair scrapes across the floor. She senses his approach and spins around so suddenly she almost bumps into him when he reaches past her to pull out the desk drawer. Startled by his closeness, she moves away quickly, grabs her jacket from the back of the chair and heads for the door. "I've got to go," she mumbles. "Thanks for the coffee." She reaches the door without looking back.

"Wait!" The single mechanical sounding word, stops Julie in her tracks. Her hand drops from the door knob. Turning slowly to face Virgil she immediately recognizes the device he has taken from the drawer and pressed to his throat. She can see from his expression, the weariness about his eyes, that, like her father, he is loath to use the Electrolarynx. Yet the fact that he is willing to do so, is a testament to the urgency of whatever it is that has forced him to do so.

He removes the photograph that she was asking about from the wall and walks over to hand it to her. Accepting it warily, she studies the faces of the older couple, and the young woman with a baby on her hip. Her eyes dart back up to Virgil, just as he presses the voice box to his throat and his words crack the hollow silence.

"The boy needs you."

And recognition of the smiling dimple-faced toddler dawns on her.

41

Virgil's story

Virgil Blue is the Keeper of the Grandfather Rocks. An honour passed down from his uncle.

Yesterday, after his failed attempt to avoid today's sweat lodge ceremony, Virgil brought the stones to his old friend on the banks of the Chilco River. Old Alphonse glanced up from the firepit he was tending when the pickup truck, tires crunching on gravel, came to a slow stop in the dying light of the day.

After the sacred stones were unloaded the two men sat before the orange glow of the growing fire, their lips unmoving as they spoke in a long forgotten language that needed no voice.

You come too late, my friend. I cannot heal you.

I come on behalf of the boy, to ask you to help me guide him on his vision quest.

I will take the journey with him.

I promised his mother I would be at his side.

It is not safe for you.

It is less so for the boy.

At any other time, preparing for a sweat, delivering the Grandfather Rocks, fire-tested and free from evil spirits within, would have been a time of celebration. A time to look inward, a time to heal. But Virgil fears his young cousin is too weakened by grief for this vision quest. Yet he knows the boy is determined, and he will attempt it on his own if Virgil refuses to guide him.

This morning the sun has not yet risen. Stars still shine between the clouds scudding across a moonless sky as he and the boy arrive on the riverbank. The sweat lodge is ready. Its willow frame is covered with a mixture of ragged-edged animal hides and colourful blankets. Barely taller than the five-foot-high domed structure, Old Alphonse works outside. A deerskin jacket hanging loose from his thin shoulders, he pushes a blunt-nose shovel into the firepit. With a strength that belies his years, he retrieves a large stone from the hot coals, turns slowly and then crouching low carries the searing hot rock through the flapped opening into the lodge.

He reappears from the darkened interior, and Virgil helps him transfer more stones inside. Then all three of them take armloads of wood from the pile next to the firepit and stack them on top of the remaining stones, filling the hole to its rock-rimmed edges. While they work tiny snowflakes appear, only to melt among the sparks lifting from the fire.

When they are finished, the old man stands before the boy. He searches his face. Their breath crystallizes on the air between them. Then, in a voice low and unhurried, Old Alphonse asks if the boy has fasted, if he has kept his body free from alcohol and caffeine for this ceremony. The youth answers with a nod, at the same time holding up his offering of a pouch of tobacco. A sinewy hand accepts, and the pouch disappears into a jacket pocket.

Virgil offers no tobacco, the expected custom. He knows too well the harm years of it have done to his own body. Instead, cradled across his palms, he holds up a polished walking stick. The staff, which he has made from a single mountain ash root, straightened and strengthened in water baths, is as long as his old friend is tall.

Both Elders remain motionless, their faces betraying nothing.

Glistening specks of snow become fat flakes that drift aimlessly between them as they hold each other's gaze. In the river below, ice-blue glacier water washes over a thousand centuries of sculpted stones. Finally Old Alphonse accepts the walking stick. Placing it on a tarp laid out on the ground, he begins to undress.

Following his lead, Virgil and Levi remove their own clothing. Once they are stripped down, the old man, wearing nothing more than a breechcloth, pushes his silver-grey braids onto his back and leans over the fire. He holds a twisted bundle of twigs into the embers at the edge of the firepit until it begins to smoke. Circling the boy first and then Virgil, he passes the smouldering sage up, down, and around their naked torsos, while a sing-song chant rises from deep in his throat. Virgil repeats the ritual for him. Before entering the lodge, they each drink from the buckets of water placed outside the low opening.

As they crawl inside, sage and cedar boughs crunch beneath their hands and knees, filling the sweltering air inside the lodge with the heavy Chilcotin scent.

Darkness engulfs the trio the moment Old Alphonse pulls down the flap to seal off the opening. Virgil's eyes slowly adjust to light. Before long the red glow from the central stone pit reveals the outline of the old man on the other side. Sitting cross-legged he tosses crushed leaves into the pit, and then with a circular motion of his hands urges the rising smoke to his face and inhales deeply. Virgil and, beside him, the boy, do the same. Water is sprinkled across the hot stones and embers. The steam hisses up, finding its way into Virgil's lungs. Beads of sweat gather on his scalp and forehead. They run down his face and drip from his chin. More and more billowing steam rises; condensation drips from the willow frame above, the hot droplets landing on bare skin. Virgil feels the dirt beneath the sage and cedar turning to mud. The heat-thick air grows increasingly heavy; it presses down on every inch of his body, it scorches his throat, his lungs. His chin drops down onto his chest. After a while he raises his head to check on the boy. Levi, his skin slick with moisture, his long hair plastered against his skull, stares trance-like into the swirling space before him. Satisfied with the even rising and falling of his young cousin's chest, Virgil turns his attention back to the stone pit. Taking a handful of leaves he spreads them across the hot rocks and burning embers. He inhales deeply as the leaves crackle and hiss in the searing heat. His body begins to rock back and forth in rhythm with Old Alphonse's humming chant while he searches the renewed surge of smoke and steam rising in the darkness. Within the dancing grey and orange shadows Virgil imagines he sees the faces of his mother, his father and brothers, smiling, beckoning. He wants to let go, to be with them, but theirs are not the visions he seeks this day. One by one the ghostly images dissolve, fading back into the churning smoke, until in the depths of the thick haze the form of a crow takes shape. The bird wings its way up, its black feathers and ebony head growing and changing as it rises into the massive head and shoulders of a black bear. Beneath eyelids as heavy as lead, Virgil watches the apparition drift toward Levi, the bear's head now morphing into the smiling face of a young girl. As if he too is seeing the same vision, the boy's arms slowly rise, he reaches up, and from his barely moving lips comes the whispered name, "Darla."

42

I don't need Mr Emerson to tell me that it's not really my face that Levi sees rising before him, only the memory of me. Still, I try to reach him with my thoughts. While his hallucination grows, I repeat over and over that I'm okay. That he needs to stop this, now.

If only Mom had listened to Mr Blue.

Yesterday, he tried to convince her to meet with Levi, to join him in a healing circle. If she had only agreed, then this sweat, this vision quest of Levi's, would not have been necessary today. But Mom stopped hearing Mr Blue the moment she understood that the woman in the photograph was his cousin, and that the child on her hip, was her son, Levi.

She fled from the cabin before he had a chance to convince her to meet with Levi, to participate in a healing circle. I wish she hadn't. I wish she knew the truth about the accident. She needs to forgive Levi, not only for his sake, but for hers, for Dad's, and for mine. If only Levi could tell her that it was my fault, not his. If only he could tell her the whole truth, about the beer can, the rose, and why I took off my seatbelt.

But of course Levi won't tell her any of that. That's just not his way. He's too proud to offer excuses and too honourable to shift blame. He only wants to give her the message he heard me tell him that night. His 'intentions are pure,' as my Gram used to say, but his method is flawed.

Mr Blue has agreed to accompany Levi on this sweat because he believes

Levi is trying to find peace, to find healing, in his 'vision quest.' He doesn't realize that what Levi is really trying to find is me on this day, this anniversary of my death. His true intention is to keep the promise he made to Mom that night, to take me home safely. He believes that if he can leave his physical body and find me in the spirit world, that he can help me pass through to my home on the other side.

I don't know why he believes that. Mr Emerson says it's an ancestral memory embedded deep in his subconscious, a memory that he's decided to trust. He's not saying whether Levi's right or wrong, only that it's not safe. I'm with him. I'm afraid that if Levi goes on too long with this, he really might find a way to join me in this in-between place. And if he does, he may not be able to leave. And it's just not his time; Levi still has things left to do on earth. The Elders were right when they told him he had an obligation to the youth of his people, who look up to him. He's lost sight of that.

Mr Blue fears for Levi, too. He keeps watch on him through visions dancing up in the darkness. I concentrate on trying to tell them both that it's time to end this. Maybe in their altered state they'll hear me. But then, intentionally, or unintentionally, Mr Blue puts a stop to it himself. His eyes roll back, and he slumps over onto the ground, his cheek slamming against the wet cedar boughs.

43

The bear slowly takes form, growing larger in the rising mist.

I'm dreaming, Julie tells herself. *It's just a dream. I can wake up anytime.* Yet she remains frozen in some ethereal netherworld, unable to turn away from the looming image, its head lifting from hunchbacked shoulders, jaws opening, exposing menacing teeth. Then from the depths of its cavernous throat, a crow flies up.

The bird wings higher and higher, until it is nothing more than a black dot in the sky. Wanting to follow it, she remembers what she's always known: *I can fly.* She feels herself become weightless as she lifts from the ground, easily, so easily. All she had to do is remember. Trees, fields, forests grow smaller beneath her, as she rises, until without warning the sound of distant banging shatters the moment. "Julie? Julie?"

She tries to ignore the intruding voice and rise once again on imaginary wings. But Ian's voice is insistent.

The dream disintegrates and her eyes snap open. Disoriented, she slowly focuses on the frosted overhead light in centre of her bedroom ceiling.

"Julie?" Ian calls from the other side of the door. "Are you awake?"

Sitting upright in bed she shakes away the reluctance to let go of slumber, and calls out quietly, "I'm up."

"Phone call for you. It's Jessie."

Fully awake now, her dream nothing more than a fragile memory dissolving in the morning light, she pushes the hair out of her eyes. Jessie calling so early?

She throws the blankets back to swing out of bed, feeling the cold fear that an unexpected phone call brings. Striding across the room, every possible disaster races through her mind: Jessie's girls? Her husband? Their mother?

The bedroom door opens before she can reach it, to reveal Ian holding the telephone out to her.

He waits in the doorway, as she takes it. "Jess?" she breathes into the receiver. "Is everything all right?"

"Sure," Jessie's cheerful voice answers. "I just wondered why you hadn't called back yesterday. That's all."

"Sorry, I completely forgot."

"That's okay. Hey, were you still sleeping?"

Julie glances down at her watch. Ten fifteen. Not early after all. "No. Well... yeah... I slept in, I guess."

She mouths *It's okay* to Ian, who turns away and heads downstairs, but not before she catches where his attention was focused. She looks down at herself, at the wrinkled cashmere sweater, the blue jeans, the clothes she had so carefully chosen to wear over to Virgil's, yesterday.

Virgil's? *Oh God!* She can't think about that right now.

She closes the bedroom door with a soft click. "I'm just having a tough time right now, Jess," she says quietly into the phone.

"Of course. I had the feeling that you might like to talk today, that's all."

"It's okay. I'll be fine." She won't tell her how. She won't tell her about yesterday's bottles of wine emptied in an afternoon and evening that she can't remember ending. She does remember answering Jess's email though, promising to call her later, as well as the many telephone calls from their mother, which, not trusting her own slurred responses, Julie had not bothered to answer.

"Mom left a number of messages on my answering machine," she says searching through the shirts hanging in the closet with one hand while she holds the phone to her ear with the other. The topic of their mother was always a good subject changer. "I haven't called her back yet either. She okay?"

"Same old, same old. Well except right now she's all atwitter about the photographs you emailed. They really made an impression on her, especially the last one of the cowboy."

Virgil? Had she sent that image to her mother?

"She's talking about going back up to your place. Her exact words were, 'Maybe spend some time getting to know that handsome old cowboy.' Can you imagine? Mom flirting with a ranch hand?"

"Oh, God," Julie says, pulling a plaid shirt from its hanger and heading back into the bedroom.

"I thought I should warn you," Jessie says. "She's actually considering flying up for Christmas."

Julie stops in her tracks. "Hah! Well, that's not going to happen. Tell her we're going away. That we won't be here for Christmas."

"Well actually, Jules, that's something I wanted to talk to you about myself. I was wondering if maybe... well it's just an idea, but what do you think about us all coming to spend Christmas week with you this year?"

Her words catch Julie off guard. "Oh, I uh... No, you wouldn't want to drive up here then. It'll be miserably cold. Snow. Who knows what the road would be like...?"

"Barry's used to winter conditions. He grew up in Revelstoke, remember."

"What about the girls? That wouldn't be fair to take Emily and Amanda away from their home at Christmas," she says dropping the shirt onto the chair by the bed.

"It would be an adventure for them."

"I, uh I don't know..."

"They miss you, Jules."

Julie slumps down on the end of the bed. "I'll have to talk to Ian. I'm not sure…"

"Just think about it, okay?"

She arrives downstairs to find no sign of Ian, or the dog. The only sound in the empty house is the hum of the fireplace fan in the living room, and the distant drone of a tractor motor outside. In the kitchen, the wine bottles, which she had sought refuge in yesterday, are nowhere to be seen. Did Ian get rid of the, what—two—three—empties? Or had she? She has no idea, no memory of cleaning up or going to bed last night. What she does remember all too clearly is fleeing from Virgil's cabin yesterday morning, stunned by his request.

How could he have asked her to meet with Levi Johnny? By the time she reached home she was seething with the knowledge of how completely foolish she had been. The crow pendant, the dreamcatcher, the photograph of Levi as a toddler with his mother, it was all in plain sight. Virgil had done nothing to hide his connection to Levi. But still, he should have told them. They had the right to know that the man who they had both come to trust—more than they did each other these days—was related to the boy who was responsible for Darla's death.

It slowly dawned on Julie that Virgil had befriended her for no other reason than to find redemption for his cousin's son. She had washed down her growing anger with a glass of Pinot Noir. Perfect for betrayal. For surely Virgil had betrayed her, and Ian.

Later yesterday afternoon, she had heard his truck motor. Had he seen her standing there in the mudroom window watching him drive his pickup past the house, moving so painfully slowly, as if reluctant to leave, as if waiting for her to call him back, before disappearing around the corner of the hill?

Now, she wishes she had. She wishes she had demanded an explanation. Maybe she should have let him finish his little speech in his cabin. Not that she would have considered going with him to meet with Levi, or agreed to join them in some 'healing' ceremony she doesn't believe in. No, only so she could have demanded to know how he could have deceived them all this time. And then it strikes her. Does Ian know? Has Ian known all along?

The screeching of engine gears draws her back to reality. From the den window she watches the tractor come to a jerking stop out in the pasture, then Ian climbing down from the idling machine. With only the dog accompanying him he walks back to the flat-bed behind the tractor and tosses bales to the waiting herd. No Virgil to help with the feeding this morning?

Curious, she goes into the living room and looks out the window. Not a trickle of smoke rises to the sky in the treetops above the cabin.

By the time Ian returns to the house, bringing Pup and the smell of hay and manure into the kitchen with him, Julie has decided not to confront him about Virgil. If he already knows, then it is one more betrayal for her to chew on. If he doesn't, what good would it do to tell him? How would she even go about telling him how she found out? No, she will just have to swallow her resentment, go back to ignoring the man's presence. It's a hollow decision, leaving her with nothing more than an empty feeling as she watches Ian warm his hands on the sides of the coffee pot.

"Virgil must have gone to town," he says. "Strange. He usually tells me when he's going to be away."

By the time they go to their rooms that night there is still no sign of their tenant. Early the following morning, Virgil is once again out in the pasture with Ian feeding the cattle. Ian returns to the house, slamming the mudroom door behind him just as Julie is getting ready to go for a hike with Pup. She looks up from lacing her boots to find Ian standing in the doorway, his face clouded, a crinkled piece of familiar yellow notepaper clutched in his hand.

Shaking his head, as if to clear it, he says, "He's leaving."

44

"I just don't understand it," Ian says staring down at the paper as if he has missed something.

Julie takes it from his hands. The message, written in the scrawled script that she has come to recognize, offers little explanation. Like all of Virgil's notes it's simple and to the point. In as few words as possible it gives notice that he will be 'moving on.'

"I just don't understand it," Ian repeats, more to himself than to Julie.

Watching his shoulders slump as he walks out of the room she is pretty certain that she understands. Virgil is leaving because she refused his request to meet with his nephew, cousin?—whatever Levi is—refused to grant him redemption. But how can she tell this to Ian, who can't even bear to hear their daughter's name spoken out loud.

She stays out of his way for the rest of the day, letting him come to terms with the sudden change. That night after finishing his supper, Ian announces that he's heading over to Virgil's. "Maybe, over a cup of coffee, I can find out what's really going on," he says pushing his plate away. "See if I can change his mind."

Julie puts her fork down on her untouched plate. "I can help feed the cattle."

"It's not about the cattle," he says frowning. "Something's changed. I don't know what, but this is Virgil's home. Why all of a sudden is he leaving?" His eyes search hers for an answer.

She looks down and concentrates on gathering up their dinner dishes. "Who knows," she replies slowly. "What do we really know about Virgil anyway? Why not just let him go?"

Ian's chair scrapes on the floor as he stands up. "No," he says headed out of the kitchen. "Something's not right."

Julie rises quickly, and follows him out into the mudroom. Her protests die on her lips as Ian reasons with himself, "Maybe it's as simple as talking him into letting me pay him for all the work he does. Hell," he says pulling his coat on, "he doesn't even have to feed cattle this winter. We can sell the livestock. He doesn't need to do any work around here if he doesn't want to. I just can't believe he really wants to go."

Less than an hour later he returns, defeated. Julie searches his face for any sign that Virgil has placed the blame on her, but in her heart she knows he would not.

"Well, he's really leaving," Ian says, shaking his head in defeat. "Won't say exactly when, just that he can't promise to stay the winter, will probably be out of here by January. He advised me to sell the herd."

At the beginning of November, the first cattle trucks come and go, the mournful bawling of their cargo trailing behind. As the transports crawl up the hill, Julie turns away from the unwanted glimpses of huge brown eyes rolling in panic—as if aware of their destination— behind air vents in the metal enclosures.

Certainly she has never been under any illusions about the ultimate fate of the cows. She has eaten her fair share of steak and hamburgers, after all. Still, seeing the first of the animals being loaded and shipped out to auction today is somehow unsettling. Over the last week she has listened to Ian consider the alternatives, cutting back the herd to something more manageable, hiring someone to replace Virgil—Virgil himself has offered to recommend someone who would be willing to take over the cabin, his chores, his role on the ranch—but in the end, Ian has decided to send the entire herd to auction. And ever since making that decision Julie has watched him grow more and more despondent. His reaction surprises her, and forces her to consider her role in all this. She, too, has alternatives. She could go over and speak to Virgil herself. See if there was anything she could do—short of his requested meeting with Levi—to change his mind. Or, she could tell Ian the truth, why she believes Virgil is going. Perhaps, if he knew, he would not be as eager to have him stay. Stuck in indecision, she has done nothing, letting the situation play out without her interference.

This evening she remains in the den watching television alone. Earlier this afternoon she had reminded Ian that today was the American election, but once again he has chosen to bury himself in his office files. Surfing from channel to channel, she can't help but think he is avoiding watching the election returns because of the thought that would hang in the air, unspoken, about how thrilled Darla would have been to experience this moment in history. *Well, I'll experience it for her.* Julie swallows back the jagged lump in her throat and concentrates on the scenes unfolding on every major channel. In city after city, swelling crowds are gathered in the streets in anticipation of finding out who will become the forty-fourth president of the United States of America. As state results are announced, there is a moment, like a collective sigh of relief, before the crowds erupt in celebration. Cameras pan the rejoicing crowds, the uplifted faces say it all. In the split second following understanding, tense anticipation turns to relief, disbelief to belief. Tears of joy flow unchecked down cheeks of all colours, races and religions. Strangers jump up and down, hugging and kissing each other, and dancing breaks out in streets across the nation. It is truly an historical moment. How Darla would have loved knowing that, as she had wondered, "Yes! This can really happen!" Julie recognizes the naked emotion in the rejoicing faces on the screen. Their joy is about more than the success of the Illinois senator's 'yes we can' campaign, about more than race, or party, or fixing the economy. It's about hope.

And in that moment comes awareness that the unbearable sadness threatening to overwhelm her is her own complete and utter loss of hope.

45

Chilcotin winter does not wait for the December solstice. It arrives on a biting north wind. For two days the arctic air howls down the lake, peaking whitecaps and misted sprays, swirling across the surface in its wake. Thin layers of ice forming along the water's edge are crushed in the turbulence and thrown to shore. The warmth inside the ranch house—where the wind's fury is nothing more than a distant moan—is testament to the solidness of the log structure. And then as suddenly as it came swooping into the valley, the windstorm abates, leaving behind a crystal-blue sky and plunging temperatures. The thermometer outside the kitchen window drops to zero, ten below, twenty below. Ice appears along the shore once again, expanding further and further out, until one morning Julie wakes to find the lake a frozen sheet of glimmering ice.

Out in the back pasture the remaining cows huddle together beneath the skeletal cottonwood trees along the creek. Tomorrow morning, the last of the cattle trucks will arrive to take the rest of the herd to the stockyards. Ian intends to follow them in for the auction.

Preparing for her first hike in days, Julie pours coffee into a Thermos. Tightening the lid she glances through the living room to where Ian is sitting staring at the computer in his office. Earlier she had asked him to join her, but as she expected, he barely acknowledged her invitation.

Ever since Virgil's announcement, Ian has shrunk further and further into despondency. Julie tries to temper her growing impatience with his reaction, yet she can't ignore that in some strange way it angers her. He is behaving as if he's lost his best friend, and perhaps he believes he has. But Julie believes that he, and she, too, for that matter, had simply read something deeper into Virgil's silences than was there. They had seen in him what they needed to see, rather than who he truly was—a man they knew little, to nothing, about.

After packing the Thermos and her camera, Julie straps the tripod onto her backpack, reminded as she does so that from the very beginning Virgil seemed to know more about them than they ever did about him. Even the can of bear spray, which she considers now, came from him. She discards it, along with the iPod music. The plus side of winter with its freezing temperatures is that there is no longer any need for them, no danger of running into bears who by now have retreated to their dens, hibernating until spring.

Today she feels safe hiking the hillsides above the south pasture. With the dog at her heels she crosses the ranch yard. The horses lift their heads from the hay manger, their jaws working at their breakfast as they watch her pass by. Ian has offered the Clydesdales to Virgil. "He should take them with him wherever he is going," Ian said. "They're really his anyway." She had not disputed it. But Virgil did; he declined the offer, informing Ian that he would find a home for them. To Julie's relief Ian has decided to keep all the horses. She has no idea what they will do with the Clydesdales, but she cannot imagine the ranch without their presence.

The cold bites at her cheeks, causing her eyes to water as she makes her way along the fenceline of the pasture. At the far end she shimmies through the bottom rungs. Startled by the havoc created by the windstorms, she skirts the edge of the timberline, where unprotected trees lay broken and shattered like so many discarded matchsticks. Just when she is certain that it's futile trying to locate the trail she and Virgil took the day they went chasing after cows, Pup, sniffing at the skiffs of snow, stumbles upon it. She follows him, scrambling over deadfalls and broken branches that litter the winding path. Deeper into wind-ravaged forest, the devastation lessens and the trail becomes easier to navigate. Despite the stinging cold, sweat trickles down Julie's skin beneath her woollen underwear as she climbs higher. Sunlight filters through the trees, glinting on the tiny ice particles that drift through the still air like fairy dust.

It takes the better part of two hours before they reach the summit. When they do she is sweat-soaked, but exhilarated. While Pup scurries around with his nose to the ground, exploring the smorgasbord of odours in the clearing, Julie searches for a good vantage point. After settling on a panoramic view, which stretches from the south pasture to the far northern end of the lake, she sets up her camera and tripod, and then sits down on a nearby stump to have coffee and wait for the sun to be directly overhead. Through the steam rising from her coffee mug, she stares down over the treetops. In the valley below, the ranch house and outbuildings appear like islands in a sea of white, and she can't help but compare this view to the first day she and Ian came out with the real estate salesman. Since that day, so much has changed, and nothing has changed. There is precious little left of their marriage except sharing meals and the polite conversation of strangers. The one thing that they have in common, the one thing that should bind them together, their daughter, is a forbidden topic. And in her heart she knows, that this, more than anything else, would be unbearable to live with for the rest of her life. Yet, gazing down into the valley, the thought of leaving this place saddens her already bruised heart. She rarely goes to town anymore. It's not the distance. She has never minded driving, in fact she used to enjoy long road trips. She could go in with Ian, who never fails to invite her every second Friday, but she has yet to accept, preferring to stay out here rather than face town, and the silent drive.

With a shiver she recalls her mother's warning about getting 'bushed.' Was she right? Is that what keeps her here? Or is it simply because she doesn't know where she would go if she was to leave Ian?

And if leaving is truly an eventuality, why wait? Especially now. In fairness shouldn't she go now, before Virgil does?

She jumps as Pup nudges her free hand.

"Hah," she says, putting down her tin cup. "You just love me for the treats." Retrieving a biscuit from her backpack she wonders what she would do without her faithful companion. And to think she hadn't wanted a dog. Then the truth hits her, that it would be cruel to take him away from here. Pushing the thought to the back of her mind, she stands and concentrates on focusing her camera.

By the time she is finished taking her shots, heavy clouds have appeared on the northern horizon. Dark and foreboding, they scud across the sky as she makes her way down the mountainside. When she reaches the bottom pasture, a black ceiling covers the valley. Fat flakes drift down, growing larger and larger in their hushed descent. "Pieces of clouds," Darla used to call them when she was little. She would run around their yard, bundled up in her snowsuit, trying to catch them on her tongue. Once again, Julie's eyes tear up, not from the cold, but from the sweet memory. No, it's not the memory, she decides, it's having no one to share it with.

As she crosses the field, in the distance, the yard light glows pink through the falling snow. Looking like a wolf in the wild, Pup forges ahead, the fresh powdered snow flying up from beneath his huge padding feet as he leads her home. Home. The thought of the fire crackling in the living room, Ian waiting for her return, brings an unexpected warmth as she hurries behind the dog. Before she reaches the ranch house her decision is made. She doesn't want to leave, the ranch, nor Ian. It's she who must try harder to make this work. She knows that their life together can never be the same as it was before, but if there is anything left to salvage of their marriage, it is she who must find it. They don't need a third person, Virgil, or a new hired hand, to keep the ranch going. She is capable. No. More than capable to help with the physical work. Together she and Ian can manage it. They can truly turn this ranch into their home.

The mudroom door swings open the moment she steps onto the back porch. Stamping the snow from her boots she smiles up into Ian's relieved eyes. Yes, tomorrow she'll go into town with him. Perhaps during the long drive, she can find a way to reach him, to remind him that Darla is a part of who they are. Maybe she can find a way to convince him that they need to share memories of their daughter, not fear them.

46

The next morning a transformed landscape greets Julie. The lake and fields lay dormant under a seamless blanket of white. On the hillsides tree branches sag under the weight of the overnight snowfall. Since dawn, Ian and Virgil have been out with the tractor and truck ploughing and sanding the hill. By the time the cattle truck shows up, the road into the ranch is clear. A few hours later the remaining cows are loaded and on their way.

While Ian gets ready for the drive into town, Julie feeds the dog. She wants to take Pup along with them today, but Ian has already discounted that idea, pointing out that the dog has become completely independent now that he can come and go through the doggie door into the mudroom. It's true that ever since the weather turned cold, Pup prefers to be outdoors, spending his nights in his kennel on the back porch and coming inside only now and then for a drink of water or a quick visit. "He's a ranch dog, Julie," Ian insisted before he went up to shower. "It's not fair to drag him into town. He'll be fine out here by himself." She knows he's right. Still this is the first time they have left him on his own and Julie is nervous about doing so.

The metallic smell of snow rushes in on the crisp winter air the moment she opens the mudroom door. Across the ranch yard Pup and Virgil's dog are wrestling in front of the barn. At the sound of her voice, Pup rolls upright in a billow of snow, and then bolts toward the porch. Left lying with his muzzle on the white ground, Virgil's dog watches him go, then stands up to shake the snow from his coat when his master appears in the barn doorway.

Julie has not encountered Virgil since that day in his cabin, but even from this distance she recognizes the same weariness in his face that was there then. Keeping her eyes on him she leans down to place the dog dish on the porch. She straightens up then backs into the mudroom and closes the door slowly. *He doesn't want to leave the ranch either.* The thought keeps her rooted in front of the door window. Uncaring if he can see her behind the glass, she watches Virgil trudge through the snow on the way back to his cabin with his dog by his side. *He doesn't want to leave anymore than Ian wants him to go,* she thinks as he disappears down the road. *Can I fix this?* She turns away, and heads upstairs, uncertain that she would, even if she could.

While Ian showers, Julie goes into the spare bedroom. The cardboard boxes, which she had chosen last night, wait inside the door. This is her first step in her resolve to try to find a way to put her and Ian's marriage back on track. Without saying anything to him, she has made the decision, as he has always wanted her to, to take the boxes of Darla's clothes in to the Salvation Army. Sorting through them last night, she had been unable to resist opening each box to pull out armfuls of carefully folded clothes and crushing them to her face. Fighting the urge to do so now, she carries them one by one to the mudroom. She leaves the box of dolls behind. Ian is right about the clothes, there is no good reason to save them. But the dolls? She cannot bear to let go of Darla's dolls.

After loading the boxes in the back of the idling Jeep, she waits in the driver's seat. When Ian comes out, loaded down with his briefcase and file boxes she rolls down her window. "I'll drive," she calls out in answer to his questioning expression at seeing her sitting behind the wheel.

"The roads might be pretty slick today."

"I'll drive slow," she promises, buckling on her seatbelt with a deci-sive click.

Ian hesitates for a moment, but then walks to the back of the car when Julie rolls up her window. Adjusting her rear-view mirror, she keeps her eye on him as he lifts the rear door. He hesitates at the sight of the boxes, their contents written on each in black marker. He loads his own boxes then climbs into the passenger seat, without a word.

Fresh snow crunches beneath the Jeep's tires, as it crawls steadily up the hill, navigating the sharp-cornered switch-backs with ease. Spending so much time in a vehicle when she was selling real estate, Julie has always insisted on the best 'rubber' money could buy, and now she is grateful for the sure-footed traction of the studded tires. By the time they reach the top road, she is confident that she is once again getting the feel of Cariboo winter driving.

When they turn onto the main highway, she relaxes. Except for drifting skiffs of snow, the road to town stretches before them, a rib-bon of black asphalt. She allows the Jeep to pick up speed, stealing a quick glance at Ian, who is already lying back against the headrest, his eyes closed in sleep. Or, she thinks, more likely in pretence of sleep—his way of avoiding the temptation to criticize her driving.

With the hum of the tires the only sound in the car she concentrates on the road. It's not his silence that she minds, it's what lies behind it. She finds herself considering Virgil's muteness. Unlike the silence between her and Ian, filled with blame and grief, anger and resent-ment, which threatens to explode if broken at the wrong moment, the silences she had shared with Virgil were tranquil, calm, in harmony somehow with the moment. With a start she realizes that she misses those moments. Like the music. She misses the music. Even in the coldest of weather, she still leaves her bedroom window open a crack, but no matter how hard she listens, the voice of a distant violin no longer seeps into her bedroom in the middle of the night.

She forces herself back to the moment, searching for the right words to start up a conversation with Ian. There was a time when that was never a problem. It seems so long ago, another life, when they used to cherish moments like these, alone in the car. She had always looked forward to long road trips, where without interference from telephones, clients, Ian's or hers, they would talk non-stop. And then when Darla was growing up, for Julie, the only truly enjoyable part of visiting her mother in Vancouver was the chance to spend seven hours in the car with her family. Seven hours filled with conversation, and laughter. And they would sing. How they would sing! Ian, with his beautiful deep tenor voice, loved to croon old Irish ballads. He would break into song the moment conversation lagged in the car. By the time Darla was eight she knew all of the lyrics to the most improbable songs—songs like "Galway Bay" or "Danny Boy," which she would sing along with her father at the top of her lungs, even affecting his feigned Irish accent. Julie had had her own travelling repertoire of old Joni Mitchell, Judy Collins and Joan Baez songs, songs she had grown up with—one legacy from her mother that she hadn't shunned. Darla's favourite was a Joni Mitchell ballad, "The Circle Game." Right up to the time she was a teenager she would ask Julie to sing it every time they drove any distance at all. They always thought of it as Darla's song.

Unwittingly Julie finds herself humming it now, mentally singing the lyrics. But when she reaches the verse about *sixteen springs and sixteen summers gone now*, her throat closes up. Beside her Ian stirs. Has he heard? Does he remember, or even think of those times? She glances quickly at him, but he turns away to face the passenger window.

Julie switches on the radio, pressing the search button until she lands on some country and western station whose music holds no memories for her, or Ian. For the next hour she forces herself to listen to the almost comical wailing laments of lost loves, lost homes, spilled whiskey and beer, but nothing about lost children.

On either side of the highway, grey clouds hang heavy over the fields, hillsides and tree tops. Less than a half hour from town snow begins to fall once again, the growing flakes spiralling in a hypnotizing vortex against the windshield.

When the accident happens, like all accidents, it happens without warning. Afterward, Julie will remember it in fragmented slow motion images. The transport truck coming toward them from the opposite direction: the commotion of snow lifting and swirling up from beneath multi-tires; the billowing clouds left in its wake as the loaded semi speeds by; her white-knuckled hands, gripping the steering as they enter the blinding whiteout.

Only later will she question whether the black blur she sees on the highway as she comes out of the swirling snowstorm could truly be a bear at this time of year. But in the moment the fleeting image causes her instinctive reaction. A reaction, which, even as it occurs, she knows is wrong. In that split second of recognizing that there is a living creature in the path of her Jeep, she is unable to prevent her foot from slamming on the brakes, her hands from swerving the wheel. Then the helpless feeling as suddenly the Jeep's tires—the best money can buy—lock and skid sideways across black ice, as easily as sliding through grease. Her mind racing, Julie tries to turn the useless steering wheel in the direction of the skid, but it's too late, out of her control. Careening toward the bank on the other side of the road, she lets go and gives into the inevitable. In the heartbeat the car becomes airborne, and sails into a silent white abyss, the unbidden thought whispers inside Julie's mind. *"Darla, I'm coming."*

Their soundless flight is broken by the grinding screech of impact. Something solid rips through the undercarriage and the windshield shatters at the same moment the airbags explode. Still the vehicle keeps moving, bucking and rolling, smashing against unyielding objects, while the unseen world spins out of control. Then as suddenly as it started it is still, the only sound the whine of the motor. Disoriented, Julie reaches for the ignition key. The deflating airbag blocks her search.

She forces it away to find herself staring through the bottom edge of the shattered windshield at a world turned sideways, a world where hundreds of white papers flutter from an upside-down sky.

Her trembling fingers locate the ignition key on the steering wheel and turn off the motor. In the ensuing silence, she feels the wind and snow swirling inside the Jeep. Only then does it dawn on her that the vehicle has landed on its side with the tailgate door thrown wide open, and that the sheets of paper fluttering down are Ian's files.

Ian?

With great effort she turns her head to the right, her jaw and face aching from the impact of the exploding airbag.

"Ian," she cries, feeling panic for the first time. "Ian, are you okay?"

The slack passenger airbag moves, and Ian's face appears above her. "Yeah, you?"

"I think so." She looks around. "We've got to crawl out the back," she says. "I'll need to go first, so you'll have room."

It takes a few moments to unfasten her seatbelt. Twisting and turning carefully, she squeezes herself out from under the steering wheel. She crawls over the seats toward the rear of the vehicle, feeling the Jeep rocking precariously as she does.

In the front, Ian suddenly drops from his seatbelt restraint. "Careful," Julie hollers back to him as she rolls out onto the ground, "the Jeep's not stable." As Ian pulls himself toward the rear of the vehicle there is a warning screech of metal and Julie screams in horror as the vehicle teeters and then rolls slowly from its precarious perch. As it flips over, Ian is tossed out like a rag doll, slamming onto the ground below, a moment before the Jeep lands on its roof in the same spot.

Razor sharp rocks beneath the snow rip through Julie's clothes, cutting her hands and tearing skin as she scrambles down into the ravine. At the bottom she pulls her way around the Jeep, her heart pounding in her throat. Relief floods through her at the sight of Ian lying face up, as if waiting for her, on the other side of the car. His glasses are nowhere to be seen and his right leg is bent up against his chest while the left, from the thigh down is lodged under the Jeep's roof. Still, he attempts a grin when she drops down beside him. "Well this is bloody stupid," he says. "My leg's stuck. I think it might be broken."

Julie chokes back a nervous sob. A broken leg. They can handle that. It could have been so much worse. Looking up at the path of destruction on the steep hillside she thinks it's a wonder that they're here at all.

"Can you move?" she asks.

Ian struggles to pull his leg out from beneath the Jeep, the pain blanching his face. "No. It's pinned."

She puts her arms under his shoulder and, bracing her legs against the metal, tries to slide him back, but it's useless. She stands up and pushes against the vehicle, but it won't budge.

From the highway above comes the sound of a vehicle approaching in the distance. But as Julie listens anxiously, it speeds by without slowing down. She is suddenly aware of the seriousness of the situation. No one can see them down here. They're going to have to get themselves out. They're damn lucky if they come through this with nothing more than a broken leg.

"I'm going to try digging your leg out," she says, and goes around to the back of the Jeep. She has to scrunch down to look inside. Empty. Everything that was once stored there for emergency, the shovel, first aid kit, jumper cables, must all have been thrown out, along with the boxes. She scans the churned-up path the Jeep took to its final resting point, frantically searching for any sign of the shovel, only to see, scattered across the hillside, hanging from tree branches, and lying on the snow like laundry waiting for the sun, jeans, t-shirts, sweaters—Darla's clothes.

She shakes away the image, she can't think about that right now. At the sound of another vehicle on the highway above, she glances up in hope. So near, and yet so far. The engine roar increases then turns into a distant drone heading toward town. Julie rushes back to Ian, drops down on her knees and starts clawing through the snow beneath his leg with her bare hands. Her fingernails rip as they scrape against dirt and rocks. The ground is too hard. She knows it's futile, but can't give up.

"Julie, stop." Grabbing at her hands, Ian tries to sit up. He slumps back, the colour drained from his face. "You're going to have to go up and flag someone down."

God, how can she leave him down here alone? she wonders, but answers, "Okay." She removes her jacket and spreads it on top of him.

"Don't," he says, "You keep it on."

"I'll be warm enough, climbing up that damn bank," she says, "while you just get to lie here and relax." Ian's attempted smile turns into a grimace. Reluctant to leave him, but fully aware of the threat of shock, or hypothermia, Julie leans down and kisses his forehead. "Like the man said, 'I'll be back.'"

She starts climbing, following the path of the Jeep's descent, grabbing at roots and branches, anything to help pull herself up. At the sound of another vehicle on the road above, this time coming from the direction of town, she scrambles faster, frustrated as it too passes by. But then, instead of fading off into the distance, the motor slows, idles and then with a roar backs up to stop on the highway directly above. As car doors open and close above, Julie screams out, "Help. We're down here."

She hollers it out over and over, even after the three faces appear on the edge of the bank, their dark eyes looking down to meet hers.

47

Hah! I always knew there must be a reason for keeping that ugly red sweater. Mom bought one for each of us as a joke, the Christmas that I was fourteen. She thought the tacky sweaters were funny. I even wore mine that Christmas Eve.

None of the other drivers heading in to town saw it hanging from the tree below the highway like a red flag. But the ladies in the blue van, on their way home to NaNeetza Valley, noticed right away that something was out of order in the landscape when they passed by. Thank heaven, the women stopped and went back to investigate. And no, don't go getting the wrong impression. I had absolutely nothing to do with this. I'm not sure that even when I was alive I could have come up with an idea so bizarre.

Now, while one of the women stays above to keep watch up on the road, the other two make their way down the hill with a shovel that Mom had asked for. I wonder if she wasn't so concerned with the accident, with getting Dad safely out of this predicament, if she wasn't in a bit of a state of shock herself, running on adrenalin, would she recognize her rescuers? Would she remember them from the summer Levi invited us all out to the local rodeo on the NaNeetza Reserve?

Would she recall how we had come upon these same three ladies working behind the concession stand counter, chatting and laughing in the way that good friends do when there's no one else around? Or how the laughter ceased the instant they realized that they were not alone, and then their polite, guarded acknowledgements as Levi introduced us to them?

And I wonder, after they get Dad back up to the highway, will Mom recognize the third woman waiting there? Will she see in her wide handsome face, the older version of the woman in the photograph at Virgil's cabin? The photograph of Levi as a baby on his mother's hip.

Without questions or directions, as if they are called to do this every day, once the two women reach Dad, they make fast work of digging under his trapped leg and sliding him out from under the Jeep.

Mom crouches down and gently lifts his corduroy pants cuff. He winces as she pushes it back. She abandons the effort but not before getting a peek at where bone has punctured skin on the front of his calf. The two women are already in action. Pulling a small hand-axe from the leather scabbard on her belt, the tallest one strides toward a stand of aspen trees. Her friend moves along the hillside, searching through the strewn debris. After they return, Mom holds Dad's leg straight while the women, using thick branches, stripped clean and shaped by the axe, expertly splint his calf from the knee to the ankle. His leg is wrapped up and bound securely before Mom can register that the pink material they used to cushion the make-shift splint is my favourite old terry-cloth bathrobe. Right on!

Getting him up that steep hill is another matter. Even from my point of view it seems it will take divine intervention. But don't get me wrong, I'm not saying that it doesn't exist, I just don't know how to call on it. But those two women, hah, they don't need to call on anything. Without hesitating, they hoist Dad up onto his good leg, his splinted leg hanging free, and throw his arms around their broad shoulders and then start climbing. Unlike Mom, who came straight down the hill, and then tried to climb back up the same way, they traverse the hillside, winding their way up as if there is a hidden path beneath their feet. Mom scrambles behind, keeping an eye on the injured leg, mouthing unnecessary warnings of 'careful, careful,' unaware that she's doing it.

Back up on the highway, a logging truck, with a full load of timber, flagged down by Levi's mother, stops on the opposite side of the road. The driver climbs down and rushes over to the edge of the bank, arriving just as the women, with Dad slung between them, struggle over the top.

"Jeeze," he says at the sight of them. "I'll go radio for an ambulance."

"Comes too slow," the tall woman says, carrying my father toward the van.

Levi's mother glances from my father's ashen face, to my mother, and I can tell right away that she recognizes them. The man and woman who had condemned her son, who had judged him without hearing him. The knowing flickers through her eyes, then disappears leaving her with an expression of nothing more than the steely resolve to do what needs to be done in the moment. She slides open the van door. Climbing inside, she folds down the rear seat, then in one quick motion unrolls a foam pad onto the van floor. She helps to ease Dad inside, then spreads a blanket and sleeping bag gently over his prone body. He's too out of it with pain to recognize her, and Mom, climbing in beside him, is too out of it with worry. Without a word, Levi's mother slides the door closed, climbs into the driver's seat and turns the van toward town. I wonder if she would be so generous if she was aware of what her son is up to right now.

Out in the forest at NaNeetza Valley, Levi is secretly building a sweat lodge. He knows that Old Alphonse won't let him do another sweat again so soon, so he's going to do it by himself. Virgil Blue is unaware of his young cousin's plan or he would put a stop to it. But Levi is convinced that he almost reached me in the spirit world last time and he intends to try again. Alone. Dangerous stuff. If I knew how to intervene I would. Now it looks like the only one who can save Levi Johnny from himself, is Mom. But she is too wrapped up in her own drama.

48

"Interesting," the doctor muses holding the X-rays to the light. "Compound fractures can be problematic," he says studying first one then the other. Satisfied he lowers them and addresses Ian lying on the ER gurney. "You can thank whoever's responsible for that strange-looking splint for keeping the damage minimal."

Julie would like to do just that, thank the women who not only rescued them, but also delivered them to the hospital hours ago. But after arriving, in the confusion of the ER attendants removing Ian from the van, loading him onto a stretcher, and rushing him through the automatic doors, she had not thought to. Only as the doors where sliding closed behind her did she turn back. But the van and the three Good Samaritans were gone.

Now sitting in the green-curtained cubical, she listens to the doctor explain that they will be taking Ian up to the operating room shortly for surgery to realign the tibia bone. "Then we'll just keep you in overnight, watch for any swelling beneath the cast," he says. Switching his gaze from Ian to Julie, he adds, "But my guess is by tomorrow he'll be good to go."

"Well, that's a relief," Julie says in the void left by the doctor's sudden exit.

"For who?" Ian mutters.

Startled by the curt response, she turns quickly to look at him lying flat on his back, his eyes closed. It must be the shot they gave him for the pain, she thinks and lets his comment go. The fluorescent light above his head casts a ghostly parlour on his already grey skin. She reaches up and switches it off. Before long his breathing becomes even and she settles back in the uncomfortable chair by his bedside.

The heavy antiseptic hospital smells unsettle her stomach while she waits for someone to come and take Ian up to the OR. As soon as they do, she'll go outside to get some fresh air.

Time can't possibly go any slower than it does for a healthy person waiting in a hospital, she thinks. In the hushed environment, every sound seems amplified, the moans or whispers from the other cubicles, the hum of machines, the squeak of nurses' rubber-soled shoes on linoleum, the minutes ticking by on the huge overhead clock, which she can see through the opening in the curtain.

And then just as she is contemplating the relative peacefulness of this 'live' Emergency Room compared to that of the constant bedlam of television dramas, a sudden eruption of pandemonium bursts through the sliding glass door. Julie stiffens at the frantic sounds of running feet, and the panicked voices of people rushing into the cubical on the other side of the curtain behind her. Something bumps up against Julie's chair and she quickly slides it away. She doesn't want to eavesdrop, yet there is no way to avoid hearing the heart-wrenching emergency—a child not breathing, French fries blocking her airway—playing out a few feet from where she sits.

How old is she?

Two years, two years... please...

How long has it been since she stopped breathing.

I don't know, I don't know. I just looked down and she was blue.

Julie can feel the panic of the unseen mother as the story unfolds, the practised calm in the voices of the doctors and nurses firing questions as they work to clear the child's airway. *How many did she eat? How long ago?*

Then the father's accusing words, *She's just a baby. How could you have fed her fries?*

I didn't! I didn't. They were mine, I just turned around, I just... the bag, she had the bag!

It seems an eternity of confusion before Julie hears a weak cry. *Oh god, oh thank god,* her thoughts echo the mother's weeping words.

Only as the air escapes from her own lungs, does Julie realize that she has been holding her breath. Beside her Ian stirs, and she turns to find the same relief reflected in his eyes. Some things don't have to be said out loud. A broken leg is nothing.

Exhausted, Julie drops the motel key and the Subway sandwich onto the night table, and then sinks down onto the edge of the bed. This morning seems so long ago.

After Ian's surgery this afternoon, she'd dealt with the police, the auto wreckers, and started the insurance claim, before it occurred to her that she hadn't eaten today. She doesn't even feel like it now, but knows she has to get something into her stomach. All she really wants to do is crawl into the motel bed and sleep. But there are still things to be taken care of.

Unwrapping the sandwich, she forces herself to take a bite then sets it back on the nightstand. While she chews she takes out her wallet and searches until she finds the piece of paper she is looking for.

Picking up the bedside phone she keys in the number. She is about to give up on the seventh ring. "Yeah?" a muffled voice demands.

"Terri? It's Julie O'Dale."

"Julie!" Terri swallows something, and then continues." Sorry to sound so short, but so many of the phone calls I get these days at supper time are telemarketers."

"Oh, are you eating? I can call back."

"No! No, of course not. I heard about your accident. How are you, Gal?"

"My God! You've heard already?"

"The 'Bush Telegraph,'" Terri chuckles. "Used to take a few days for gossip to make the rounds out here, but now with the Internet, it's hours. Heard Ian broke his leg. How's he doing?"

"Good, he's good. Thanks. He'll be staying in the hospital overnight, but he's okay. The Jeep's a write-off, though. It looks like it could take a day or two to straighten things out here with the insurance, buy another vehicle."

"I can just imagine."

Julie hesitates. "That's why I'm calling," she continues. "Pup is out there alone. And well, I hate to admit it, but I have no idea how to get a hold of Virgil. I don't even know if he has a telephone."

"Oh that man," Terri sighs with exasperation. "Yeah, he's got a satellite phone all right, but he never turns the damn thing on. Anyway Girl, don't worry. You're covered. Soon's I heard the news, I went over to your place to tell Virgil. He already knew though. Seems his cousin, Marilyn Johnny, was one of the gals from NaNeetza Valley who helped you out."

Virgil's cousin? Julie searches her fragmented memory for the faces of the women. But all she recalls of the silent drive into town is the back of three heads in the front of the van, each with a thick braid of raven hair hanging between squared shoulders. She hadn't been oblivious to the fact that they were First Nations, but one of them was Levi's mother? How could she have missed that?

The next day, when Julie arrives at the hospital to pick Ian up in the 'loaner' Jeep, which they will use until their new one arrives, the afternoon sky is a clear, crisp winter blue. Her breath forms white vapour puffs as she walks the short distance from the 'patient pick up' area to the front doors.

Up in his room on the second floor, Ian is waiting slumped and round-shouldered in a wheelchair, his leg encased in a cast from below his knee, down to his ankle. As she pushes him to the elevator, he is silent and morose, and, in Julie's eyes, looking as if this broken leg has turned him into an old man. Perhaps it's because, before they left, the doctor had advised them that Ian will be in a cast for at least two months, and that for the next while, he'll need to come in once a week to check on how the bone is healing.

It will be five days before their new vehicle arrives, so there's no reason for them not to return home today.

Downstairs in the hospital lobby, Julie pushes Ian's wheelchair toward the entry doors. Without warning he locks the brakes, causing the chair and Julie to come to a sudden stop. "I can walk from here," he says, pushing himself up.

Julie has learned that arguing with Ian when he is in such a determined state is useless, so she hands him his crutches. Once he is up and balanced between them he swings his lanky body with surprising agility, out the door and across the sidewalk, reaching the curb before Julie can catch up to him. When she does, she directs him to their waiting vehicle, unlocks the door and slides back the passenger seat as far as it will go. Ian shrugs her away as she tries to help him climb inside. But after he backs himself onto the seat, he allows her to lift his cast and gently guide it onto the foam squares she has placed on the floor.

"How's that?" she asks.

"Fine," Ian sighs. "Don't fuss, Julie..."

The highway is bare, not a sign of ice or snow on the road, as they head west. Still, Julie drives cautiously, taking each corner with extra care, trying to smooth out the ride in order not to jar Ian's leg. Half an hour from town, patches of snow appear in the fields and forests flanking the highway. As the road drops away on her left, she slows down even more, keeping an eye out for the spot where they went over the bank yesterday morning.

For miles it seems hopeless, everything looking so unfamiliar. Just when she believes she will never know exactly where their accident occurred, in the distance, a disturbance on the side of the highway appears. As they approach the churned-up shoulder—evidence of the struggle the tow truck had winching the Jeep up to the road—she slows to a crawl. She leans forward to look past Ian, who is also peering over the edge of the bank. Down below there is no sign of the debris, the boxes, tools, papers—no sign of Darla's clothes—which had littered the slope yesterday. "I wonder who cleaned up all the stuff?" she muses, pulling back onto the highway.

There is no response from Ian. After fifteen minutes of taciturn silence, as though no time has passed since she spoke, he asks, "Why?"

"Why what?" She glances at Ian. How vulnerable he looks without his glasses, she thinks, returning her attention to the road.

"Was it intentional, Julie? Going over that bank...?"

"What?" she demands, her foot reaching for the brake. "What are you saying?" As the car slows down she turns to him.

Staring out the windshield Ian murmurs, "Why did we go off the highway?"

"There was something on the road," she says, her voice rising at the implication of his words. "For God's sake. I swerved to avoid an animal."

"There was no animal."

Pulling over to the side of the road she brings the car to a jerking stop, snaps it into park and turns to him. "Ian," she says to his jaw-clenched profile. "Ian, look at me."

When he doesn't respond she reaches over and takes his chin in her hand, forcing him, like an errant child, to face her. "Listen to me," she says. "I hit the brakes when I shouldn't have. That's all. I had absolutely no control; there was nothing I could do. We skidded on a patch of black ice." She stops, her hand dropping away from his chin, as the full impact of her words hits her. Out on the highway an empty logging truck passes by, the Jeep rocking in its passing airstream.

Looking down at her hands resting in her lap, Julie says, "I'm sad that you believe I'm capable of that."

"What am I to supposed to think? You never, *never*, go into town with me. All of a sudden you want to? You insist on driving?" He waits for a moment, and then in a low voice adds, "I *heard* you, Julie. I heard what you whispered as we went over the bank."

Her head snaps back up. "What? You heard what?"

Ian shakes his head, but holds her gaze, the pain of the words he won't repeat, obvious in his naked eyes. Had she really spoken them out loud? Had she truly given voice to the thought, to the strange relief she felt in that moment of inevitability? Resigned she starts the motor, leaving the unuttered words lying heavy between them.

49

At home, Ian's sullenness becomes a third presence. Julie tiptoes around it during the days, shutting her bedroom door on it with relief each night. Nothing she does seems to please him. Her suggestion to make up the cot in his office, so he wouldn't have to hobble up and down the stairs, is rejected. His favourite baked treats remain untouched. Whenever she brings him coffee in his office, he barely acknowledges her presence, and more often than not, she finds him slumped in his leather swivel chair staring outside.

This morning is no different. Setting down the steaming mug on his desk and picking up the cold one, she wonders how his eyes can take the relentless glare of sunlight reflecting from the frozen land-scape. She has to squint just to look out at the lake, a solid sheet of ice now, shimmering beneath a brittle blue sky. A winter wind has swept the snow away from its surface, leaving behind an opaque tapestry of cracks and swirls.

"I'm going out to check the generator," she says to the back of Ian's head. When there is no response she leaves his office, shutting the door behind her.

Since returning from town the communication between them has been almost non-existent, their conversation in the car left unresolved. Yet it has never left Julie's mind. Was there any truth in his implied accusation—does she have an unconscious death wish? Placing his mug in the sink, she shakes her head against the thought.

Outside, the crusted snow crunches with her every step as she walks over to the shop. The last few night's temperatures have dropped to well below minus twenty Celsius, struggling to climb to ten below during daylight hours.

Against Ian's objections she has taken over his chores. She feels a certain satisfaction in bringing in the wood and keeping the fires going, and looks forward to the physical activity. "There's no need for a fire," Ian grumbles every time she bundles up to face the bone-numbing cold, "just let the propane kick in." But Julie enjoys the comforting warmth of the ever-burning central fireplace. Not to mention the excuse to get outside. Hiking is out of the question these days, with Ian wanting to know her every movement if she leaves the house.

After checking the solar energy levels and finding no need to turn on the generator, she goes back inside and retrieves her camera from the mudroom. Trudging across the front yard down to the lake she feels Ian's eyes on her back. Resisting the temptation to turn around and look up at his office, she stops at the shoreline and stands in the hushed silence listening for the ice to 'sing,' a phenomenon new to her.

She'd heard the strange, otherworldly sounds, for the first time the day after she brought Ian home from town, when she'd gone down to check the thickness of the ice. Stepping out onto the dark surface and finding it cement hard, she had taken a few cautious steps when she heard an eerie moaning beneath her boots. Retreating quickly to solid ground she had listened in wonder to the music-like tones reverberating from somewhere under the frozen surface.

Whenever she is outside now—or at night through the crack in her window—she finds herself listening for the random percussion-like sounds emanating like music from beneath the ice.

She does so now as she removes her mittens and shoves them into her jacket pocket, but all she hears is the screeching whine of a motor trying to turn over. The stubborn engine catches and the hum of an idling vehicle comes from the direction of Virgil's place.

Julie raises her camera and focuses on the horizon at the end of the lake where trees cut into a sky so blue it looks painted on. She adjusts against the light of the whitened landscape, wondering if it is too bright, but when she lowers the camera and checks the digital image, she is pleased with the results. Her fingertips burning, she takes a few more shots then hurriedly pulls her mittens back on. As she heads back to the house the distant engine hum turns into the sound of a vehicle in motion. She looks over her shoulder to see a strange pickup truck emerge from the north road. It turns into the ranch yard and pulls up a few feet from her.

The driver's window rolls down, and Terri Champion hollers above the engine noise, "Hello, on this glorious Chilcotin day!"

"Hello to you, too," Julie says walking over to the truck. "What? No snowmobile?"

"Heck, you need a lot more snow than this piddley few inches for that. But don't worry, it'll come." She turns the motor off and rests her elbow on the window. "Just thought I'd pop by to check up on you two, see how you're making out."

"We're good," Julie assures her. "Come on in for coffee."

"I just had some at Virgil's. One cup of his is enough to do a soul for a week." Her barking laugh is punctuated by a low moaning sound coming from the lake.

"Did you hear that?" Julie asks.

"Just another voice of old Mother Nature." Terri takes off her sunglasses and grins. "Like your 'talking trees.'"

"I wish I'd never told you that," Julie laughs. "Really though, what causes those sounds?"

"It's just the ice expanding and contracting. The stress cracks can cause quite a chatter. The bigger the lake, the louder the chatter."

"Sometimes it sounds almost like music."

"Yeah, but music ya gotta learn to listen to. It changes with the thickness of the ice. Right now it's safe walking anywhere down at this end of the lake, or ice skating, if you've a mind to. Another week of this sub-zero weather, and you'll be able to drive a Mack truck across her. Heck, I could land my ski-plane here, I've done it before. Just gotta steer clear of the north end. Too many underwater springs down there."

"Springs?"

"This lake isn't called Spring Bottom for nothing, Gal. Even in the coldest part of winter you can't trust the ice at the other end of the lake." She studies Julie's face for a moment, then adds, "But I'm sure Virgil's told you that."

Sensing something more behind Terri's words, Julie tells her that Virgil is leaving.

Terri nods slowly. "Yeah. I kinda figured that."

"Did he say something?"

"No. You know Virgil. He doesn't waste any words, either with that contraption of his, or on paper. No. It's all the boxes stacked in a corner. Either he's giving a whole lot of stuff away, or he's moving. So what's up?"

Julie raises her hands to her mouth and blows warm air into her mittens, then says, "Why don't you come up to the house, and I'll make you tea." She smiles, and adds, "In a china teacup."

Sitting at the kitchen table, keeping one eye on Ian in his office and her voice low, Julie tells Terri the story, starting with the first time she met Virgil in the garden, and ending with the last time she saw him at his cabin.

"I had no idea until then," she concludes, "that his cousin is Levi Johnny's mother." Then taking in Terri's unsurprised expression, she asks, "You knew?"

"I doubt if anyone in the Chilcotin doesn't know that," Terri says gently. "I just assumed you did, too."

"No, I didn't. Don't you think it's something he should have told us?"

Terri lowers the delicate teacup. "All I know is that Virgil Blue is not a deceptive man. He's about nothing if he ain't about truth. I'm guessing that he believed you knew."

After Terri leaves, Julie marches across the living room to Ian's office. He remains hunched over his desk, his back to her when she throws the door open.

"Were you aware that Virgil and Levi Johnny are related?" she demands.

The office chair slowly rolls away from the desk. Ian lifts his casted leg off the stool it's resting on, and swinging it to the side, he swivels the chair around to face her. He leans back against the headrest, pushing his new eyeglasses onto his forehead. Squeezing his eyes shut, he pinches his nose, and then replaces his glasses. Meeting Julie's gaze, he says quietly, "Yes."

"How long have you known?"

Ian shifts uncomfortably in his chair.

"How long?" Julie repeats.

"Since August, since the day you met him in the garden. He thought we knew."

"He thought we knew?" Confused, a flood of questions rushing through her mind, Julie shakes her head in an attempt to clear it. Struggling to keep her voice from rising she asks, "It didn't bother you?"

"Yes, of course it *bothered* me, at first. I only found out when I went over to his cabin that day, after you two met—after he realized we didn't know. He offered to leave, if you remember. But by then, well by then, I knew him, I relied on him. I was relieved when you said he could stay—I decided that it shouldn't make any difference. Being related to someone isn't a crime, Julie. He isn't responsible for..." he swallows, and looks away, speaking into the distance. "He isn't responsible for our 'troubles.'"

Troubles? She lets the trivial word hang in the silence. When his eyes finally meet hers again she chooses not to pursue it; instead she asks, "You didn't think it was something that, he—you, for that matter—should have told me?"

"I considered it, but decided against it when you voiced your opinion about keeping him away from you. I didn't count on you two spending any time together."

Ignoring his statement Julie says, "I wish you'd told me." Turning to leave she suddenly remembers their conversation about the dream-catcher in Virgil's window—well, her conversation, Ian's ignoring. She is about to ask why he didn't take the opportunity then to tell her, but changes her mind. It makes no difference now that Virgil is leaving. What does make a difference is the depth of Ian's deception, and the revelation of how little she knows him.

"So how did you find out?" he asks behind her.

Without turning back Julie answers, "It doesn't matter."

For the rest of the week she fills her days polishing and dusting every wooden surface inside the house, stacking wood and splitting kindling beyond what they will ever use, shovelling snow—making work, using physical activity as an excuse to keep her body moving in order to avoid thinking. It isn't working. At night she lies sleepless wondering if they can go on like this forever. Forever staying in a relationship that has deteriorated so much that their marriage is nothing more than an 'arrangement' now. Forever pretending that they are anything more than two people occupying the same space, separate, yet together, bumping into each other coming around corners, mumbling apologies for the contact of strangers, forever sleeping in separate beds, separate rooms. They are less than friends, less than strangers, not in love, not in hate, worse yet, indifferent. She wonders if it's easier for those whose marriage erodes slowly over time, instead of being severed in a moment like theirs was, severed while they still loved each other, leaving them unable to talk about the one thing that links them. Every night she battles with this one-sided conversation, coming to the same conclusion: forever is too long. But with Ian temporarily disabled, now is not the time to force the issue.

When they head into town for Ian's first visit with the doctor she still hasn't told her family about the accident. In her email correspondences with Jessie she has avoided mentioning Ian's broken leg. She doesn't want to give her mother any excuse to come up to 'help' out. Somehow the woman always seems to know when things are kept from her, and Julie doesn't want to put her sister in a position of having to keep a secret. Every day she dreads receiving a phone call about Christmas, which Jessie has warned her about, but so far her mother has been silent. Surely in winter weather, she would not just show up like she did this summer, would she?

In town, after an hour's wait, it takes the doctor less than five minutes to inform them that he is satisfied with the knitting of Ian's tibia. Relieved, Julie drops Ian off at his office then heads to the car dealers. After picking up their new vehicle she spends the rest of the afternoon wandering around the stores. Christmas is only a month away, and she should start thinking about gifts, especially for her nieces. Last year she avoided the holiday altogether, sending no presents, and she vows she will not do that to them this year. Yet three hours later she has purchased nothing, and goes to pick up Ian, telling herself that she will order from the Internet and have the gifts shipped.

At the office she finds Ian sorting through the contents of two cardboard boxes. Inside one are the first-aid kit and emergency tools, which had been thrown out of the back of the Jeep during the accident last week. In the other box, water-stained and wrinkled, are the lost statements from his banker's box.

"Where did these come from?" she asks.

Ian shrugs. "Who knows? The receptionist found them outside the office door on Monday."

Ian doesn't really need these hard copies, of course, he has everything backed up on the computer, but someone has gone to a lot of trouble retrieving all this from the accident scene. Saying nothing about her suspicion about who that someone might be, Julie glances around. Glad to see no sign of any other boxes she remains silent about them, too. She doesn't have the heart to bring up Darla's clothes.

The day fades into night before they are halfway home. Julie drives below the speed limit, constantly scanning the roadsides illuminated by her headlights for any sign of animals.

As they turn off the highway onto the dirt road leading to the ranch Ian breaks the silence.

"I talked to a realtor today," he says.

As if possessing a mind of its own, Julie's foot comes off the gas pedal. She catches herself before reaching for the brake. Forcing herself to keep her eyes on the road she asks, "A realtor? What for?"

"About selling the ranch."

"Selling? Why...?"

"We're not ranchers, Julie."

"We don't have to be ranchers to live out here. You said that from the beginning. We don't need to run cattle, or put up hay. But we could. We could do it if you really want to."

"The place is just too much for the two of us."

Julie slows the car and glances over at his profile illuminated by the dashboard light. "Many people have made lives out here, 'just the two of them,'" she argues, "in conditions, I'm certain, that are a whole lot less luxurious than what we have."

"It's too isolated."

"Terri Champion says there are people living deep in the bush out here who never go into town."

"These roads are too treacherous."

"You think the odds of an accident are less in town, in the city? Come on, accidents happen everywhere, Ian. That's hardly a reason."

"The realtor's coming out next week," Ian says as if she has not spoken.

50

Once, in Mr Emerson's English class, we played 'Six Degrees of Separation.' He was discussing a John Guare play, based on the concept that every person on earth can be connected to any other person by six acquaintances or less. He ended up letting us spend the whole hour of class time experimenting with it one afternoon. He was so cool that way. When I told Mom about it, she said that she was familiar with the concept as 'Six Degrees to Kevin Bacon.' Anyway, if she wasn't so hung up right now on Mr Blue being related to Levi, and his connection to me—two degrees of separation I would say— she might get that it's possible to connect anyone on earth to me in just a few more steps, so what's the big deal.

Right now, I can see that by tomorrow, there will be only one degree of connection between Mr Blue and the people I love, Mom, Dad, and Levi. Tonight they all lie alone in their beds, none of them sleeping.

Levi has finished building his sweat lodge. The small domed structure is hidden in the bush out at NaNeetza Valley, ready for the solitary sweat he has planned for tomorrow. Split wood is stacked by the firepit along with stones from the river. The problem is those stones. Unlike the Grandfather Rocks, which Virgil is the keeper of for his people, these stones are dangerous; they could easily explode in the heat if there are any cracks, air pockets or water hidden inside. Fortunately Levi's mother has put a kink in his plans for tomorrow night. Marilyn Johnny knows her son. Levi is not a deceptive *person, and lately he has been skulking around the house, disappearing for unexplained periods of time. When he returns, he avoids meeting her eyes. She doesn't know what he's up to, but she senses that he needs to see his cousin, Mr Blue, before he does something stupid.*

Just as Mom guessed, it was Levi's mother and her friends who went back to the accident site and collected all the stuff from the hillside, then dropped it off on the porch at Dad's office in town. Not all of it, though. Levi's mother insists that tomorrow he is to take the rest, my clothes, which she has folded and packed carefully, over to Mr Blue's to be returned to Mom. Giving away a loved one's possessions is an important part of letting go, she tells Levi, and my mother needs to do it herself. Levi can't deny his mother. But tonight, with the boxes of my clothes waiting next to his bed, he can't sleep. The nearness of my things only reinforces what he believes is his spiritual obligation to help 'see me home.' He lies awake thinking about his 'vision quest,' which he is now forced to put off for one more day. He wishes that Virgil could join him in his sweat, but he knows that he can't ask his cousin again. So Levi has led Virgil to believe that his 'vision quest' was completed. Levi doesn't feel that it is too far a stretch from the truth. He believes when he does his own sweat, he will find a way to help me reach my spirit home. Once he has, he promises himself, he will return to school, to hockey, to the real world. But right now, he lies wondering if tomorrow he will be able to look into his cousin's all-knowing eyes, and keep this secret from him.

At the ranch house my mother, too, is lying awake staring in the darkness. And down the hall from her my father does the same. Dad has taken a sleeping pill and will soon be able to quiet his mind—a mind full of chatter about selling the ranch, about their unfinished conversation in the car, and about me.

Mom won't sleep at all tonight. Convinced that the only reason Dad wants to sell the ranch is because of her, she is moving closer to the decision that she believes is inevitable. I hear the mental turmoil in her mind as clearly as if she is speaking out loud. She has to stop my dad from throwing away his dream. She has to find a way to fix this before it's too late. And the way to do that, she believes, is to convince Virgil Blue to stay. In the morning, while Dad is once again ensconced in his office, she intends to go over to Mr Blue's cabin and try to change his mind about leaving.

If only my parents would talk to each other. But Mom and Dad have forgotten how. The longer they let it go on, the harder it's become to find their way back to the place where they can. I don't remember the last time I saw them hug, or kiss each other. Certainly not since I've been here in this in-between place. Not a long time for me, but too long for people who have forgotten that they love each other. If they're not careful they might never remember.

And Levi is so stuck in what he believes about my 'spirit life' that he's stopped living his.

Mr Blue is the only one who holds no illusions. Rising early, he now sits at his kitchen table in the dim light of dawn, writing his truths on yellow-lined paper.

51

Leaving the house proves to be more difficult than Julie anticipated. All morning it seems, a restless Ian has been underfoot. Every time she is set to head out, there he is, hobbling through the rooms on his crutches, on one errand or another, before finally settling in his office.

Now, slipping out the back door, Julie closes it gently behind her. She stands on the porch for a moment and inhales deeply, breathing in the crisp smell of fresh snow in an effort to clear her sleep-deprived mind. The temperature outside has risen to just above zero, warm compared to the frigid temperatures of the last few weeks. An overnight snowfall has left the lake an untouched carpet of white, so bright it seems luminous in the late morning sun. The dry snow squeaks beneath her boots with each determined step across the yard. Pup, excited at the prospect of going for a walk, circles her, then bounds toward the north road, turning back after a few yards to be certain that she is still coming.

She hurries after him, anxious to be out of view of the house before Ian realizes she is gone. Once on the road, and hidden behind the stand of trees, she slows her pace. Two sets of footprints in the snow, man and dog's, tell the story of Virgil's morning journey to the barn to feed the horses, and his return home. She follows the tracks to his driveway, where she hesitates, and for the first time contemplates his reaction to her arrival. Will Virgil even open the door to her? Invite her in? She wouldn't blame him if he didn't. She has treated him poorly. Ian's right, the fact that Virgil is Levi's cousin has nothing to do with their 'trouble.'

Pup, confused by her immobility, sits at her heel. He looks up at her, his head cocked to one side, as if asking her to make up her mind. Squaring her shoulders in renewed resolve, she says, "Come on."

Banishing the conflicting voices in her mind—arguments that she mulled over and over, in last night's seemingly endless hours—she heads down the driveway. She owes this to Ian, to at least make an attempt to convince Virgil to remain, before it's too late. Beg him if she has to. She will apologize, do whatever it takes to change his mind. She couldn't save her daughter, can't save her marriage, but maybe she can save Ian.

Up ahead, Virgil's dog starts barking, then a moment later appears at the side of the cabin. Pup bolts forward, yelping his own greeting. The two meet by Virgil's snow-covered pickup truck and then, barking and playfully nipping at each other, race around to the front of the cabin. *Well at least Virgil is getting fair warning of my approach.*

When she comes around the corner the dogs jump up from wrestling in the snow, shake the powdered white from their thick coats and watch her climb the porch steps. On the way to the door, Julie glances at the window, but sees only her own reflection in the glass. She can feel her heart racing, the blood pounding in her ears as she lifts a gloved hand and knocks. There's no response, no sounds of movement inside. She waits for a minute then tries again, resisting the impulse to pound harder. She leans closer, turning her ear toward the door. Perhaps he's in the washroom, or the back bedroom, and she *should* knock a little harder. She raps once again. When there's still no response she has mixed emotions. A small part of her is relieved, a very small part. The other part is disappointed, saddened at the thought that Virgil may be sitting inside, deliberately ignoring her.

She's certain that he must be home. The footprints leading to his door, his pickup truck at the back covered in a few inches of new snow, are evidence enough. *Well, he has no obligation to answer his door, no obligation to indulge me anymore.* She's no longer the man's landlord, and clearly not his friend. He owes her nothing. Still she waits longer, hoping that he might change his mind. She considers going over to the window to place her hands on the glass and peer inside, and then imagines seeing him standing at the kitchen sink staring back at her. She starts to knock again, when it suddenly occurs to her that she has gone about this the wrong way. She should have taken a cue from him and written a note. Yes, that's exactly what she should do, go home and explain everything on paper and then slide it under his door. Just as she decides to return home and compose something, the door creaks open to reveal Virgil Blue squinting against the light as he finishes pulling on a plaid flannel shirt.

Julie takes a quick step back, less startled by the thought that she has woken him from a nap at this time of day, than by his appearance. He's aged since the last time she saw him. It's more than the fact that he's lost weight. It's the intensified weariness about his sunken eyes, the sallow complexion, which emphasises the faint remembrance of pockmarks on hollow cheeks.

All of this registers in Julie's mind during the seconds it takes for Virgil to focus on her and give mute acknowledgement to her presence. She opens her mouth to ask if he's okay, but something in his eyes stops her. "Can I come in and talk to you, Virgil?" she asks, then adds quietly, "Please?"

He moves to one side and allows the door to swing all the way open.

"Thank you," she says stepping past him. The musty scent of smoke-cured logs and barn odours, welcomes her inside. Virgil closes the door behind her. Buttoning up his shirt with one hand, he ushers her to the kitchen table with the other. Gratefully she pulls out a chair and sits down. Removing her jacket, she hangs it on the back of the chair as Virgil gathers up a stack of yellow-lined notepads from the tabletop. He takes the bundle over to the roll-top desk. While he stores them in a drawer, Julie takes the opportunity to look around the dimly lit interior. As Terri Champion had said, the evidence of a pending move is undeniable—the boxes stacked in the far corner, the bare walls. Even the bookshelves have been emptied, as well as the cubbyholes on the roll-top desk. A small, square, post-it note is stuck on the side of the desk. Similar notes are attached to other items of furniture, the recliner chairs, the side of the TV; there's even one stuck on the edge of the table. She leans closer to check what's written on it, just as Virgil turns back to her. She straightens quickly, feeling her face redden at being caught snooping. But Virgil doesn't seem to notice. He goes over to the wood stove and feels the side of the blackened coffee pot. Satisfied, he removes two mugs from the warming oven above and places them on the table along with a bowl of sugar. He retrieves a jug of cream from the fridge and then pours the coffee in both mugs. While he does, Julie takes the time to compose herself, glad for the ordinariness of the ritual.

When he finally takes his seat across from her, he brings an empty notepad and pen with him, placing them on the table. Sipping the bitter-strong coffee, Julie tries not to wince. She needs this. After last night's long sleepless hours, her brain will welcome a good jolt of caffeine. Still, she adds more cream, and then cupping the mug in both hands straightens up in her chair.

"I want to thank you for looking after Pup," she says. "And for keeping the fire going in the house while we were in town after the accident. Well, for all you do for Ian, for us."

Virgil looks up from his coffee mug, and nods.

"We saw Ian's doctor yesterday," Julie continues, forcing herself to speak slowly. This has to be done right. "Ian will be in a cast for a few months. If all goes well he'll have a walking cast by Christmas. Sometime in January, February at the latest, he should be back on his feet. I came to tell you to, well, to ask you to stay. I..." she stops to watch Virgil take up the pen and write something on the notepad. He turns it to face her.

I'll try to stay until he is healed.

"Thank you," she says, looking back up. "But what I really meant to say is that you don't have to move. Ever. There's no reason for you to leave." She hesitates, and then adds, slowly, "Because when Ian is better, I will go."

Virgil scribbles on the pad. *Where?*

"I have no idea. Back to town, to Vancouver. Somewhere, I'll figure it out by then. All I know right now is that I have to go."

Even upside down she can read the single scribbled word. *Why?*

"Why?" She repeats his laconic question. There are so many reasons why. Some of which she cannot even explain to herself. Staring into her coffee mug as if the answer is there she swallows back an unexpected lump in her throat. "Our marriage is over," she says with a shrug. "We're just one more statistic, one more relationship that couldn't survive the loss of a child."

When she glances back up, his eyes are still on her. Perhaps it's because there's no judgement, no expectation lurking behind those dark eyes, that she continues. "The truth is that we both harbour too much blame, too much guilt for there to be room for anything else between us." And then as if talking to herself, she is quietly recounting the evening of Darla's death, the mistakes, the missteps, both hers and Ian's. All of the facts, the truth and the imagined, spoken out loud for the first time, spill out of her, taking on a reality of their own. And as she unburdens herself a sense of peace that she hasn't felt in a long time fills her.

When she is done the sound of the fire in the wood stove behind her has died down. Outside the dogs' playful wrestling has ended and they wait somewhere in faithful silence.

"I'm sorry," she says finally. "I didn't mean to dump all that." She meets his eyes. "The real reason I came over here is to ask you, to beg you, to please stay. This is your home. There's no reason for you to leave. Ian's talking about selling. Once I am gone there'll be no reason for him to do that, no reason for either of you to give up on this place."

Shaking his head slowly, Virgil writes something on the pad again and turns it around.

I cannot stay, it reads. *I will be gone by spring.*

"No, please," she says, her head jerking back up. "It's because of Levi, isn't it, because I wouldn't meet with him? I'm sorry that I..." she stops mid-sentence and watches Virgil's gnarled hand move deftly across the yellow-lined paper. She leans forward and reads the words as they take form on the page.

Levi is all right, Virgil writes. *He's returning to school, to hockey, after Christmas. He has found peace with his grief.*

Julie sits back, the meaning sinking in. *Really? Well, good for him.* The acrimonious thought catches her off guard, and she chastises herself. This is not how she'd expected this to go.

Last night and this morning she had considered the possibility of agreeing to meet with Levi, agreeing to the healing circle Virgil had requested in order to convince him to stay. The truth was that since her own accident with the Jeep, every time she recalled the complete loss of control, which she had experienced as they slid sideways across the black ice, she thought about that other accident, when Levi was at the wheel. On the way over here she believed that, if Virgil asked her again, she was prepared to meet with his young cousin, prepared to give him the chance to redeem himself. Yet, now after Virgil's words, she feels a disquieting resentment, like a small animal gnawing inside, to the idea that Levi has found peace with Darla's death. *Where is my compassion?* Before she can sort her conflicting thoughts, the dogs start barking and a car door slams behind the cabin.

Ian? Would he have hobbled outside to drive over here with a broken leg just to search for her? Well let him, she thinks, pushing her chair back from the table wearily. Perhaps he can convince Virgil to stay. She has failed.

Virgil gives no indication of hearing anything outside. Instead, as if she had spoken out loud, he writes: *Maybe meeting with the boy would help you to find your own peace.*

Shaking her head she stands up. Virgil rises with her and reaches back to open the top drawer of the roll-top desk. He removes the Electrolarynx, places it to his throat and says, "Julie."

It's the first time Virgil has said her name, she realizes, the first indication that he even knows it, or that she is anything more than some intrusion on his solitude.

Suddenly, footsteps pound on the porch outside. A shadow moves across the kitchen window and the sound of a single knock breaks the silence. Julie turns toward the door just as it pushes open. Daylight floods in, silhouetting the figure standing in the open doorway, balancing two cardboard boxes. He steps inside, shouldering the door closed, and saying, "Hallo, this place." The boxes lower. In the dim light, Julie barely recognizes the face of Levi Johnny.

52

Somewhere between Virgil's look of surprise at Levi's sudden appearance, and the heartbeat of recognition between Levi and Julie, is her awareness of the synchronicity of this moment. Here they were speaking about the boy, thinking about him, and as if summoned, he appears. Like other eerie coincidences in her life, she realizes that a split second before the door opened, she saw this coming, experienced it like a déjà-vu. In some deep part of her being, she has always been aware that their paths would cross eventually. Face to face with him now, she recalls that the last time she really saw Levi—through anything except the fog of grief—was on the night of the accident, when she had glanced back from the top of the amphitheatre as she left the high school. And with that memory, comes her last vision of Darla, her smiling face looking up so trustingly at Levi as he tucked the yellow rose behind her ear.

She shakes the image away and searches the changed face of the man-child standing before her. If she had run into him anywhere else, Julie isn't certain that she would have recognized Levi. Like Virgil, the weight has dropped from his tall athletic frame. His hair has grown longer. Dark and glistening, it's pulled back tight against his scalp into a ponytail, leaving his thin face sharp, angular, older-looking, no sign of dimples in his sunken cheeks. An unexpected ache for this lost boy tugs at her heart. She glances back at Virgil and sees in the concern flooding his face, his realization that he is mistaken—Levi is not all right. This is not a soul at peace.

Virgil is the first to speak. "Welcome, young cousin." His crackling mechanic words shatter the rigid silence. And then, placing his Electrolarynx on the table, he turns his attention to the stove, stoking the dying fire as if nothing is amiss.

The hypnotic moment broken, Levi sets the boxes down inside the door. "Mrs O.D.," he says straightening up, his voice barely audible.

"Levi," she hears her acknowledgement as if from a distance.

"These are for you," he says, indicating the boxes. "Darla's clothes."

Taken aback, she opens her mouth then closes it again. There is no need to ask. She knows exactly where they came from. Levi's mother. The question is why? Why would she inflict this pain on her once again by returning them.

As if she had given voice to her thoughts, Levi responds. "My mother, she says you will want to complete their journey."

At the stove, Virgil slides the cast-iron lid back in place with a jarring scrape. Turning to face them, he gestures Julie and Levi to sit down at the table.

Julie starts to protest, to say she must leave now, but the plea in Virgil's eyes stops her. A plea for the boy. *I can't do this*, her instincts scream. But her body betrays her, and she lowers herself to her chair. Levi takes the seat across from her.

Not knowing what is expected of her, not certain she can give it if she did, she studies a coffee stain on the tabletop. A chair scrapes across the floor and she senses rather than sees Virgil join them at the end of the table. Her heart thudding in her ears, she raises her head and meets Levi's eyes. For the first time since she has known the boy, he does not glance away, his gaze, steadfast and unwavering, holds hers. After what seems like forever, he says gently, "I see you, mother of Darla."

Something inside Julie cracks. A sob rises in her throat, and with it, the question that only now does she allow to surface. "Why?" she chokes. "Why wasn't she wearing a seatbelt?"

And there it is. The question that has gnawed at her heart from the moment she learned that her daughter had gone through the windshield. Darla, whom she and Ian had always jokingly referred to as the 'seatbelt police,' was never unbuckled in the car. A seatbelt would have saved her; it had saved Levi. Why wasn't she wearing one that night?

"She was," Levi replies, his voice gentle. "She took it off..." he hesitates. His eyes flicker away, they focus on a spot somewhere beyond Julie, but not before she sees his inner struggle, his desire to spare her from more pain.

"Took it off? Why? Why would she do that?" She wants to know. She doesn't want to know.

"She took it off to pick something up off the floor," he says slowly, as if remembering each measured word.

"To pick up what? What could have been so important?"

"Nothing," he answers, his voice barely a whisper. His gaze shifts back to meet Julie's once again, the sorrow pooled in his eyes "The accident was my fault," he tells her. "I lost control of the car when I hit the brakes."

"Why? Why on earth did you slam on the brakes?" she demands.

"I'm sorry," Levi says simply, offering no excuse, no reason, and no answer.

At the end of the table, Virgil starts to write on the notepad, then giving up, he drops the pen, picks up the Electrolarynx, and holds it to his throat.

Looking from Julie to Levi he asks, "Wasn't there more to your daughter's life, to your friend's life, than how she died?" He repositions the device. "Shouldn't the memory of her, of the time you shared on this earth, be a joy, not a burden?"

As the mechanical-sounding words echo in the silence, Julie's tired mind wrestles with their meaning. And a glimmer of truth finds its way into her heart.

"Levi," she says with a sigh. "Please, get on with your life. You don't need my forgiveness to do that. But if you do, then I forgive you." Even to her own ears the statement sounds hollow, insincere.

"Thank you," Levi says. "But Darla's spirit is not home yet."

Before Julie can grasp what he is saying, Levi adds, "She needs you to know that she is all right."

Julie jerks back from the edge of absolution. "What are you talking about?"

"She told me to tell you that she is okay."

"What do you mean, 'she told you'?" Julie demands, unable to stop her voice from rising. "When? When did she say that?"

"After the accident."

"The police said she died instantly. Are you saying that they lied?"

"No. Darla's spirit told me."

"Her *spirit* told you?" Julie jumps to her feet, shaking her head. "If her *spirit* could speak," she says, yanking her jacket from the back of the chair, "why wouldn't she speak to me?" She turns away and heads to the door.

"Maybe she does," Virgil's robotic voice says behind her. "Maybe your head isn't quiet enough for your heart to hear."

His words stop her. Her shoulders slump and without turning around she reaches for the doorknob. "I'm sorry," she says. "I can't do this."

"That bear," Levi calls after her, as she pulls the door open, "She doesn't want to hurt you."

Julie hesitates in the doorway. *Bear?* What does that have to do with anything? Had Virgil told him about her run-in with the black bear this summer. But when she glances back over her shoulder, the expression on Virgil's face denies it.

Her mind reeling, overtired and confused, she hurries out, closing the door behind her, but not before hearing Levi say, "Darla, she is the bear."

53

Pup jumps up and follows Julie when she comes outside and rushes down the porch steps. As if sensing her mood he remains close by her side, until she reaches the end of the driveway. When, instead of turning toward home, she heads north, the dog hesitates and then bounds forward to catch up to her.

Levi's and Virgil's words follow her, too. Trudging through the snow she tries to ignore them. But they won't let her alone.

She quickens her steps, trying to stave off the threatening tears. They come anyway. These are old tears, they belong to a lost daughter, to a lost marriage, to Ian. She weeps at the image of the man she once loved so much, alone and unable to share his constant sorrow. She weeps too, for Levi, for her failure to reach out to him. She weeps for their three broken souls, all connected by their love for Darla, and hopelessly disconnected from each other.

And some of her tears belong to Virgil, to the truth she read in his eyes today, that he is unwell, yet his illness is something he wishes to bear alone. And the truth behind his words to her—that somehow along the way she has allowed Darla's memory to become a burden.

By the time she reaches the north end of the lake she can barely see to put one foot in front of the other. She trips on a frozen rut beneath the snow and stumbles forward. Unable to stop herself from falling, she comes down hard, her hands scraping on ice and gravel. Wearily she pushes herself up, then sinks back down onto her knees in the middle of the road, drops her head into her hands and gives into her utter despair. At her side, Pup whimpers and pushes himself against her. Blindly Julie reaches for him and, hanging on to him like a lifeline, buries her face in his warm coat and sobs. Held back for too long, the unleashed sorrow engulfs her. Kneeling in the snow, she allows her too long held-in-check grief to take over, crying until she is spent, until her shaking and drained body can give no more.

When she looks up again, stars are appearing in the late afternoon sky. She is exhausted, so tired that the temptation to just lie down and fall sleep is overwhelming. But the dog squirms in her arms and licks at her cheeks, forcing her back from the edge of despondence. She pushes herself to her feet, wiping her face with the back of her sleeve. Through blurred vision she looks down the lake at the ranch house on the distant shore, barely visible in the fading light.

Ian will be worried. It's time to go home. It's time for them to speak truthfully. Before he makes any decision about selling the ranch, it's only fair that she releases him from their broken marriage. It's too late for them, too late to find a way past the brittle sorrow that they both wear like armour. But it is not too late for Ian to keep his dream.

She looks down the road, at the winter shadows closing in from the forest. She's forgotten how early, and how completely, darkness takes hold of the land once the sun passes over the western ridge. Turning, she heads across the marsh. It will be much easier to follow the shore-line back—keeping the lights of the ranch house in view—far quicker than trudging through the snow on the road.

Picking her way through the reeds and frozen bulrushes, she quickly crosses the marsh. Along the way Pup investigates every tiny animal track in their path. When they reach the lake Julie brushes away a patch of snow with her boot and sees that the ice is rock solid. Still, she hasn't forgotten what Terri told her about the springs at this end of the lake. The dark patches further out on the ice attest to their presence. She climbs back up onto the shallow bank and, under the shelter of trees where the snow is only a few inches deep, follows the shoreline toward home.

Still, it's slower going than she expected and she has to watch her footing with every step along the uneven ground. After a few hundred yards, a rabbit, his winter white coat blending with the terrain, hops out from the underbrush ahead. Sensing her presence the rabbit freezes on the edge of the bank, and then darts out onto the ice, only to come face to face with the dog. The frightened rabbit bolts, zigzagging back toward the marshes, with Pup in hot pursuit. Julie opens her mouth to call him, and then decides not to. He'll come back.

As she continues along the shore, fine powdered snow drifts from overhead branches, floating like dust motes through the air. Out on the lake, gusts of wind skitter across the ice, lifting the dry snow in swirling eddies across the frozen surface. Julie glances back over her shoulder to check on the dog, who has given up on the chase and is now following a fresh scent. Suddenly a gunshot-like crack shatters the silence, and the dog stops in his tracks. Crouching low, he heads back toward Julie with his tail between his legs, as if the sounds emanating from the ice are in pursuit.

Like music, the sonic pings carry through the air, bounce off the ridge and echo across the frozen valley. Drawn by some inexplicable urge, Julie steps down from the bank and walks out onto the ice. Ignoring the warning voice inside her, she moves forward. Tempting fate with every step, unable to stop herself, she keeps putting one weightless foot in front of the other. She hears Pup whining somewhere in the distance, feels the dry snow turning to slush beneath her boots. Still, she walks as if in a trance, further and further out onto the lake's frozen surface, drawing closer and closer to the dark patches. And then, out on the ice, one of the dark patches moves. Behind a curtain of lifting snow, the black image rises like a mirage, its outline growing larger, shifting and changing, until it gives form to an illogical shape. But it can't be. It's only a trick of her sleep-deprived mind, a hallucination brought on by exhaustion, and by Levi Johnny's words. But even as she denies it, the black shape becomes the hulking form of a bear. The beast appears so real, that Julie imagines she can see each snorting breath turn to crystallized vapour. She squeezes her eyes shut, closing them against the impossible vision. Yet when she opens them the apparition is still there. Strangely unafraid, she moves toward it, admiring the beauty of the animal rising on its hind legs to stand upright.

Pup's whines turn to furious barking, and then to howls that lift to the heavens. And still Julie keeps going. The voice screaming in her head turns into Darla's. *Go back!*

But it's too late. Beneath Julie's feet the lake groans in protest. In the split second before the ice gives way, Julie sees it coming, as clearly as if this has all happened before. But she is powerless to stop it. It happens in less than a heartbeat. In one moment her world is filled with afternoon twilight, swirling snow, the image of a bear, and Pup's howling pleas, and the next, she is plunged into a black nothingness. Before her brain can make sense of what's happening, the shock of cold hits and the frigid water sucks her deeper and deeper. She kicks frantically against its icy grip. Her lungs screaming for air, not knowing if she is up or down, she struggles until she feels her head break though the surface, feels air on her face, hears Pup's howls. In a panicked gasp she sucks in water, and is pulled back under, her heavy jacket, her boots weighing her down. She searches madly for them, trying to kick them free, but cannot locate her own feet. Struggling against the inevitable, feeling the penetrating cold sapping her strength, paralyzing her body, she gives one last futile kick. Her head bumps up against something solid. Her heart and lungs ready to explode, she reaches up, blindly searching with unfeeling fingers for the opening in the ice above her.

And then suddenly, in the black silent depths a pinpoint of light appears, and a peaceful warmth, a lightness of being, floods through her. She stops struggling. There is no more fear. No more urgency. Surrendering, she reaches toward the light and sinks slowly down into the murky depths.

54

"You have to go back."

"Darla!"

"You can't stay here, Mom."

"Oh my God! Darla, where are you?"

"I don't know how to explain it." Where is Mr Emerson when I really need him? "I can only tell you that I'm here, somewhere on the edge of forever, waiting for you to let go, to let me move on."

"Oh, Darla, I'm sorry. I'm so sorry I couldn't save you."

"I didn't need to be saved, Mom. Nothing you, or Dad, or Levi, could have done would have changed my date with destiny. My life, my purpose, on earth, was over."

"So is mine now."

"No, it's not; you have to go back to your life."

"Please. Let me stay with you. I don't want to return to a world without you."

"You're never without me. The only thing that separates us is time." How can I explain that here, in this in-between place, time is not linear, but concurrent, eternal. That our lives on earth are nothing more than a breath in eternity? I can't.

"I'm ready now, Darla, I'm not afraid to die if only I can be with you."

"It's not your time, you still have so much to do on earth."

"Please, no. It's too painful."

"Pain is the price we pay for love during life's journey. No one escapes it." I no longer question these thoughts manifesting themselves as I need them. Neither does Mom—the reversal of our roles is as natural as if it has always been this way. Maybe she knows more than she realizes.

"If you give up now, if you don't pull yourself back up onto that ice, Levi will be lost forever."

"Levi? I forgave him."

"He didn't ask for your forgiveness. If he needed that he could have told you about the rose."

"The rose?"

"The reason I took off my seatbelt." He didn't tell Mom because he was afraid that it would hurt her too much. But I would rather she blamed a rose for what happened, than Levi. So I tell her about the yellow rose falling out of my hair, taking off my seatbelt to reach for it, splashing the beer over Levi, causing him to brake. I tell her everything that Levi couldn't bring himself to. "Levi needs much more than your forgiveness, Mom." And then I tell her about his determination to help me reach the spirit world. About his secret sweat lodge, the danger in his plan—the danger hidden in the rocks.

"You are the only one who can stop him. The only one who can release him from his promise to bring me home safely."

"It's too late."

"It's not too late. You can go back and stop him."

"Please, let me stay with you."

"I know you would die for me, Mom. But will you live for me?"

55

Her eyelids slowly flutter open. The vague memory of a dream she doesn't want to let go of slips away into the murky green light. Through a veil of watery half-vision the green hues turn into curtains. Beyond an opening in those curtains, a large wall clock takes shape, its minute hand soundlessly clicking off the seconds. She lets her gaze stray downward, to the blankets covering her—their warmth radiating throughout her body—and to the head resting in folded arms on the edge of the bed.

"Ian?" Her voice comes out a hoarse whisper.

His head jerks up. His silver hair sticking up at odd angles, his swollen eyes searching her face, he chokes, "Oh God! Julie, you're awake." He reaches up to touch her cheek.

"Where am I?"

"In the hospital."

"How...?"

The curtain snaps back and a white-coated doctor steps in. "Well, back with us, are you?" he asks picking up a chart at the foot of the bed.

Ian reaches for his crutches, but is waved to stay in his seat by the doctor. "This won't take long," he says removing the stethoscope from around his neck and placing it in his ears.

While she's being examined Julie searches Ian's face. Beyond the relief etched into his furrowed brows, she senses something different. And then she realizes that the difference is not in him, but in her. Something is missing. The resentment, the bitterness she has carried for so long is no longer there. Looking into Ian's eyes, she is filled with comforting warmth that goes beyond the warmth being forced into her body by the intravenous tubes, the heated blankets.

"That was pretty clever of you," the doctor says replacing the stethoscope around his neck. "Hoisting yourself up onto the edge of the ice like that."

Julie looks from Ian to him. She has no idea what he's talking about.

He pulls another instrument from his pocket and clicks on the light. "If your jacket sleeves hadn't frozen to the ice," he says leaning forward, "you would certainly have slipped back under when you lost consciousness."

Trying to make sense of what he's saying, she lets him move her head from one side to the other to peer into her ears. Satisfied, he gently lifts one of her eyelids and says, "Look into the light."

And the fragmented memories come flooding in with his words. She tries to sort through the vague details of the dream, the hallucination, whatever it was, as the light moves from one eye to the other.

The doctor straightens up, clicks off the instrument and replaces it in his pocket. Julie only half hears him speaking about hypothermia, about bringing her core temperature up a few more degrees. She glances beyond him at the wall clock. Nine o'clock. Morning? Night? She has no idea how long she has been unconscious. Her last clear memory is of walking out onto the frozen lake, in a blur of swirling snow.

"We'll just keep an eye on her for a few more hours," the doctor says to Ian. "But I'm pretty certain they'll be no reason you can't take her home in the morning." He smiles down at Julie. "You're a lucky lady."

After he leaves, she turns toward Ian. "I went through the ice."

"Yes," he says. He leans down to press his lips on her fingertips. But not before she sees the unasked question in his eyes. *Why?*

"Ian?" she whispers to the top of his head, "I need to ask you something."

Without looking up he squeezes her hand.

"If there were no me," she asks, "would you still sell the ranch?"

His lifts his head, his red-rimmed eyes searching hers. "If there were no you," he says, "I would be devastated."

Julie swallows back the lump in her throat. "I don't know why I walked out onto that ice," she says holding his gaze. "I can't tell you in all honesty that it wasn't on purpose. But I can promise that you will never have to worry about me doing anything like that again."

Ian lowers his head, saying, "We don't need to talk about this right now."

She places her hand onto his face. "Darla was there," she tells him. "When I was under the ice... Darla spoke to me."

She feels him stiffen. Feels him withdrawing into wherever he goes whenever their daughter's name is mentioned.

"Listen to me, Ian," she says gently. "I don't want to leave the ranch, or you. But what I can't do anymore, what I won't do, is continue on without being able to share Darla's memory. Isolation is more than a place. We can't go on together, out in the Chilcotin, or anywhere else, without Darla's memory being a part of who we are."

Ian slumps back in his chair, dropping his head into his hands. Julie reaches over and strokes his hair. "We need to celebrate her life, the time she spent with us, instead of dwelling on her death. I need to be able to say her name out loud, without fear that the reminder is too painful, for you, or for me."

Ian raises his head, his face a mask of anguish. "I don't need reminding," he chokes. "I go to bed every night with her name in my mind and wake up every morning seeing her face." He brushes away a tear. "And every time I look at you, I am reminded that if I had been there that night, if I had not made such a stupid meaningless choice, Darla would still be alive."

"It wasn't your fault," she says. "I'm sorry, so sorry that I held onto my anger at you for so long. Anger is easier to deal with than grief, I guess. But it wasn't anyone's fault. Not yours, not mine, not Levi Johnny's. Nothing any of us did would have changed what happened. I know that now. Your being home, or not being home, the door being locked or unlocked, made no difference. Darla made me see that.

"We need to move on, Ian, for Darla's sake, for ourselves, we have to let go of all the useless remorse. Our love for Darla didn't die with her. *That* we can hang onto."

Ian pushes himself up and takes Julie in his arms. His face pressed against hers, he whispers into her hair, "I miss her so much."

"I know," she replies, and for the first time the tears she feels flowing down her cheek belong to them both.

There is so much more to say. But now is not the time. Perhaps someday she will be able to tell Ian about how their daughter—a wiser, older, more complete Darla, she realizes now—convinced her to make the choice to live. Through the clearing fog of memory, she recalls begging to see her one more time, and an answer coming from somewhere in the darkness, 'look into the light.' And when she did, the pinpoint of light grew and Darla appeared. Wearing the costume from the play that night, a yellow rose pinned into her hair, she had smiled so peacefully that Julie felt the lightness of acceptance replacing the hot stone of sorrow she had carried for so long. A dream? Perhaps. But the promise she made to Darla within that dream, she will keep—the promise to return to life, not simply to endure, but to live with purpose.

With a start, she tries to sit up but there is no energy in her body. She reaches for Ian's hand, asking, "How did I get here?"

"Virgil and Levi," he says. His fingers interlock with hers, he explains how Virgil's dog had become so agitated by what they thought was a pack of wolves howling, that they had followed him out to the road and spotted her tracks in the snow. They took the van to investigate, and Pup's howling had led them to where she lay, half in and half out of the frigid water. With Virgil on one end of a rope, Levi had tied the other end around his waist and crawled across the ice to her.

She has no memory of being pulled out, carried to the van, or of Virgil stripping her of her wet clothes to wrap her in a sleeping bag.

"Your body temperature was so low, the hypothermia so set in, that you barely had a heartbeat by the time they found you," Ian says, his voice catching. "Virgil crawled into the sleeping bag with you to warm you while Levi drove back to the house."

"I called the Champion ranch. Thank God your friend Terri was home," he says, pushing a hand through his hair. "Twenty minutes later she landed her ski-plane in front of the house. You were in the hospital emergency room less than an hour after you were pulled from the lake."

As the story unfolds Julie realizes that she owes her life to the three of them, especially Virgil and Levi. Levi? She owes him even more. She struggles to sit up again. "Where are they? I need to speak to Levi."

"What you need is rest."

"No! I have to see him. It can't wait. We've got to find him."

"Don't worry, he's right here—out in the waiting room with Virgil and Terri. You can thank them all later."

"Please, Ian," she begs, "go out and ask them to come in."

"Are you sure?"

"Yes, it's important. It can't wait. Please."

Reluctantly, Ian gives into the urgency in her voice. Before he leaves, she asks him to raise the head of the bed. She needs to be able to look into the boy's eyes.

Waiting nervously she begins to question her own memory. How was it possible for Darla to have told her so much in the brief time she was under the ice? Was it nothing more than a dream, an illusion brought on by her oxygen-deprived brain? She tries to recall the exact words, the sound of Darla's voice as she spoke to her. Spoke? No, not really, her voice had not come from outside of Julie, but from somewhere within. It had all seemed so real moments ago, but now she is beginning to doubt. Had she only imagined it all?

And then in a moment of clarity it comes to her that it doesn't really matter. Levi is in trouble, she saw that the moment he walked into Virgil's cabin. Whether she only imagined her encounter with Darla or not, she will keep her promise to release him from his.

Ian returns to her side, and right behind him the boy appears between the opening in the curtains, followed by Virgil and Terri. The strain of the day's events etched on their faces, they stand timidly at the foot of her bed.

Terri is the first to speak. "Well, Girl, that's not exactly how I planned to take you on your first flight over the Chilcotin."

"Next time I promise I'll stay awake."

"Darn tootin,'" Terri replies, failing to conceal the catch in her throat.

Julie leans back on her pillow. "Thank you," she says, looking from one to the other. "Thank you all for my life." Her gaze rests on Virgil's face. She is unable to read if the expression in his dark eyes is relief, or exhaustion. "The healing circle?" she asks him. "Is it possible to do one here? Now?"

Following his mute acknowledgement they all join hands around her bed. Julie meets the boy's tortured eyes. She smiles softly at him and says, "I see you, Levi Johnny, friend of Darla's."

56

The heady aroma of roast turkey and mincemeat pie permeates the ranch house air. The haloed sparkle of multicoloured Christmas tree lights shine from the darkened living room as Julie carries the glistening, oversized bird into the dining room. She sets the heavy platter down ceremoniously in front of Ian—who is wearing a walking cast now—at the head of the table.

"Just a second, everyone," she says, rushing over to the corner where she has set up her tripod. Ignoring the mock groans, she focuses the camera and then quickly takes her seat. The delayed flash goes off and the chatter around the table resumes. Julie catches the reflection of the scene in the plate-glass windows, just as she had on their first night in this house. *How things have changed since then.* As if reading her thoughts her sister, Jessie, winks at her, while her brother-in-law, Barry, banters with Ian about the correct way to carve a turkey. Julie smiles and looks down the table, at her nieces, Emily and Amanda, sitting in their red velvet Christmas dresses, eyes wide at the enormous size of the drumsticks, which have been promised to them.

Until the moment the girls had arrived, and she held them in her arms again, smelled the child's innocence in their hair, Julie had no idea of just how much she has missed them, how much of Darla lives on in them. Now, watching their grandmother lean over to fuss with the ribbon in Emily's hair she is reminded of how her mother used to fuss over Darla's hair in the same way. Now, satisfied with the newly straightened bow, she looks up, meets Julie's eyes and asks, "Grace?"

Julie nods, and lowers her head. Why not? She has a lot to be thankful for. It makes no difference what name is used, God, the Universe, the Holy Spirit, the Great Spirit; she knows there is something larger to give homage to.

With eyes closed, she listens to the rote words of gratitude for the abundance of food, for time spent with family, and then looks up with a start, when her mother concludes with, "And we give thanks for the memory of our beautiful Darla, who is with us all now. Amen."

At the other end of the table, Julie catches the flicker that crosses Ian's face. He still struggles with hearing their daughter's name, she knows, but he is trying. That's all she can ask. He meets her gaze, then returning her smile, he looks over to his mother-in-law and says, "Thanks, Mom." Then he pushes his chair back, stands up with the carving knife and fork in hand and commences "butchering"—according to Barry's teasing—the turkey.

Heaping platters of food are passed from hand to hand, and in the din of the rising conversation, Julie leans to her mother and asks, "Do you remember how excited Darla was about the Obama campaign, Mom?"

"I certainly do."

"Can you imagine how thrilled she would have been over the results—about the inauguration next month?" Julie says, spooning mashed potatoes onto her plate. "She would have been especially excited to share that with you." She passes the bowl of potatoes to her mother. "So I've been thinking," she looks back to the head of the table, "well, Ian and I are wondering, if you'd like to stay for a few more weeks after Christmas so we can all watch the inauguration ceremony together."

Her mother's hand freezes mid-air. She recovers quickly, accepts the bowl, smiles, and says, "Nothing would make me happier, Dear."

"Good, it's settled then."

For a few moments the only sound is the clinking of cutlery against china. "Maybe that handsome cowboy, your Mr Blue, would like to watch it with us," her mother says. "I must say that I'm quite disappointed that he didn't join us tonight."

Julie smiles at her mother's complete about-turn of subject. But she too is sorry that Virgil couldn't, or wouldn't, share Christmas dinner with them. It wasn't from lack of trying. She had invited him, knowing as she did so that it was a long shot, that he would never be comfortable at a table full of strangers. His absence was neither her choice, nor Ian's.

During the last month, she and Ian have each, in their own way, come to terms with their relationship with Virgil. Julie knows he is still leaving, but in her heart she knows it has little to do with her and Ian, and more to do with Virgil's own solitary journey. It is obvious now that Virgil is sick. Yet, she respects his unspoken request not to probe. Each time she sees him now she is aware of the subtle changes. More than once she's come upon him in the barn standing between his Clydesdales, pressed up against one or the other as if drawing strength from them. Each time, not wanting to intrude on the private moment, she waits in the shadows until he resumes his chores. Every morning and evening now, she joins him in the barn to help feed and care for the horses. Although it has never been acknowledged, she is aware that he is teaching her to take over his role. There are no notes between them anymore, and no unnecessary words spoken by Julie whenever they are together. They have little need for words now. Everything that needed to be said between them was said that day in the hospital in the healing circle around her bed.

She recalls with wonder the brief ceremony and the unexpected calmness of mind and body she was left with when it was over. As everyone was leaving she had asked Levi to stay behind for a moment. When they were alone, the boy had listened without any indication of judgement or rejection as she described her meeting with Darla while she was under the ice. "She's almost home now, thanks to you, Levi," she had told him. "Your promise is fulfilled." Only when she went on to tell him that she knew about the rose, and about the sweat lodge hidden in the bush at NaNeetza Valley, about Darla's warning of the danger waiting in the stones, did a flicker of surprise cross his face. "There's no need to do the sweat, the vision quest, anymore, Levi," she had said quietly. "It's time to go back to your life, to school, to hockey."

He remained expressionless, motionless, for a moment before giving his head a nod so brief that Julie was not certain it was agreement. Had she convinced him? She had to be certain. "Darla asked me to give you a message." She had no idea if the words had any meaning at all, or whether they had sprung from her own imagination, until she saw Levi's reaction, the dimples that appeared on his cheeks, when she repeated, "She said to tell you, that 'you make her heart come glad.'"

"Aunt Julie?" five-year-old Emily's voice breaks into Julie's reverie.

She smiles at her youngest niece, "Yes, Sweetheart."

"Amanda said that you might give us some of the dolls in that big box in the closet upstairs."

"Did not!" her sister cries, nudging Emily in the side.

"Did too," Emily whines. "You said Darla doesn't need them anymore."

In the startled silence that follows, Julie feels everyone's eyes turn to her.

She puts down her fork. "Of course she doesn't," she says smiling at the girls. "I'll tell you what. Tomorrow, you can both go through them and choose as many as you want. You can even take the whole box home with you if you like. I'm certain that's exactly what Darla would want."

57

Virgil's story

In the darkened cabin, dying embers glow through the wood stove's cast-iron grill. Moonlight streams in through the window above the kitchen sink, pooling on the chrome tabletop, and illuminating the yellow notepads neatly stacked there.

Forty years of his life in these handwritten pages, one notepad for each year he has spent in the Chilcotin, for every year since he changed his name to Virgil Blue.

He sits at the table writing by the light of the moon. When he is finished, he places the final yellow page on the tabletop beside the letter addressed to his sister.

His chair scrapes across the wooden floor as he pushes it back, and he stands in the shadows surveying the room. His affairs are in order. His remaining possessions are packed and ready to go, their destination clearly marked on each box. It's time.

Earlier this evening, he had walked over to the barn to be with his horses. Sensing the final farewell, the Clydesdales had shifted uneasily in their stalls, snorting their sadness while he stroked their muzzles.

On the way back to the cabin he had stopped in the ranch yard and looked up at the house. While the yellow light from the windows cast long shadows on the snow, the muffled sound of Christmas music and laughter had drifted out into the silent night. And he had smiled. All was as it should be.

He glances down at his final note. Certain that she will be the first to discover him gone, the first to find these notepads, he imagines her sitting at this table reading his life, and trusts her to carry out his wishes. Trusts that she will see that these pages, and the letter to his sister, with his explanation as to why he cannot keep his promise to return to his childhood home, are delivered.

Outside the full moon and the northern lights brighten the night sky. Down on the lake, reflecting the silver light, the dock, imbedded in the ice, and the willow chair, wait for him. He reaches up and removes the pendant from around his neck. He rubs his thumb over the smoothness of the intricately carved ebony crow, then lays the pendant across his final note to her.

Turning to the counter, he opens the black case lying there, and carefully removes his violin and bow. His gnarled fingers pluck at the strings until the instrument is in tune. When he is satisfied he goes over to the door. Frigid midnight air billows in around him as he opens it for the last time. Then, with his dog at his side, he heads down to the dock, where he will lift the violin to his chin, and play himself home.

58

The lilting strains of "O Holy Night" evaporate like smoke as she rises up from a dreamless sleep. A memory of tonight's music, or could it possibly be Virgil playing his violin in the middle of this Christmas night?

Fully awake, the music nothing more than a dream, she lies with her eyes closed, straining to recapture the soulful melody of a distant violin. But the only sound in the room is Ian's even breathing beside her. She opens her eyes. Careful not to disturb his leg, she gently untangles herself from his arms and rises from their bed. Drawn across the master bedroom floor by the memory of the music, and by the brilliant light spilling in the patio door, she pushes it open and steps out onto the balcony.

Outside the landscape is as bright as day. She gives an involuntary gasp at the shock of frigid air, and at the illuminated scene greeting her. Above, a full moon shines down from a star-filled sky; at the far end of the lake, the northern lights dance across the horizon. She stands for a moment, captivated by the beauty, the magic of the frozen night, and then turns to hurry back inside. Placing a hand on Ian's shoulder, she gently shakes him, until she feels his sleeping body respond to her touch. His eyes slowly open and meet hers, and in his unguarded look she sees the reflection of the love that has never really left them. "Come," she whispers, "there's something I want to show you."

And without question he rises. Grabbing the quilt from the foot of the bed and wrapping it around their shoulders, Julie leads him across the room.

"Incredible," Ian gasps as they step out onto the balcony. Standing in his arms, watching the light show play out in the northern sky, Julie can't help comparing this moment with the first time she experienced this celestial phenomenon, last summer, the night she first heard Virgil playing the violin. She can almost hear it now.

She looks over toward the bay, where the shimmering moonlight illuminates Virgil's dock. The light and shadows create the illusion of someone sitting there in the willow chair. A trick of the light? The vision seems so real she imagines the blurred outline of Virgil playing his violin as he had on that summer night. But the shadows are still, no music fills the air tonight, and Julie is filled with the sadness of knowing it will never happen again.

At that moment, a howl breaks the frozen silence. A wolf, or dog, baying at the moon? As the mournful cry echoes down the lake and disappears, an involuntary shiver grips Julie; she wraps her arms tighter around Ian and melts against him.

In the hushed silence he leans down and places his mouth against her ear, "Come spring," he murmurs, "we'll build that dock."

"Yes," she whispers, her hands finding bare skin beneath the quilt. "I'd like that."

59

A white aura begins to glow around their bodies. As it grows and brightens, just as Mr Emerson promised I would, I remember that I know—that I have always known, and forever will know—exactly what that white light is. It's so simple that I can't imagine I ever forgot. Thanks, Mom, for reminding me.

There's no need to regret this goodbye to her, to Dad, to Levi, to everyone I love, because as soon as I pass through I will meet them on the other side. It's so easy when you understand the truth about time having no meaning on our journey to Love.

In a single luminous flash, the light fills the universe before me, and in that light a figure takes form. Wearing his cowboy hat, carrying his violin in perfectly formed hands, he appears smiling and unhesitant, as he enters the glow radiated by the couple, and the twin brothers, waiting for him.

Welcome home, Virgil.

ABOUT THE AUTHOR

DONNA MILNER is the author of the internationally acclaimed novel, *The Promise of Rain*, a *Globe and Mail* Top 100 pick for 2010, as well as *After River*, which was published in twelve countries and translated into eight languages.

Born Donna Jonas, in Victoria, British Columbia, Donna spent her childhood in Vancouver. As an adult she relocated to the town of Rossland in the heart of the BC's West Kootenay, and ten years later moved to the central interior city of Williams Lake. She now lives in an off-the-grid, eco-friendly, lakeside home in the Cariboo woods with her husband, Tom, and their dog Beau. She is currently working on her fourth novel.

Learn more about Donna and her books on her website: www.donnamilner.com

ACKNOWLEDGEMENTS

I am forever grateful to family and friends for their ongoing support and encouragement, and for always being there, ready and willing to read early drafts. In particular, I would like to thank Tanya LaFond, Aaron Drake, Joanna Stiles Drake, Diane Jonas, Bonnie and Keith Coulter, Angela Menzies, Joyce Aaltonen, Juliee Thompson, Verena Berger and as always, my husband, Tom. I am so blessed to have you all in my life and as a big part of my 'writing life.'

I also wish to acknowledge Jane Gregory and the good people at Gregory and Co, as well as Vici Johnstone at Caitlin Press—thank you all for your ongoing faith in me.

And finally, to an old Chilcotin cowboy, for the 'borrowing' of his colourful name, my thanks to the late Virgil Blue—the most interesting character I never knew.